THE EXCEPTION TO THE RULE

BY

BETH RINYU

This book or any portion thereof may not be reproduced or used in any manner whatsoever without the express written permission of Beth Rinyu, except for the use of brief quotations embodied in critical articles and reviews.
Cover design & Formatting by: LKO Designs
Editing by: Judy's Proofreading
Proofread by: Judy's Proofreading

ISBN-13: 978-0615739229
ISBN-10: 0615739229

DEDICATION

I'd like to thank my family, friends, co-workers, and all the people I met along the way during this process that helped to keep me motivated...you guys know who you are!

.

PROLOGUE

My mother's beautiful blond hair was draped over her shoulders as we cuddled together under my Strawberry Shortcake bedspread. She was reading a story from my favorite book filled with fairy tales. The stories always included a handsome prince and a damsel in distress who would overcome any obstacle and fall in love. Of course, at five years old, before life proves otherwise, you really believe this could happen. This had become our routine whenever my dad was working the night shift.

"And they lived happily ever after..." My mother's voice was soft and gentle. I leaned my head on her shoulder and felt so at ease as I breathed in her freshly shampooed hair.

"Do they always live happily ever after, Mommy?" I asked.

"Yes, they do." She smiled down at me with her warm brown eyes.

"Do you think someday I could be a princess and find a prince?" I asked.

She pushed my hair from my face and smiled. Her perfect porcelain complexion accented her ruby red lips, and as I looked up at her in admiration I thought—*I have the prettiest mom in the world.* "Oh, Kat, you're already a princess and yes, someday you will find a very handsome prince and live happily ever after." She kissed me on the forehead and hugged me tightly before turning off the lamp on the nightstand. Pulling me closer, I closed my eyes and listened to the blustering wind howling outside my bedroom window.

"I love you so much, Mommy."

"I love you too, sweetie, more than anything in this world."

"More than you loved your mommy and daddy?" I asked.

"Yes, more than anything," she said.

"Well, I don't think I will ever love anyone more than you or Daddy."

"When you are older and have children, you will see–it's a love like you've never known." I could almost see her smile even in the darkness.

I nuzzled closer to her and petted her long silky hair. "Good night, Mommy."

"Good night, sweet girl…"

CHAPTER 1

Twenty-three years later

It was my boyfriend, Jake's, thirtieth birthday and I had planned on taking him out for a nice romantic dinner, something we hadn't done in a long time, since we had both become so busy with our careers. So, I was ecstatic when my last patient canceled, allowing me to slip out of work a little earlier than usual.

Jake and I met five years ago and had been together ever since. We were semi-living together. I spent most of my nights at his house, making sure I slept at home a couple of nights a week to appease my dad, who was very old-fashioned in his way of thinking and didn't believe in living together before marriage. He seemed to totally overlook the fact that I was a grown woman. In his eyes, I was still his little girl—but, in his defense, I was his only child. My mother passed away when I was eight years old, so it had been just me and him for the past twenty years.

I hated to see my dad upset and never wanted to disappoint him. Every time we would get on the subject of my living arrangement, he would call me Katrina. I knew when he used my full name, he was either trying to be funny, or he was displeased over something. Otherwise, he called me Kat, like everyone else.

Jake's present was in the back of my car, I wanted to drop it off at his house, so it would be waiting for him when he came home from work. Jake was an up-and-coming lawyer at a big law firm in Philadelphia and a workaholic. He commuted well over an hour each day, so I was pleasantly surprised to see his shiny new Lexus in the driveway already.

Admiring the landscaping job that the two of us had diligently worked on all weekend as I made my way to the front porch, I used my key to enter his house. The humming of the refrigerator was the only sound to be heard as I placed his gift on the kitchen table and quickly peeked into the living room, finding no sign of him. Wanting to surprise him, I tiptoed up the stairs and looked in one of the spare bedrooms that he used as an office, hoping to find him—but it was empty. I crept down the hall to his bedroom, where the door was half-closed and slowly opened it. I had to do a double take even though I didn't want to. My stomach clenched and my eyes instantly burned with tears—Jake was in bed with another woman. He looked up, quickly pushing away the girl who was on top of him and jumping out of bed.

"Kat!" he yelled, running after me while trying to put his pants on at the same time. I ignored him as I ran down the steps two at a time, unable to get out the front door fast enough. I gagged on the stinging bile rising from the back of my throat, tasting the sourness of my lunch from earlier today. Making it out the door just in time to throw up in the forsythia bush, I cringed when his hand touched my back, trying to comfort me.

"Don't touch me!" I shouted and pushed him away.

"Kat, please, don't go, can we just talk?" he pleaded as I got into my car.

I wasn't hearing anything, wanting to get as far away from him as I possibly could, I slammed on the gas and backed out of the driveway. Speeding down the street and driving for some time, I finally pulled over once I felt like there was enough distance between us. I put my car in park and began to sob hysterically. *How could he have done this to me? I had dedicated the last five years of my life to him. Just a few weeks ago we were talking about getting engaged.*

***

As the weeks passed, I focused all my energy into my work, trying my best to get the image of that dreaded day out of my head. I wondered if she was the first woman that he had cheated on me with or if that was just the first time he got caught. A heaviness rose to my chest just thinking about it. I had lost all respect for him and even more importantly—trust. I was now content with the commitment I had made months ago to go on a nine-month medical mission in Africa. This was so out of character for me—I was normally such a homebody, but I now felt a sense of urgency to get away from Jake's *I'm sorry* flowers, phone calls, emails, and everything else that reminded me of him.

Before I knew it, the big day was here, and I would leave for my journey in just a few short hours. I had been procrastinating about picking up the last of my things from Jake's house, but I couldn't put it off any longer. I strategically planned it so he would be at work and I wouldn't have to see him. My plan was foiled when I pulled up to his house and saw his car in the driveway.

After just finishing my morning run, I knew I probably looked a mess. I glanced in my rearview mirror, adjusting my thick wavy hair into a more presentable ponytail. I didn't have any makeup on and was thankful that I had just hit the beach a few days ago, which gave my face a healthy suntanned glow.

Jake opened the door before I even made it to the front porch. "Good morning," he said, acting as if everything was normal between us. I tried my best not to look at him but couldn't help myself. He still looked so handsome with his wavy dirty blond hair and hazel eyes. "Do you want some coffee?" he asked.

"No, just my boxes."

"I miss our morning runs," he said, noticing my running attire.

"Jake, can you please just get my boxes so I can go?"

"Can we just talk for a minute? You're leaving for nine months, and you haven't talked to me in weeks. I think we really need to talk about what happened, Kat."

"There's nothing to talk about. You cheated on me, we broke up—*the end*." I tried to keep my emotions in check, but my heart was secretly aching.

"That was a mistake, and it will never happen again—I love you. I've been miserable without you these past weeks." He placed his hand on my arm and pressed his forehead against mine. "Will you please give me another chance to prove to you how much I love you?" He sounded like he was pleading one of his cases.

I still loved him, but I had to remain true to myself and not give in. "No." I removed his hand from my arm and yanked my two boxes from the kitchen table. I took his house key from my key ring and threw it on the kitchen counter.

"Kat, please," he called as I struggled to get the front door open. Totally ignoring him, I marched down the driveway, throwing the boxes in my trunk as he followed behind me.

"So that's it—you're just going to leave without even talking to me?" he asked.

"What do you want me to say, Jake? That I'm humiliated, that you hurt me more than anyone has in my life, or that I can never trust you again?" I closed my trunk and walked over to the driver's side of my car.

"I'm sorry, Kat." He grabbed my elbow and pulled me closer.

"Yeah, I am too. Sorry that I actually thought you were the one for me. Now, let go of me!" I got into my car and slammed the door. Within minutes of driving away, all the tears I had been holding in were flowing down my face.

I pulled into my driveway and stared at my dad's perfectly manicured lawn—the place I had called home for my entire life. I looked in my rearview mirror and wiped the last of the tears from my big brown eyes. I didn't want to have to explain to my dad that I was shedding more tears over Jake. Dodging the automatic sprinklers, I made my way to the front porch. "Be right there, Dad," I shouted as I walked into the house, carrying my boxes.

"Hurry up, breakfast is almost ready," he shouted back.

I went into my bedroom and placed the boxes on the floor, I tried to pull it together as I sat on my bed and studied every inch of my room. This was the place where I had gone for the past twenty-eight years, whether it was getting over a broken heart, being sent here for punishment, or to pull all-nighters cramming for exams. The bright yellow walls accented by my denim blue comforter, my blue throw pillows and blue lamp gave my room a calming effect. I was suddenly reminded of all the different colors my walls had been throughout the years, and how my dad had the unfortunate task of painting them every time I went through a new phase. There was only one picture that had withstood all my different stages. It was that of a little ballerina. It had been given to me by my mother when I first started taking dance lessons at three years old. My love of dance continued until college, when I had to make a choice between that or a career in medicine. Since the chances of becoming a great doctor were far better than becoming a world-famous dancer, I decided to hang up my ballet slippers for a stethoscope.

The smell of bacon permeated from the kitchen, finding its way into my bedroom, tempting my empty stomach, and I couldn't ignore it any longer. My feet hit the hardwood floor, and I made my way down the long hallway, taking in every portrait that lined the walls, as if it were my first time looking at them. First was a picture of my mom and dad when they had first started dating. Next was their wedding picture, their love for one another was so apparent just looking at it. The one that always caught my eye, causing me to do a double take, was of my mother and me. It was taken the Christmas right after I turned eight years old. I wore two pigtails in my thick, unruly hair and a Mickey Mouse sweatshirt. What was left of my mother's once thick and beautiful long blond hair was hidden under a hat. The paleness of her skin was enhanced by the dark circles under her eyes. All the chemo and radiation had taken its toll on her already petite frame, and I probably weighed more than her in that photo. Through it all, she always had that same angelic smile on her face, always trying to stay strong for everyone else. As I grew older, I imagined how many times she must have secretly cried herself to sleep. She kept her spirits up until the end–and the day that picture was taken had been no exception. That turned out to be the last photograph of my mother and me. Three weeks later, she lost her long fight with breast cancer at only thirty-four years old. I kept the memory of that day etched in my mind forever. Whenever I began to miss her I would think back to that day and feel like we were right there together again, sitting under that Christmas tree.

I took a deep breath before heading into the kitchen where my dad was making his famous omelets. This had become our Sunday morning tradition ever since I could remember, so I was pleasantly surprised to be having this on a Thursday.

"Kat, please tell me you weren't crying over him again," Dad said.

Anthony Vallia, my dad, was old-school Italian. He had a strong belief in hard work and commitment to getting what you wanted in life. These were qualities he instilled in me very well. He was a newly retired police officer who had dedicated his life to me and my education. In short–he was my hero. He was always afraid I'd miss out on things that other girls my age got to experience with their moms, so he did a great job making sure that I didn't, by fulfilling both roles.

He was tall, rugged and very well built, taking care to keep in shape by hitting the gym each day. He was the type of man who could jump into an action movie and take over the lead. His dark brown hair now had just a touch of gray around the edges, and I was always envious of his hazel eyes with flecks of gold, preferring them to my plain old brown ones.

"I'm fine, Dad." As I poured myself a cup of coffee, I realized how much weight he had lost and immediately became angry with myself for becoming too busy with work and pining over Jake to recognize this.

"Swiss or cheddar?" he asked.

"Swiss and you may want to put some extra in yours," I answered, taking a sip of my coffee. "What's with the supermodel skinny look–have you been hitting the gym a little more?" I tried to mask my concern with humor.

He looked down at himself. "Hey, the ladies like the lean look."

"Well, don't lose any more or you'll disappear." I walked over to the stove to flip the bacon, and he tapped my hand lightly, signaling to get away from his culinary masterpiece.

"Well, you're one to talk, you can afford to put some meat on your bones too, kid."

I decided to drop the subject because I wasn't going to get anywhere. Another trait of his he passed down to me was stubbornness. Unfortunately, he had just a tad more in him, which never allowed me to win any argument, unless he let me.

I sat down at the table waiting for my omelet, sensing a new appreciation for my home, and what it was going to mean to be away from it for so long. Most people can't wait to move away from their hometown and make their mark in the world. I guess I was a lot different. Sure, I wanted to make something of myself. I felt like I had already done that by achieving my lifelong dream of becoming a pediatrician. I was well aware of how fortunate I was to be doing something I absolutely loved for a living. Thankful every day to my father and the sacrifices he made for making that a reality for me. I couldn't ever imagine myself living anywhere but the tiny little bayside town I grew up in, just outside of Cape May, New Jersey. It was a secret little gem with some of the most beautiful sunsets that not many people knew about, keeping the summer crowds to a minimum. My parents had stumbled upon the place by accident when they had first gotten married. They were vacationing in Cape May and decided to go for a drive—one wrong turn and my mother was hooked. They bought a one-story, three-bedroom, fixer-upper just before I was born, restoring it into something out of *a Better Homes and Gardens* magazine.

I was excited about leaving but through the excitement, there was still some apprehension. Being in a remote village in Nigeria where sickness prevailed was hardly a dream vacation and to be leaving the country for nine months was drastic for me. I wasn't much of a traveler, and this would be the first time that I was even leaving the East Coast.

"These are my best omelets yet," Dad said, placing the plate in front of me.

"I'll be the judge of that," I said as I took the first bite. "I've had better," I joked.

He smiled and lightly smacked my arm with the dishtowel he had hanging on his shoulder.

"Nine months will fly by, Kat," Dad said as if he was sensing my apprehension about leaving. "Besides, it will give you a chance to forget about that bum." My dad, who once treated Jake as a son, now despised him for what he had done to me.

"Oh, come on, Dad, you were the one who practically had me walking down the aisle with that bum."

"That was before I knew he was a bad guy," he said as he buttered his toast, not missing a beat. I nearly spit my coffee out, laughing at his police mentality. "He wasn't the one, you will know the one, and once you find him nobody will ever be able to replace him." The conversation was quickly becoming more serious.

For him, I knew my mother was the one. They grew up in the same neighborhood and had known each other their whole lives. By the time high school came around he didn't see her as the shy, pigtailed, freckle-faced girl, and she didn't see him as the scrawny, awkward boy, always getting in trouble for being the class clown. They married a few years after high school graduation and the rest was history. I often wondered why he never had any interest in finding anyone new. Even though he dated from time to time, he was never serious about anyone. I sometimes wondered if I was the reason why. But he always seemed so content with the way things were. Ironically, I was the one who wanted him to find someone.

"Well, I don't know if I will ever find the one, and I am perfectly okay with that," I lied. I wanted to find true love and have a family more than anything. The dream of becoming a mother was equally as strong as my dream to become a doctor. I loved children and couldn't wait until I had my own one day. But that dream would have to be put on hold for now.

"Oh no, Kat, it will happen when you least expect it–trust me," he answered.

I got up from the table and began to load the dishwasher. I was scrubbing away at a frying pan going over my to-do list in my head, much to my surprise, it was pretty much all checked off. I just had to throw some last-minute things in my bag and I was set.

Dr. Charles Morgan, one of the doctors who would be accompanying me, was picking me up for the airport at 7 p.m. Charles, my mentor, was around the same age as my dad, and I respected him and his knowledge immensely. I had become very close to him and his wife, Claire. They never had children, but Claire had such a motherly way to her, which I found very comforting. They had become an extended family to me. The fact that he was coming, helped to put my mind greatly at ease.

The two other doctors joining us were Tricia Aller and James Wiltshire. Tricia and I had met a year ago when we both joined the same practice. We were the youngest in the group, alongside three older stuffy gentlemen doctors. It was like a breath of fresh air having someone my age to relate to, and we became instant friends. She was so bubbly and her appearance was just as cute as her personality. She had beautiful green eyes and short spiky brown hair that was perfect for her small face and petite frame. She and I were to be roommates and I was relying on her positive outlook to help get me through my bouts of homesickness.

James was another pediatrician at our hospital. He too was around the same age as Tricia and me. I had gotten to know him fairly well over the past year and became fond of his jokester personality. He and Tricia always exchanged jokes, and she was too naïve to see that he was actually flirting with her. They had great chemistry, even though she was only 5'2" and he was almost 6'5". He was an above-average looking guy with light brown hair that he wore a little longer all around. He didn't look like your typical clean-cut doctor, but he was able to pull off the longer-hair look very well. He had big brown eyes and a boyish way about him. The matchmaker side in me thought that he and Tricia would make the perfect couple.

The day flew by and before I knew it the clock on the fireplace mantel was chiming seven times. The butterflies were released from the cage inside of my stomach when I looked out the window and saw the car that would take us to the airport in the driveway. The moment I had been dreading most about this trip was finally here–saying goodbye to my dad.

My dad and Charles were deep in conversation over last night's baseball game as I stood by the front door with my bags in hand, waiting for them to be done with their chatter. I looked at myself in the full-length mirror waiting for my presence to be acknowledged, noticing for the first time the perfect light blond streaks that the sun had left in my dirty blond wavy hair. Why couldn't my hairdresser get that right shade of blonde, no matter how hard he tried? As I examined myself from head to toe, I realized once again, my dad was probably right about putting meat on my bones. I was 5'5" and just about 100 pounds, which only made my already tiny bustline, look even smaller. Although people would tell me how pretty I was, I never believed it. I was never the type of person who beamed with self-confidence, and I was envious of those who did.

"Hey, Kat, are you ready to get this show on the road?" Charles asked, as if I hadn't already been standing there for the past five minutes.

"I guess so," I answered hesitantly.

"I'm going to take these to the car." Charles grabbed my bags and shook my dad's hand before walking out the door.

"Well, it's time, kiddo," my dad said, embracing me tightly.

I was unable to keep the promise I had made not to cry, allowing the tears to roll down my face. "I love you, Dad."

"I love you too, but call if you're planning on coming home early, so I can get the ladies out of the house," he teased, always using humor to get him through tough situations.

"Deal." I forced a smile.

I gave him one last hug and kiss as I headed out the door, turning around before getting into the car to take one last look at my house and my dad standing on the front porch. I etched it into my mind right along with the Christmas picture of my mother and me.

The last thought on my mind as we pulled away was of Jake–would I ever fall in love with someone, the way I had with him? I sighed heavily, hoping this trip would serve its purpose and mend my broken heart.

CHAPTER 2

After what seemed like a never-ending flight, we finally touched down at Lagos International Airport. I slept for quite some time on the plane and woke up feeling refreshed. This was Charles' third time coming here, so we were heavily relying on him. As we walked out of the airport and into the night, I was surprised that it wasn't as oppressively hot as I had expected—not much different than the heat and humidity back at home in the summer months. There was a strange smoky smell in the air as swarms of mosquitos greeted us. The taxi pulled up and we loaded our bags. The twenty-minute taxi ride seemed never-ending down dark, narrow, bumpy dirt roads. Charles sat in the front seat having a conversation with the taxi driver, who spoke broken English, sounding like they were long-lost friends as I sat in the back seat crammed between Tricia and James, already doubting my decision to come.

We pulled up to a large one-story building surrounded by four other buildings, very similar in size and structure. Charles explained in detail what every building was used for.

"So what do you guys think about your new home for the next nine months?" Charles asked with a grin.

"Ugh," was all Tricia could manage as she grabbed her bags and headed into one of those buildings with James not too far behind.

Charles chuckled at Tricia's out-of-character reaction. "I guess she's a little cranky from that long plane ride," I said, laughing.

"Well, Kat, what do you think?" he asked.

"Actually, it's not as bad as I had expected."

We entered a big windowless room with painted cinder block walls and a familiar musty scent that didn't take me long to recognize—it was the same smell as my attic at home. Tricia and James were talking to a tall lanky man sitting behind a desk who seemed to have a French accent. Charles automatically took over the conversation, getting us the keys for our rooms. He handed me a keychain with a big number nine on it. I made my way down the narrow hallway, taking in each number on the door, finally reaching door nine, feeling like a contestant on *Let's Make a Deal*. I slowly opened the creaky door, afraid to see what was going to be behind it. It was an average-sized room with two single beds and a nightstand between them. Just like the large entryway, there were cinder block walls along with the musty scent. There were two small windows on each side of the small closet and a large dresser that sat on the far wall. The small bathroom consisted of a pedestal sink, a toilet, and shower stall.

I placed my bags on the bed furthest from the door and sat down to take everything in. The bed was as stiff as a board, making me painfully realize that the comforts of my nice tranquil bedroom really were a million miles away.

Tricia entered the room and broke my daydreaming. "Yuck!" was all she could muster. Her sunny disposition, upon which I was depending, had disappeared.

Ironically, it was I who tried to spread the cheer about our new abode. "Where's your sense of adventure?" I asked jokingly.

"I think I left it somewhere over the ocean," she answered.

My second wind I had gotten when I got off the plane suddenly diminished. I was overcome with exhaustion, and when I looked down at my watch it was 11:20 p.m. Charles had set my watch for me with the correct time while we were on the plane, and I already lost track of what time it would have been at home. I cringed at the thought of the uncomfortable bed, but I was so tired, I could have probably slept on a bag of rocks.

I walked over to my bags, fumbling through them for a pair of pajamas while Tricia got up to answer the knock on the door. "Well, I can see you two are getting all settled in," Charles said, walking into the room.

"Pretty much." I looked around.

"Just remember, bottled water, even to brush your teeth—and no ice," he warned.

"Can we take a shower with that bottled water too?" Tricia asked with disgust in her voice.

"She's still grumpy. Maybe we'll get our old Tricia back after a good night's sleep." I grinned.

"Good night, girls," Charles said, shaking his head and laughing as he closed the door behind him.

We changed into our pajamas and lay down on our beds. The room was oppressive. Even with the windows open and fan on, it felt as if no air was circulating. I tossed and turned forever, trying to get comfortable and drown out Tricia's snoring. When I closed my eyes, I imagined myself walking along the bay, beachcombing, before finally drifted off into a restless sleep.

***

Tricia was already dressed and putting clothes away when I woke up. "Good morning, sleepy head, one hour until orientation!" she said in her Mary Poppins voice, which proved my theory–all she needed was a good night's sleep.

"Oh shoot, that's right." I jumped out of bed and ran immediately into the shower. I maneuvered the faucets trying to find the hot water, only to discover, it wasn't very hot at all, and smelled of sulfur. I showered as fast as I could, not feeling much cleaner than before I had gotten in. After pulling my wet hair back into a ponytail, I brushed my teeth with the half-empty bottle of water that Tricia had left on the sink.

"That was quick," Tricia said as I walked over to my suitcase to grab my shorts and tank top. I dressed and we headed on our way. The large one-story building from last night was a lot busier in the morning light. Not that you could tell it was morning, the only sign of natural light was coming through the small window located above the entryway door. Tricia and I flawlessly maneuvered our way through the crowds of people and exited the building. The heat I had been expecting yesterday hit me in the face immediately. The moisture in the air made the humidity at home feel refreshing.

"I feel like I'm in the sauna at my gym," Tricia said fanning herself with her hand.

I looked down at the paperwork we had been given which included a map of the village. "I think we have to go over to this one." I pointed to the building right next door.

The building was almost identical to the one where we were staying. In fact, all the buildings were pretty much the same. They were all one story, white exteriors with red roofs and very few windows. There was a small room off to the side where we were told to report, with a Hispanic-looking woman seated behind a long wooden table.

"Hello," she said with a Spanish accent. "Can I please have your names?"

We gave her the information as she looked through a huge accordion file, pulling out our paperwork, and handing us each a paper-clipped stack of papers with our names on it. There was also an ID badge containing our names and pictures that we had submitted months ago. She went over each page in detail, explaining that they would try to assign certain patients to us, but it was very hard to stick to a day-to-day routine due to the overwhelming number of people in need. She informed us that there were other villages nearby that may need our assistance if their medical team became overwhelmed, but for right now this was where we would be most needed. We were officially starting tomorrow, but she suggested that we use today to familiarize ourselves with our surroundings.

We walked back outside and into the stickiness. Just downhill was the small village where we'd be working. We made our way slowly down, apprehensive of the conditions that awaited us. When we reached the bottom, we saw a series of well-constructed huts and some actual buildings with several large medical tents intermingled amongst them. There were some homes that looked as if they were constructed of clay and others that looked like battered shacks, made of whatever material could be found. I had only seen these types of living conditions on TV and in *National Geographic* magazines, so to be here experiencing it in person was very surreal for me. There were practically as many goats walking around as people. We passed several boys chasing a soccer ball in an open area as two women dressed in traditional colorful African garb, each holding babies on their hips, looked on. There was a group of school-aged children gathered in a circle intently listening to an older woman sitting in the middle reading them a story. The villagers seemed to be content with their lifestyle, seemingly unaware of the disease that prevailed. Most of them seemed unaware and unfazed by our presence. Others would just nod their heads and smile.

We finally reached the medical building. Inside was a series of beds in open wards with curtains in between each bed to divide them.

There were about twenty-five beds per ward, an intensive care unit, a small laboratory, an emergency department, several offices, and a small pharmacy. The electricity was supplied the same way that it was to the building that we were staying in, by large generators.

"Hello, Dr. Vallia and Dr. Aller," an older Asian gentleman said as he approached us, reading our IDs. He introduced himself as Dr. Chen and shook our hands.

It seemed as if every bed was filled, and it suddenly occurred to me just how seriously in need these people were. "Well, Dr. Chen, we were told that we didn't need to officially start working until tomorrow, but it seems like you have your hands full. Is there anything that we can do to help out?" I asked.

"That would be most helpful. But first let me familiarize you with some things." He led us to a large storage cabinet, showing us where all the supplies were kept then gave us a brief tour of the facility. We walked through the rows of beds, where he explained that each bed had a number by which each patient was identified. I began to think of how impersonal it was to be referred to as a number instead of a name. Then I heard Charles' voice telling me not to get attached emotionally while I was here. I tried to dismiss my prior thought, until I focused my attention on a little boy who looked to be about seven years old. He seemed so scared and lonely, and I immediately began to wonder if he was alone. Many of the children here were orphans, losing their families to the diseases that ran rampant. Dr. Chen caught me staring at the little boy, confirming what I already knew.

"That's Akin, he has malaria. He lost his father about a year ago to it, and his mother just passed away last week," Dr. Chen said.

I walked over to the little boy's bed. I could see dried-up tears staining his face, and my heart sank when I thought of him suffering all alone.

"Hi," I said. He looked at me with big brown doe eyes and smiled. I knew he couldn't understand a word I was saying, but just my presence seemed to put him at ease. Charles' words were already out of my head. I had become emotionally attached within the first few minutes of being here.

"He has a list of medications that need to be administered yet today, if you would like to tend to him," Dr. Chen said. "At this point we are just trying to keep him comfortable and keep his fever from going any higher."

"Comfortable? Will he recover?" I asked.

He explained to me the type of malaria the boy had contracted, which I already knew from my medical studies, was the worst form to have. Eventually all his major organs would shut down. My heart dropped as I looked at him, now knowing his fate. I grabbed his chart hanging on the edge of his bed and started reading it over. He had just turned eight years old two months ago. Everyone in his family was gone—he was alone in this world. I quickly gathered his meds and gave him a smile. "This will just be a little pinch." He clenched as I administered the IV into his fragile little vein. It would only be a matter of minutes before the medication would take effect and lull him to sleep, so I sat by his bedside until his eyes closed and his labored breathing became more relaxed.

I was amazed at how quickly the unofficial first day of work flew by. The number of patients I had seen in one day was more than I typically would see in a week back home. I couldn't believe that there were so many sick children in one place, basically covering every age group. I made one last round, checking on everyone I had seen for the day, saving my last stop for my favorite patient. I smiled as I looked in at little Akin lying in his bed, even though my heart was aching for him. Here was a little boy who should be out enjoying life, playing baseball or learning to ride a bike, but instead he was lying in this bed waiting to die. I knew this was part of my job, the part that I was hoping I would never have to see, but being in this place, a child dying was an all-too-common event. Still groggy from the medication, he managed a smile back. I sat by his bedside for a little longer just watching every breath he took, hoping my presence gave him a sense that someone did care. I finally got up when I saw that he had fallen into a deep sleep. Checking his IV one last time, I caressed his little face gently, whispering, "Good night, sweet boy," with a heavy heart and tears in my eyes.

CHAPTER 3

The weeks were flying by and before I knew it, I had reached my two-month milestone. Little Akin was still hanging in there, having a better reaction to the medication than expected. I didn't want to get a false sense of optimism, so I decided to hope for the best but expect the worst. I was starting to get accustomed to my routine, my rock-hard bed, and sulfur-smelling showers. I was even finding myself thinking of Jake less. The thing that I couldn't get used to was talking to my dad just once a week. I looked forward to our weekly call more than anything. It made me feel like he was in the next room instead of halfway across the world, even if it was only for five minutes. He always assured me that everything was fine. I had never been able to gauge his mood, even by looking at him. He was always good at masking when anything was bothering him. He told me that he had gone for his physical, which was long overdue. It made me happy that he had kept his promise to go. I would hang up each time feeling the same homesickness as always, but quickly snapped out of it once I began focusing on work.

I had finally felt like I had a good night's sleep for the first time since I'd arrived. I woke up feeling refreshed, even though it felt like it was already 90 degrees. The bags that had taken up residence under my eyes for the past week were finally gone, and my suntanned face was glowing. I brushed my teeth and decided I didn't want to wear my hair back today, even though I knew I would regret it later in the day in the hot blazing sun. I slid my ponytail holder on my wrist, knowing It would only be a matter of time before it went into my hair.

Tricia was already dressed and pacing the floor waiting for me. We were attending a seminar that was mandatory for all available staff. "Ready?" she asked in her bubbly voice.

"Can't we just skip this?" I asked as I walked out of the

bathroom.

"Be happy—you're having a good hair day!" Tricia said, touching my hair briefly as we exited the room.

We walked into the large windowless meeting room that was already filled with people, finding two seats together in the second row. The seminar was to give a brief overview of the current statistics of outbreaks, the area's most in need, and to answer any questions that we might have. The guest speaker was Dr. Julian Kiron, a pediatric oncologist. He had been here several times to assist in pediatric cancer outbreaks that had been occurring recently, and was well known in the medical world as one of the most up-and-coming doctors in his field. I had read many articles about him and was curious to see the face behind the name. Although I had heard he was a dynamic speaker, I really wasn't very interested in hearing anything he had to say today—my mind was a million miles away.

Tricia read over the agenda for the seminar while I used mine to fan myself and shoo away the bugs. I just wanted to get this over with so I could go and check on Akin. As I looked around at the other attendees, I focused my attention on a strikingly handsome man making his way across the room as everyone stopped him to talk. He was well over six feet tall with a perfect body, appearing to be in his early thirties, with very strong features and perfectly pitched lips. His jet-black hair was a stark contrast to his crystal blue eyes that could be seen even from across the room. Tricia mumbled something to me, but I wasn't paying attention to her, I was too focused on this stranger who had just entered the room.

The room became silent as a short, heavy-set woman approached the podium and introduced herself as Dr. Courtney Jones. I got butterflies in my stomach when the handsome blue-eyed stranger took the empty seat next to me. I tried to focus as best I could on what was being said as I checked off every item on the agenda in anticipation of it being over. I rested my head against the back of the chair and rolled my eyes whenever someone would slow down the process and ask a question.

"Bored?" the handsome, blue-eyed man sitting next to me leaned over and whispered.

My stomach fluttered. *God, the color of his eyes is so intense. They don't even look real!*

"Huh?" I replied, taken off guard. "Oh, well, I just have a ton of other things I could be doing right now," I whispered as I finally regained my composure.

His boyish double-dimpled grin made me melt, and I felt myself instantly smiling back. "Well, it's almost over," he said.

"Yeah, just one more stuffy doctor's boring speech to sit through. I'm sure he's so full of himself that he'll probably drag it out forever, talking about how great he is."

His smile turned into a lighthearted chuckle. I really didn't think it was that funny, but obviously, he found some humor in it. Tricia slapped me lightly on the arm to pay attention, but it was of no use–I was much more interested in this beautiful man sitting next to me. I caught myself glancing at him once more–suddenly this seminar wasn't so boring after all.

Dr. Jones gave a brief history of Dr. Kiron's achievements, which most of us already knew. "It gives me great pleasure to introduce Dr. Kiron," Dr. Jones announced.

I was shocked when I saw the handsome blue-eyed man sitting next to me approach the podium. My face heated, and I knew I was probably turning beet red as I sank in my chair, wanting to find a way to escape from my humiliation. He flashed me an endearing smile before he began to speak.

"He's gorgeous!" Tricia remarked.

Dr. Kiron's voice was just as lovely to listen to as his face was to look at. He seemed poised and confident. I couldn't stop staring at his eyes, and a few times, I was certain he had noticed as he glanced over my way. His speech finally ended and I had no clue what it was even about, I was still in awe over Dr. Kiron.

"Wow, I never expected him to be so young," Tricia said, finally spotting James, who was seated all the way in the back, probably sneaking in somewhere during the middle. "I've got to talk to James," she said, speeding off to get to him, leaving me behind to make my way through the crowd.

I stood there trying to plan my departure, catching a glimpse of Dr. Kiron standing by the exit, fielding questions from people as they were leaving.

"Need some help?" I asked, noticing Dr. Jones dragging the podium back to the corner of the room and putting chairs back into place.

"Sure, if you got the time to spare," she answered appreciatively.

I looked back at the crowd of people bombarding the exit and Dr. Kiron. "Looks like I'm going to be here a while!" I said, wanting to avoid the crowd and the embarrassment of facing him again.

She thanked me about a million times after we had put everything back into place and then ran off to do her rounds. I was just about to exit myself when *he* entered the room. Dr. Gorgeous, Handsome, Beautiful–take your pick.

"Hello," Dr. Kiron said in his charismatic voice.

"Hey," I answered, pushing my hair behind my ears, something I always found myself doing when I was nervous. "That really was a wonderful speech–not boring at all." I tried to redeem myself for my prior comments. The truth was, I hadn't heard one word of it because I was too busy staring at him the whole time.

"Thank you. So, I didn't brag too much about myself for your liking?" he asked sounding somewhat smug.

"Oh sorry...I didn't–it was really good." My face burned. He looked more like a model than a doctor, and I was pretty sure he knew it. "I'm Katrina Vallia." I extended my hand.

He took my hand very gently. "It's a pleasure to meet you, Dr. Vallia.

"I thought that I had left my tape recorder in here, but I guess not," he said, giving the room the once-over.

"Oh, that really stinks," I said.

"Not a big deal. I have about ten others in my room," he replied.

I clenched my notebook to my chest. "Well, it was so nice to meet you," I said.

"You too, Dr. Vallia."

I was melting once again in his smile. "Kat," I blurted out of nowhere.

"What was that?" He looked puzzled.

"My friends call me Kat–I mean, you can call me Kat." *What am I saying? I sound like such a fool.*

I managed a smile and headed out the door while he stayed behind.

"Hey, Kat!" he hollered.

"Yes?" I pushed my hair out of the way as I turned around.

"Hopefully I'll see you around." The same beautiful smile adorned his face.

"Sure," was all I was able to get out with a shaky voice. I walked out of the room into the bright sunlight grinning from ear to ear, feeling like a teenager.

Tricia's voice broke me from my euphoria. "There you are! We need you in infirmary C." She grabbed my hand as we briskly walked over.

"What's going on?" I asked.

"It's Akin. He's not doing so well."

My heart sank. In the back of my mind, I kept thinking that by some miracle he would overcome this, and now any hope had been washed away. Over the past few months, he had become my first priority. I had been taking care of him adamantly every day, sitting with him for hours after my rounds were done just so he would know that someone was there. Even though we didn't speak the same language, it seemed as if there were no barriers between us.

His eyes were half-closed when I made it to his bedside, unable to stand the sight of the flies crawling over his face, I sharply shooed them away. He appeared much weaker than he had just ten hours ago when I had last seen him.

"Hi, Akin, it's Dr. Kat." His dry little lips managed a tiny smile when he saw me.

"How is he?" I asked Charles, who had been attending to him.

"We're not able to get the fever down, he has an underlying infection, and his kidneys are shutting down." I looked back at Akin and then at Charles, who had been up half the night with emergencies.

"Charles, get some sleep, you look exhausted. I'll stay with him." Charles looked at me both sympathetically and disapprovingly.

"Kat, I told you that you can't get too close to any of your patients here. It's only setting you up for heartbreak."

"I'm okay," I said, looking away. "Now go get some rest."

Charles put his hand on my shoulder as he walked away. I pulled a chair closer to Akin's bed and took his hand. "I'm right here, Akin," I whispered. He managed another little smile at the sound of my voice. I began to tell him the bedtime story that my mom would tell me when I was a little girl. He listened, smiling every now and then. I knew that he couldn't understand my language, but the sound of my voice seemed to comfort him. As he drifted in and out of sleep, I made sure to keep checking his vital stats. When his heart rate began to drop, I knew that there wasn't anything else that could be done for him. My throat burned and tears filled my eyes. *I am not going to do this. I promised Charles.* That promise was broken when Akin took his last breath and the tears began to flow down my face.

"Hey, are you okay?" I looked up to find Dr. Kiron, standing beside me.

I nodded and tried to gain my composure. "This is my fault. I was warned about getting too close with anyone." I tried to mask the uneasiness in my voice as I wiped the tears from my eyes.

"You're only human. Besides, there are always exceptions to the rules," he reassured me.

I looked at him, puzzled. Seeming to sense my confusion, he explained. "There's always someone or something that will make you feel so strongly that you will go against everything you are taught or planned. He was the exception to your rule."

I nodded as I wiped the final tear streaming down my face. "Brave boy," I said in a whisper, looking down at Akin's tiny body lying in the bed.

"What?" he asked.

"His name was Akin, which means 'brave boy.' I couldn't think of a more fitting name for him," I said, turning back to Dr. Kiron looking directly into his eyes.

"This is the hardest part about this job."

"Well this is the first patient that I've ever lost. I usually just work at getting them better," I answered. "But I can only imagine, being an oncologist you must see your fair share of heartache."

He nodded.

"I'm just glad that I was here with him, so he wasn't alone. This poor little boy had no one."

When the coroner came in to take Akin away, I didn't want to cry again and look like a babbling fool to Dr. Kiron, so I stood just outside the curtain gathering my thoughts. I was shocked when I looked down at my watch and realized that it was already 6 p.m. I had spent the entire afternoon with Akin. I heard Dr. Kiron giving the time and cause of death then came out from behind the curtain writing something on his clipboard.

"Thanks for doing that for me. I just couldn't handle seeing them take him away."

"No problem," he said, still writing on his clipboard.

"Well, I'll see you, Dr. Kiron." I pushed my hair behind my ear again.

I started to walk away when I heard him say, "Julian."

"What?" I turned back to look at him.

"My friends call me Julian." His smile showed off his perfectly placed dimples.

"Okay, Julian, I'll have to remember that." I returned his smile as I walked out into the hot sticky evening, feeling overwhelmed with emotions. Thinking of Akin and feeling so sad and at the same time, imagining Dr. Kiron's beautiful blue eyes, which strangely helped me smile through the tears.

CHAPTER 4

The short walk up the hill from the village to my room seemed never-ending, for which I was somewhat grateful. It allowed me time to clear my head. I knew that Tricia was probably back at the room, and I had to mentally prepare myself for her sunny outlook on life. After today, I couldn't think of anything sunny at all, until Dr. Kiron's face flashed into my mind. *Must stop thinking about him. He's just like Jake, incredibly good-looking, absorbed in his career and more than likely a ladies' man.* It was as if Mother Nature sensed my mood, all of a sudden, the skies opened up and a torrential rain began to fall. Oddly enough, I didn't walk any faster. Instead, I stopped and stood in the rain, letting the moisture envelop me. The smell of the rain here was not the same sweet smell of a thunderstorm back home. It was more of a stale muddy stench, but even that didn't bother me tonight. As I stood there looking at the dark quiet village just at the bottom of the hill, the rain drops hit me on the head and rolled down my face. I knew I had to get past the heartache I felt for these people. I had a job that I was sent here to do, but just for tonight, I couldn't help but sense the sorrow that surrounded this place. When I felt like I had finally gained enough composure to deal with the world, I continued my walk back to my room. I was totally exhausted and ignoring my hunger. The only thing that gave me comfort was the thought of my rock-hard bed.

I turned my key in the door, still prepping myself for Tricia. To my surprise and contentment, she wasn't there, instead I found a note on my pillow with little smiley faces on it:

Kat,

James and I are at the cafeteria grabbing a bite to eat if you care to join us!!

Love – Tricia xoxo

Even her handwriting seemed cheerful. Normally I loved her sunny persona, but tonight no one could break me free of my melancholic state of mind. Then I immediately thought of the one and only person who could—my dad. I grabbed the towel hanging on the bathroom door and dried my hair as best as I could, slicking it back in a ponytail. After throwing some cool water on my face, I looked at my watch and quickly did some calculating in my head—it was roughly 1 p.m. at home. I was hoping I would be able to catch him between his errands. I exited my room and walked down the narrow dark hallway. There were only two phones and normally a line waiting to use them, but tonight there was no sign of anyone. I dialed the familiar number on the keypad and was becoming a little despondent when he didn't pick up by the third ring. Relief swept over me when I heard my dad's voice on the other end after the fourth ring.

"Hello?" he answered in a hurried voice.

"Hey, Dad, whatya doing?" I asked as I stomped on a fire ant crawling beneath me.

"Just laying some tile in the bathroom. Kat, is everything okay?" He sounded surprised to be hearing from me on a Thursday instead of our usual Sunday call.

"Yup," I said, hoping he wouldn't sense I was lying. But it was too late—he already knew.

"Kat, what's the matter?" he asked, concerned.

It was as if I were just waiting for him to ask the magic question so I could unload all my emotions. I told him all about Akin and how helpless I felt over not being able to save him. My dad listened intently to me. I didn't pause once to take a breath, and by the time I was done, I felt like a huge weight had been lifted off my shoulders.

"It's a whole different world than what you are used to," he said. "It doesn't make you a bad person because you feel for these people. It would make you a bad person if you didn't," he continued. He had a knack for always reaffirming what I already knew deep down inside.

"Thanks, Dad, now tell me about this tile," I said, trying to shift to a happier subject.

"Well, I was going to surprise you, but you caught me. I'm re-tiling your bathroom."

"Oh, is it the terracotta?" I asked excitedly.

"Can we leave something as a little surprise?"

"I guess," I answered with laughter. "What made you decide to take on this project?"

"I had a little extra time before my doctor's appointment this morning, so I went into the tile shop right across the street from his office, and here I am laying tile."

The tile talk had completely gone out of my mind when I heard my dad mention he had a doctor's appointment. "I thought your doctor's appointment was the other day?"

"I just had to finish some tests," he said in a dismissing tone. "Can't wait for you to see this tile," he continued, trying to change the subject.

"Dad, what type of tests?" I was persistent.

"Just routine blood work, Kat. Nothing to worry about."

"Are you sure that was all?"

"I promise you, that was all."

Even though I hoped he was telling the truth, something in the back of my mind told me that there were little bits of information that he was leaving out. I felt so helpless, being so far away and not knowing exactly what was going on. Growing up, the only time he would ever take a sick day from work was to care for me when I had gotten sick. He never complained when he wasn't feeling well, so for him to be downplaying a situation wouldn't surprise me.

"Well, Dad, I'll let you get back to your tile, I'll call you again on Sunday, love you!" I blew kisses into the phone.

"Love you too, Kat," he replied.

As the line disconnected I listened to the dial tone for a few seconds before putting it back on the receiver. I was probably being paranoid, but the thought of anything being wrong with my father scared me to death. I tried to put it in the back of my mind. I had to give him some credit; I'm sure if something were wrong he would let me know. I headed back to my room, not paying attention, walking right into Dr. Kiron's rock-hard chest.

"Oh, I'm so sorry," I said, looking up at him and realizing how much taller he was than me.

"Are you okay?" he said, grabbing my elbow.

"Yeah, just not paying attention," I said, somewhat embarrassed. I gave him a smile and apologized again, continuing on my way.

"Hey, Kat!"

I turned to look at him with butterflies in my stomach.

"Are you hungry?" he asked.

"Well, actually I kind of am."

"I was getting ready to go grab something, do you care to join me?"

My head was saying, *no, Kat, just walk away, this is the type of guy that you traveled miles away to forget,* but my heart was screaming, *yes!* "Sure," I answered quickly. *I was hungry after all, so what was the harm of having some company to eat dinner with?*

We walked to the cafeteria, which was the next building over, as I tried to think of conversation without sounding stupid. The rain had stopped and there was a warm breeze swaying the trees back and forth. He held the door for me as we entered the large room identical to all the others—windowless with cinder block walls. I scanned the area quickly, looking for Tricia and James. Only one of the tables was occupied with five people, none of which were them. I stood back as one of the men from the table got up and walked over to Dr. Kiron to shake his hand and introduce himself. After a brief exchange, we walked over to decide what to eat. The cafeteria was set up very much like a primitive version of the one from my high school, except the food in my high school cafeteria was much better, which wasn't saying much.

"Well, this all looks so appealing," I joked.

"Oh, come on, this looks great," he said, laughing as he took a spoonful of what looked like some type of meat with noodles, dropping it back into the silver pan that it was in.

"I think I will just go with salad," he said, laughing.

The food here was flown in weekly and was anything but appetizing. I found myself basically living off the four large boxes of power bars that I had brought with me. I felt myself get in a bit of a panic when I opened my last box the other day. Even though I was starving, I couldn't bring myself to eat that horrible noodle concoction. I was way too hungry to be satisfied with a salad. So instead, I opted for one of the huge slices of chocolate cake that were out for dessert.

"Wow, that's a healthy dinner." He chuckled. I laughed too as I licked some of the icing from my finger. We sat down at a smaller table, located on the other end of the room from where the others were sitting, and much to my surprise, the cake was pretty good.

Dr. Kiron leaned back in his chair and intertwined his fingers behind his head. He made no attempt to hide that he was assessing me up and down, making me feel a little uncomfortable. "So, how long have you been here for?" he asked.

"Two months," I answered, taking a mouthful of cake.

"Well, you get used to the food after a while," he said.

"Somehow, I don't think so." I crinkled my nose.

I began to talk nonstop, something I always did when I was nervous. We talked about where I was from, what college and medical school I had gone to, where I had done my residency, and of course, I told him all about my dad. After a while, it dawned on me that I didn't come up for air. I apologized for being such a chatterbox, but he never looked bored by anything I was saying. He listened closely and in fact, even seemed amused. I did manage to find out that this was his third time here, and he had been to an array of other countries as well. He grew up in Upstate New York and Chicago was now his home when he wasn't traveling the world. He was on staff at Chicago Pediatric Hospital, which I already knew. He had an older sister who lived in Colorado and his parents lived in Florida. The only thing he did fail to mention was his age, which I was somewhat curious to know.

"Can I ask you a personal question?" I asked taking another bite of my cake, which I had been neglecting with all of the talking I had been doing.

"Sure," he said.

"How old are you?"

"Was that all? That's nothing personal, thirty-two," he said, exposing his adorable dimples again.

"Wow." I took a sip of water. "You're only four years older than me, and I haven't achieved even one percent of your accomplishments."

"It's just a lot of hard work and perseverance," he said. "Sometimes I feel like I live at the hospital, but that's the price you have to pay. Can I ask you a personal question now?" he asked.

"Um, sure," I replied nervously.

"Where the heck does a tiny girl like you put all that cake?"

I began to laugh. "Oh, I have a massive sweet tooth. I think my body has been fooled into thinking that sugar is good for it," I joked.

I found myself captivated once again by his piercing blue eyes as he gazed at me while I wondered if he realized just how sexy he was.

"So how does your boyfriend feel about you coming here?"

Geez, he didn't waste any time finding out what he wanted to know.

"Don't have one," I replied.

"Really?" He raised his eyebrows as if surprised by my answer.

"How about your girlfriend?" *Two could play this game.*

"Don't have one," he said almost mimicking me.

"Oh, let me guess you have three or four," I joked.

His smiled widened as if he were entertained by my sarcasm. "Umm, no, I don't do the girlfriend thing."

"Oh, are you gay?" I asked.

He choked on the sip of water he had just taken. "No, I didn't say that. I just don't have committed relationships with *women*. I don't have time for that with my job."

"Oh, got ya," I said, getting the message he was trying to convey. Which was he just had sex–no strings attached. Yes, he was just like Jake, but at least he didn't try to hide it.

"Well, I better get going," I said, feeling a little uncomfortable with where the conversation was headed and not wanting him to think that I had any plans on being his next one-night stand.

I got up and pushed my chair in while he remained seated. He was sitting back in the same position that he was in when we first sat down; leaning back in his chair with his fingers intertwined behind his head. "Good night, Dr. Kiron," I said bashfully.

"Julian," he corrected me.

"Okay, good night, *Julian*," I said sounding a little more sarcastic than I had intended. He didn't seem to mind–in fact I think he liked it. As I walked away, I could feel his beautiful eyes burning into my back. When I reached the door, I couldn't help but turn around to look at him. He was still gazing at me–his blue eyes were intense even from across the room. I stood in the doorway for a moment and gave him a quick smile before exiting. Yes, Dr. Kiron was beyond handsome and made my stomach do somersaults. My head was telling me to stay as far away from him as possible. My heart on the other hand…

CHAPTER 5

I woke up exactly two minutes before my alarm was set to go off, fumbling to turn it off to avoid hearing the most dreaded sound of the day. I stretched my entire body before getting out of bed while Tricia was still snoring away. I decided to be a little selfish and have some uninterrupted time in the bathroom before I woke her. It was like playing a game of *Twister* in the morning with both of us getting ready at the same time. I figured she would appreciate an extra five minutes of sleep anyway.

Once I finished up and was dressed, I took a seat on Tricia's bed, giving her a gentle nudge as she turned over and mumbled something incoherent.

"Wake up, sleeping beauty," I said, laughing at her.

"What time is it?" She sat up in a state of confusion with her short spiky hair sticking up all over the place.

"It's time to get up," I answered.

Tricia flung her feet over the side of the bed, sitting up next to me. "What happened to you last night?" She ran her fingers through her short hair.

"I spent the day with Akin, I wanted to be with him when he—" I couldn't get the word out.

"Oh, Kat, I'm sorry," Tricia said, grabbing my hand.

I felt a little guilty about leaving the part about Dr. Kiron out, but it was just too early in the morning to be bombarded with questions.

"I'll wait for you," I said as she gathered her clothes and headed into the bathroom. As I sat on my bed, I closed my eyes and thought about the sadness of yesterday, bracing myself that Akin probably wouldn't be the last child I would see pass away while I was here. I thought about Dr. Kiron and how this was his third time coming here, I couldn't imagine myself ever returning to such horrible devastation. It took a special kind of person, and I knew I clearly was not that type.

I was so deep in thought that I didn't even hear the water turn off, surprised when Tricia walked out of the bathroom fully dressed.

"Ready?" I asked, handing her a power bar and a bottle of water.

"Let's go," she said enthusiastically.

We arrived to set up for the long day ahead. There was already a line of people waiting to receive their much-needed inoculations. The building was packed with individuals coming in and out of the medical ward, and Tricia and I wasted no time, working diligently for hours administering one shot after another. Tricia took advantage of the little lull in the action, telling me about the problems she had encountered with a patient yesterday. I listened closely offering her some advice, when I looked up to see Dr. Kiron standing patiently at the table. This time I was the one who was checking *him* out from head to toe.

"Hey, Kat, sorry to interrupt, but have you seen Dr. Tylo anywhere?" There was a shortage of OB/GYNs on staff and Dr. Tylo was one of the few.

"No, sorry I haven't." I tried to hide my reaction from Tricia kicking me under the table.

"Well if you do, can you please tell him he's needed in seventeen?"

"Sure, is everything okay?"

"Just a baby that's about to be born in a few hours, and the mother needs to be examined, that's just not my specialty."

"No problem," I answered.

"Oh, Julian, by the way, this is Dr. Tricia Aller." I felt Tricia staring at me in anticipation, waiting for an introduction.

Tricia immediately jumped out of her seat to shake his hand, and for the first time since I had known her, she was speechless. Dr. Kiron flashed his beautiful dimples at her as he shook her hand.

"Well, I'll see you guys later." He gave me an extra smile before being whisked away by another doctor who had been impatiently waiting for him the whole time we were talking.

"Kat? Julian?" Tricia began with her interrogation. "Did I miss something? When did you become on a first-name basis with Dr. Kiron?"

"I was going to tell you, I swear."

"Well," Tricia said, raising her eyebrows. "I'm waiting!"

"Well after you ditched me for James yesterday," I laughed. "I got stuck in the crowd waiting to exit and then I ended up meeting him."

"Okay and just from that chance encounter he's now *Julian?*" She raised her eyebrows.

"Well not exactly," I replied hesitantly. "We had dinner together last night, or should I say I had cake." I figured I wasn't going to get away without giving her all the details, so I bit the bullet and told her every last one. Tricia was completely absorbed in what I was saying, asking questions every now and then.

"Wow," she said once she was satisfied with all the information. "Well he would be a quick fix to help you forget about Jake," she added.

"Oh please, Tricia, he only asked me to dinner because he felt bad about how upset I was over Akin."

"I don't know. The way he looked at you seems to be a little more than sympathy."

"Keep dreaming," I said, turning around to help a patient who had just walked in.

The afternoon picked up with more people coming in. Tricia and I didn't really have any extra time to further discuss last night, which I was very appreciative of. I didn't want my little encounter with Dr. Kiron to be blown up into something it wasn't. Even though seeing him today did release some butterflies in my stomach.

"Thank God its five o'clock, our sentence is over." Tricia put her head down on the table.

"I'm starving," I said, realizing that we hadn't eaten anything but our power bars all day. "Let's go get something to eat."

We packed up all the supplies and placed them in the lock box. James was just finishing up for the day as well. He was planning on joining us for dinner when he suddenly disappeared, and Tricia ran off to find him. I gathered my belongings and was waiting patiently for the two of them to return when I caught a glimpse of Julian entering the building. I tried my best to convince myself that the butterflies I was feeling in my stomach once again were really hunger pains. He seemed to be absorbed in a deep conversation with two other doctors, wrapping up his discussion as he approached me.

"You're still here?" he asked.

"Yeah, just finished up." I couldn't help but focus my attention on the huge raised blister on his arm. "What happened to your arm?"

"Oh, I think a spider got me." He glanced down at it as if it weren't a big deal.

"When did that happen?" I asked moving closer to examine it. It was blue in the center and ringed by redness.

"I don't know, I guess sometime today." He dismissed it.

"You have to treat that, it looks like it's getting infected."

I automatically ripped open one of the antiseptic pads that was on the table and began cleaning the wound on his arm. He looked at me as if he was taken a little off guard by my abrupt reaction but didn't resist. Once I was comfortable that it was thoroughly clean, I applied a compression bandage tightly around it.

"Thanks," he said as he looked down at his arm and then settled his gaze back on me.

Tricia and James' bickering broke the awkward silence. "C'mon, James, we're going to die of starvation waiting for you," Tricia complained.

James seemed to be paying her no mind and quickly came walking over to where Julian and I were standing. "Kat, please make her stop complaining." He rolled his eyes at Tricia.

"Dr. Kiron, this is James," I said, still trying to get accustomed to calling him Julian.

"Nice to meet you," Julian said, extending his hand.

"You too, Dr. Kiron," James said.

"Please, call me Julian," he responded as he looked over at me as if to remind me as well.

Julian possessed such an allure. Besides being stunningly good-looking, there was something about his personality that attracted me like a magnet.

Tricia's grin was a mile wide. "What happened to your arm?" she asked noticing the bandage.

"Just a spider bite, it's fine. Kat took care of it."

"Oh," Tricia said, raising her eyebrows at me. I looked away trying to ignore her.

James invited Julian to have dinner with us. He declined, explaining he needed to head over to one of the other villages, which was an hour away, to tend to some patients. I was a little disappointed at first but then my head started winning the latest battle over my heart, knowing it was probably for the best.

"Wow, that's a long drive to be going alone in the dark," Tricia said to Julian as she looked at me.

"Nah, I do it all the time; I'm used to it," he said, brushing her off.

"But still, I bet a little company wouldn't hurt?" she continued. I shook my head and gave her a dirty look, knowing where she was going with this.

Julian looked from the cabinet that he was taking supplies from and asked her, "Why, are you volunteering to come?"

"Umm, no, I mean not me, but maybe Kat would like to join you." If looks could kill, Tricia would have been dead by the expression on my face.

Julian closed the cabinet door, double-checking everything on his list. I was hoping that he wasn't going to take her seriously. "Did you want to go, Kat?" he asked.

I was always bad with answering questions when on the spot. I was especially bad when I had two beautiful blue eyes looking at me. "Um, sure," I blurted out.

"Okay, I'm leaving in about five minutes, after I load all this up," he said, grabbing boxes of equipment that he had taken out of the cabinet. James gave him a hand carrying the stuff, while I waited until they were well out of earshot.

"Tricia, what is wrong with you!" I said in a loud whisper.

"Why?" she chuckled.

"For one, I am starving and two, I'm tired!" I answered.

She walked over to her bag that was sitting on the table and took out a power bar. "Here, this is probably better than anything you would eat in that cafeteria anyway, and it's my last one." She sounded like she was doing an honorable thing by giving it to me.

I snatched it out of her hand and took a big bite. "Mmm, it's so good." I rubbed in the fact that I was eating her last power bar until we suddenly broke into laughter. I quickly retreated, letting her know that I was still not pleased with her.

"Oh, Kat, where is your sense of adventure?" she asked as my smile disappeared.

"It's in bed, where I should be going in a couple of hours, not to another depressing village, for God knows how long with some guy that I hardly even know."

"So, you get to know him. You wanted help getting over Jake, didn't you?" Tricia raised her eyebrows.

"Yes, I want to get over Jake on my own, not by getting

involved with some guy who's just like him!"

"Why do you think that?" Tricia asked

"Oh please, Tricia, look at him, he's only thirty-two years old and already a very successful doctor, and need I state the obvious—totally gorgeous!"

"Well, he certainly doesn't seem full of himself," Tricia said.

"Yeah, well you didn't have dinner with him last night, he actually came out and told me that he doesn't have relationships with women he only—"

Tricia signaled for me to be quiet when the door opened. "Oh, it's just you," she replied upon seeing just James entering.

"Oh sorry, who did you expect?" James asked sarcastically.

I sat and watched in amusement as Tricia and James bantered back and forth. I was just as guilty as Tricia. I was the one who was always trying to get her to see James as more than just a friend, but I had a valid reason for my persistence—she and James made the perfect couple. I, on the other hand, had nothing at all in common with Julian besides the fact that we were both doctors. He wasn't satisfied with just being a *doctor,* he wanted to be the best at what he did, whereas, I was perfectly fine with being Dr. Kat, community pediatrician.

"Are you ready?" Julian asked as he came back in to grab the last of his supplies.

I nodded and gathered up my belongings as Tricia stopped her chattering with James for a brief second.

"Bye, Kat, have fun!" she shouted with a full-faced grin. My only response to her was a shake of my head and a quick flip of my middle finger. James was clueless, looking at the two of us as if we were speaking some foreign language.

I stepped outside for the first time since early morning. Julian was loading his last box into a black Jeep and talking to one of the villagers who spoke very good English. They finished up their conversation as the man looked over at me.

"Nwanyi marama," he said to Julian.

"Yes, very," Julian replied.

I felt a bit uncomfortable and at the same time curious as to what the man had said to him. I tried repeating the word over and over in my head to make a mental note and look it up when I got a chance. It was of no use, it was totally out of my head within seconds.

I got into the Jeep and put on my seat belt. "You know that's really kind of rude?" I said to Julian when he got in.

"What?" he was clueless.

"If you have something to say about me, then you should at least have the common courtesy to say it in a language I understand."

A smile stretched across his face and he began to laugh. "Only if I was saying something bad and trust me, it wasn't bad." He raised an eyebrow at me. *Why did he have to be so handsome?*

I suddenly got a second wind. Maybe Tricia was right and a change of scenery would help break up the momentum of this humdrum place. The sun was setting in the distance. It was almost as beautiful as the ones at home, but nothing could compare to a Cape May sunset. The sky would light up in vibrant shades of pink and peach as the sun slowly disappeared into the bay signaling the end of another day. Just thinking about it made me smile.

The ride to the village was long and bumpy. This time Julian did all the talking, pointing out different areas of interest along the way. It all looked the same to me, but he swore that certain areas in the thick of the trees were beautiful waterfalls. I decided to take his word for it. I wasn't going to take a chance of getting eaten by a wild animal. He found it very humorous when I expressed that opinion to him.

"What's so funny? This is Africa, right? You know, lions, gorillas?"

"No, you are absolutely right, you're just funny," he said. "You better watch out, the monkeys have been known to jump down from the trees onto your head," he said, trying to sound serious. He began laughing even when I looked up through the open top of the Jeep and instinctively covered my head.

"Not funny," I said unable to hide my smile. "So, how many patients will you be seeing tonight?" I asked, trying to get a gauge on what time we would be back.

"Two. A seven-year-old and a ten-year-old. They're brothers."

"Oh, what type of cancer do they have?" I hoped that I could handle seeing this.

"Brain tumor."

"Both of them?" I asked, shocked at the coincidence of two brothers both having a brain tumor.

Julian then explained to me about the recent cancer outbreaks that had been affecting children in this region of Africa. He said that there was research being done to find out if it was an environmental issue. I was a little bit embarrassed when he started laughing. "Did you not hear a word in my speech the other day?"

"Well, you know, it was hot and crowded in there, and I was worried about Akin," I rambled on.

"R-i-g-h-t..." he said as he smiled as if he wasn't buying it.

"What? I was!" I smiled back.

It was just starting to get dark when we arrived at the village. This one seemed much more primitive than the one we were working at. There were no regular buildings at all, just huts. They didn't seem too well-constructed either. It looked as if the first heavy rain or wind would destroy them. The medical facility was a large tent, and the villagers didn't seem as friendly either. Julian grabbed some boxes from the back as one of the villagers came running over, grabbing the rest. This hospital was set up similar to the other but didn't have nearly as many beds. They only had three nurses on staff and two other doctors.

I followed Julian as he walked over to two little boys who I assumed were his patients. It was heartwarming to see a huge smile appear on the older boy's face as soon as he saw Julian.

"Dr. Julian," he said in broken English.

"Hey, Rapula, how are you feeling today?" He gave the boy a high-five.

He shook his head signaling that he was not well.

"Well, I brought this pretty lady with me today to make you feel better. This is Dr. Vallia," he said, introducing me to the little boy.

"You can call me Dr. Kat," I said, smiling at him.

I took both of the boys' vital stats for Julian as he prepared to administer them chemo. I was amazed how he took the boys' minds off what was going on by talking to them and telling them jokes. They apparently understood English pretty well, laughing at every punch line. Seeing the connection he had with these two boys was astonishing. He sat with them for another hour longer, ensuring they didn't have any negative effects from the chemo. Rapula pulled out a deck of UNO cards from the side of his bed. Julian indicated to me that he taught them how to play.

Tau, the younger boy, looked at me and then his older brother.

"Dr. Kat, play?" he asked in his best effort at English.

"Sure, but I have to warn you, I'm awesome at this game!"

Rapula dealt the cards. To my surprise, I was really having a good time. I expressed my excitement after finally winning the fourth round.

"I think she cheated," Julian joked to the boys.

Their laughter was contagious. My heart melted upon seeing how they were not letting cancer break their spirits. I knew that Julian had a lot to do with it as well. He truly had a gift, and tonight with these two boys, I had just witnessed why he was such a great doctor.

CHAPTER 6

"**Y**ou were really great with them," I commended Julian on the ride home.

"Thanks," he said.

The intense rain made the drive back even longer. It pelted the canvas top on the Jeep, sounding more like golf balls than raindrops. I kept up the conversation just enough, but I didn't want to distract him too much from driving. The narrow dirt roads were totally dark, and I was thoroughly impressed with how well he was handling driving in these conditions. I finally began to ramble on some more when I noticed the rain letting up.

"So, do you think they'll be okay?" I asked.

"It's hard to tell right now. If the tumors could be shrunk to a reasonable size and then removed, they have a great chance."

"Well, that sounds pretty hopeful."

Julian looked at me with doubt in his eyes. "It would be hopeful if there was someone here to perform the surgery."

"Oh," I said, losing my optimism. "Doesn't seeing all of this cancer make you scared to have kids some day?"

"No," he answered quickly. "I don't plan on having any."

He explained to me that he was the type of person that likes to give one hundred percent to whatever he does. He knew with the demands of his career, he would never be able to give that to a family, and he didn't want to feel any guilt over doing his job. I admired him for firmly knowing what he wanted out of life and not letting anything stand in his way. He was totally committed to his career. I certainly loved my job too, but I wouldn't let it interfere with having a family someday. Did that make me less of a doctor for feeling that way? Seeing how passionate he was about his career made me second guess a lot of my thinking.

"Wow, well that's great that you have a plan in place."

"Yup, I'm going to die a lonely old man," he joked. "What about you, Kat, you don't have a plan?" he asked, sounding more serious.

"Not really. I know I want to have kids someday. For right now, I'm pretty much happy with where I am with my life." I felt a little inadequate saying that to someone who was always striving to be more.

"So, there you go," he said. "You know what you want from your life someday. You have a plan too."

"Well, I guess you can say that. It's certainly not as grandiose as yours, but I suppose I do," I answered with a little doubt in my voice. The thought of me having a plan sounded a little ridiculous to myself. Half the time I couldn't even figure out what to wear to work in the morning. Forget planning out the rest of my life.

"What are you talking about? Being a mom is the most important job in the world," he said. "There's nothing wrong with wanting to have kids. It's just not for me," he added.

I opened up and shared the details of my breakup with Jake.

"Nothing justifies cheating. If he was unhappy with the way things were going then he should have confronted you about it or just broken up with you."

I was a little surprised by that statement. I just assumed that he wouldn't have a problem with being unfaithful, given his attitude about relationships. I could tell that he was speaking from experience, so I decided to come right out and ask him. He told me that he had been dating a girl all through medical school. To his surprise, she was cheating on him with his best friend, while he was away doing his fellowship.

"Geez, that's horrible," I said, feeling instant anger toward the girl who broke his heart.

"So, I guess he's not your best friend anymore," I asked, already knowing the answer. If I hadn't already, I could tell by the expression on his face.

I had to wonder if his past experience had something to do with his whole attitude on relationships.

The rain had completely stopped by the time we got back. Julian parked the Jeep in front of the medical building, and we walked up the hill together. I hadn't the slightest clue of the time, when I looked down at my watch, I was shocked to see that it was almost 2 a.m. Julian seemed unfazed when I told him the time, leading me to believe that getting very little sleep was a normal occurrence to him.

"Well, thanks for the company," he said when we entered the quiet building.

"Anytime. It was fun."

"Good night, Kat."

"Good night," I replied, turning the corner heading toward my room.

***

I hit the snooze button several times on my alarm but could no longer ignore it. Tricia was already up and gone. She and James had left extra early to go to one of the other villages. I slowly dragged myself to the bathroom, hoping a nice long shower would wake me up. To my dismay, it did absolutely nothing. After quickly dressing, I looked at the clock, I was happy to see that I had enough time to head to the cafeteria and get some much-needed breakfast.

"There you are," Charles said as he headed down the hallway while I was locking my door.

"Are you headed for breakfast?" I asked, happy to have a familiar face to eat with.

"Well I was going to skip breakfast today, but since you talked me into it, what the heck."

I was so hungry and planned on eating whatever they had to offer. That was until I saw that the eggs looked half-cooked, so I decided to go with the oatmeal and some fruit instead. Charles followed my lead and grabbed the same thing.

"So, what's going on, Kat? I feel like I haven't gotten a chance to catch up with you in a while," Charles said as we took a seat.

I told Charles about the exciting day I had had yesterday, helping Julian with his patients.

"He really is an amazing doctor," I said.

Charles looked over his coffee up at me. I knew that look, it was the same one my dad would give me when he disapproved of something. Sometimes the similarities between the two of them scared me.

"What?" I asked, knowing that he was trying to say something with his eyes.

"Kat, don't set yourself up for another heartache," he advised in

45

a fatherly tone.

"What are you talking about?"

"He's around your age, nice-looking, and you haven't stopped talking about him since we sat down," he answered. "I just don't want to see you get hurt."

"Thanks, but I have no intention of falling for Dr. Kiron." I smiled, appreciative of his concern.

I decided that I would stop the talk about Julian, changing topics to my apprehension over my dad's health. Charles reassured me that everything was probably okay, and I was just being paranoid. It comforted me when he told me that he would have his wife Claire go over and check on him.

"How is Claire?" I asked.

"She's okay, keeping herself busy while I'm gone. She hasn't found a new husband yet." He laughed.

"Well, she better not be finding a new shopping buddy," I said with a smile.

Claire and I had a monthly ritual. We would spend an entire Saturday shopping from early morning to late at night. She and I had become so close. I was very fortunate to have her and Charles in my life. They were like my second parents.

"I don't think you have to worry about that, you're the only one who's as crazy as her with the shopping."

"Well that's good. Please give her my love," I requested.

"I sure will," he said, taking another sip of his coffee.

I looked at him and couldn't help but think what a wonderful dad he would have made. I finished up my oatmeal, which was now cold from all the talking I had done, but I was so hungry, I didn't even mind. I wondered what would await me today as we walked over to the medical facility, breathing a sigh of relief when I saw I was scheduled to work the walk-in clinic with Charles. Anything of a serious matter would get referred to one of the doctors doing rounds or on call. I was still so tired. I couldn't handle anything that would drain me emotionally. The day went by quickly. Charles and I were the perfect team. It was always such a learning experience when I worked with him. I looked at my watch–a half hour to go. I was already looking forward to tomorrow–my day off and my weekly phone call to my dad. Even though I had just talked to him a few days earlier, I still missed hearing his voice. I wrapped up with the last of my patients and hung out, waiting until Charles was done with his last walk-in.

"Are we ready to get out of here?" Charles asked as his last patient exited the building.

"Waiting on you."

"Care to join me for dinner?" he asked.

"Of course," I replied.

We walked through the village and up the hill. Charles had wanted to clean up before heading to dinner, and I had decided to do the same. We were so engrossed in our conversation that I almost missed seeing Julian standing right outside of our building talking to three other men. Two of them were older and one looked to be about the same age as him. I gave him a quick smile, not wanting to interrupt his conversation, and he immediately stopped talking to acknowledge my presence. I introduced Julian to Charles as Julian introduced us to the three doctors that he had been speaking with. The two older doctors were pediatric oncologists from France, and the younger one was a pediatrician from England. Charles jumped right into the conversation, clearly in his element being around all these medical professionals from around the world. I, on the other hand, was not. I excused myself, letting Charles know I would meet him in the cafeteria.

"Hey, Kat," Julian yelled, running toward me.

"Yeah," I answered, turning around.

"Those two doctors from France have a surgeon lined up to operate on Rapula and Tau." There was sheer excitement in his voice. "They're here working on the funding to fly them to France so they can do the operation."

"Wow, that's great!" I answered.

"I just have to check on them tomorrow and maybe do another round of chemo." I could see the happiness on his face.

"I still say they wouldn't have made it this far if it weren't for you."

"Did you want to go with me again tomorrow? I'm leaving early in the morning," he asked, trying to avoid my compliment.

"Sure!" I instantly blurted out. I just couldn't say no after seeing the eagerness in his eyes. It didn't even matter that tomorrow was my much-needed day off.

"Okay, be ready by seven," he yelled as he walked backwards

toward the others in the group.

I smiled over the enthusiasm on his face. He was beaming when he told me the news. This was his world. He existed just to be a doctor and nothing else. This again made me feel a little inadequate for not doing the same. After my excitement for Julian finally wore off a bit, it dawned on me that tomorrow was my phone call to my dad. I was unsure if I would be back in time to reach him, so I decided that I would check in with him after dinner.

***

"Kat, really, you need to start eating more," Charles said, looking at just a small spoonful of what was supposed to be pasta primavera on my plate.

"I am," I said, pointing to the two large chocolate chip cookies on the napkin beside it. Charles shook his head at me in disapproval, again, so much like my dad would have.

"So, what's at seven tomorrow?" he inquired.

"What?" I played dumb as I took a sip of water. I hadn't even realized that Charles was paying attention to my conversation with Julian.

"Julian told you to be ready by seven," he clarified.

"Oh, that." I filled him in on what was going on with the two boys, explaining to him that Julian had asked me to come along with him while he checked on them.

"Isn't tomorrow your day off?" he asked again in a fatherly tone.

"Geez, are we still eating breakfast, or am I just having déjà vu?" I joked. "Charles, I'm fine. Did you ever think that maybe this is a great learning experience for me?" I asked in a more serious tone.

"You're a smart girl. I just remember how hard it was for Claire and me," he said.

"What are you talking about?" I asked. "You and Claire are one of the happiest couples I know."

"Oh, now we are, sure, but not when we first were married." He began to tell me about when he and Claire were first married. He was just finishing up his residency and Claire was a second- grade teacher. They thought they could handle the craziness that came along with being a doctor. Much to their dismay, they couldn't, and it finally took its toll on Claire. They separated for almost a year, until he got into a practice and his schedule started becoming a little more consistent.

I was shocked. Claire had never mentioned that to me, and we talked about everything.

"You know, they say the only thing harder than being a doctor is dating one or being married to one," he said.

"I don't know why we are even having this conversation. I told you this morning, there is nothing, nor will there be anything, going on with Dr. Kiron," I said in a very matter-of-fact tone. "Now let's change the subject, so I can eat my cookies in peace."

After we finished dinner, I headed over to the phone area waiting for one to become available. I sat down on the bench listening to some woman speaking in a foreign language, closing my eyes and daydreaming about being home and sitting on the beach. I missed it so much–the smell of the salt air, and the sound of seagulls flying overhead. There was something about touching the sand and smelling the ocean that restored your soul. I missed my house and lying in my bed on warm summer nights, listening to the crickets through the open windows. It's funny how you don't realize how many things you take for granted until they're gone. My eyes peeled open when the woman seemed to be wrapping up her conversation. I jumped from the bench when she placed the phone on the receiver and smiled as she walked by me.

I was so happy when my dad picked up on the first ring. I explained to him why I was calling him on a Saturday and filled him in on the last few days here. I told him all about Julian and what a great doctor he was, and after a while, I found that I was rambling on about him again.

"Well, you certainly sound in better spirits from the other night when I spoke to you," he said. "Would this oncologist have anything to do with it?"

"Geez, Dad, between you and Charles," I scoffed.

"Okay, but I bet he's handsome, right?" my dad chuckled. It astounded me how he could read me like a book, even when I was miles away.

I began to laugh. "Yes, he's very handsome."

"How did I guess that?"

I decided to get to my real reason for calling, the one that he was trying to avoid. "Have you gotten the results from the tests you had done?"

"Not yet," he replied in a dismissing tone. "I'm fine. You have me on my way to the grave over a few little tests," he added.

"I'm sorry if I'm being a nag, Dad, but I'm just worried about you."

"Well don't worry, I'm fine, I promise you," he reassured me.

"All right, I'm taking your word for it then."

We said our goodbyes, and I hung up the phone, still having a very uneasy feeling. I made the walk down the dark hallway to my room for some much-needed sleep, hoping to hear the sound of the ocean in the far-off distance or some crickets chirping a familiar tune in my dreams.

CHAPTER 7

I was ready promptly by 7 a.m., timing it perfectly when I almost walked right into Julian, who was just exiting his hallway as well.

"Good morning," he said. I couldn't help but notice the small piece of toilet paper he had stuck to his face.

"Did we have a little trouble shaving this morning?" I teased.

He rolled his eyes at my sarcasm.

It always seemed much more laidback on Sundays, not the usual influx of people. It wasn't as if there was less of a need for medical assistance just because it was Sunday. It was just an observation that I had made over the past few months of being here. This morning was unusually quiet, with hardly anyone around. Julian must have finally realized what day of the week it was due to the lack of chaos.

"Oh, Kat, I'm sorry. I totally lost track of my days—it's Sunday, isn't it?" Sunday was the normal day off unless you were on call.

"That's okay," I said, reassuring him that I really did want to go as we walked out of the building.

The sun was just beginning to rise, and it was one of the most breathtaking sights I had ever seen. The entire sky was lit up with different tones of yellow. I had no idea that so many shades even existed as it gradually meshed from dark to light in perfect unison. The trees in the background looked as if they were painted into a majestic picture of yellow hues. This was the first time I had witnessed any of these sunrises since I had been here, so I stood for a few more moments just taking it in, until Julian broke me from my awe-like state.

"Are you hungry?" he asked.

"No, I'm good," I answered, reminding myself of how stressed I was over eating my last power bar this morning.

"Are you ready or are you still looking at the sky?"

"Nope, I'm done, I just can't believe that something as beautiful as that sky exists in this place."

"What? There are lots of beautiful things here."

I found that pretty hard to believe. Besides this sunrise and him, I hadn't seen anything of beauty. All I saw was dust, dirt, depressing windowless buildings, and sickness everywhere you looked. If there was anything else, then I had yet to see it. I had found that my whole attitude about this place was bad. I was counting the days until I could go home, but it seemed like when I spent time with Julian my outlook changed ever so slightly. Maybe that's why this morning was the very first time I noticed the beautiful sunrise. There was just something about him. It wasn't just his good looks. It was his personality, the way he carried himself, and his carefree way. I found myself being drawn to him a little more each time I was in his presence.

We arrived at the other village a lot quicker than the last time. Time always went by fast when I was talking uncontrollably, which I found myself doing again the whole ride there. I did manage to find out a little bit more about him in between my talking. His dad was a retired college professor and his mother was a teacher. He spent his childhood summers in Cape Cod with his grandparents. He was an avid baseball player and had many baseball scouts interested in him during high school. He injured his shoulder, requiring surgery and relinquishing any hopes of a career in baseball, but he had his good grades and intense interest in medicine to fall back on. As I listened to him, I thought about how different his childhood was from mine. He had both parents raising him, a sister, and grandparents. He spent his summers away from home, which probably helped prepare him a lot better for being away. Just by listening to him I knew that things were a lot easier for his parents with putting him through college and medical school. Whereas, my dad scrimped, saved, and worked every overtime shift possible to make sure that I had the best education possible. There was only one common parallel that I could see between us. His dream of becoming a baseball player was probably as great as mine to become a dancer. In turn, both of us opted for a career in medicine instead.

Even the dismal village from the other night looked a little brighter in the early morning light. Julian was immediately greeted by an African man and woman. The man was completely bald wearing tattered looking khaki pants and a white button-up shirt that looked equally worn. The woman was dressed in a plain tan skirt with a white top.

The man approached Julian, speaking in some dialect I didn't understand. Julian nodded, and I wondered if he had really understood what the man was saying.

"Dr. Kiron," the lady said with very broken English. "Thank you for saving my babies." She squeezed his hand with tears in her eyes.

It then became clear that these were Rapula and Tau's parents. I couldn't even imagine having one child with cancer, and here these poor people had two, in a third world country, totally dependent on the goodwill of others. Julian graciously accepted her appreciation while gently warning her that there were still many obstacles to overcome. I listened to him explaining to this woman that there was still a chance that her boys might not make it with just the right balance of knowledge and compassion. The lady shook her head as if she understood, but she didn't want to hear that her boys might not pull through. This was so typical of any mother. I thought about the diversity in culture between this place and home, but one thing remained the same, the love of a mother for their child. The woman thanked Julian once more before ending the conversation.

There seemed to be only two doctors as we entered the medical facility who were running around crazily attending to patients. Julian immediately headed over to Rapula and Tau while I was feeling like I should assist one of the doctors with the influx of patients. I quickly retreated when Julian called me over.

"Rapula asked where the pretty doctor was," Julian laughed.

"How do you know that he wasn't referring to you?" I teased.

He smiled and shook his head. Rapula and Tau were in their beds just the same as the other day. There seemed to be more of a spark in their eyes. They both smiled in unison when I said hello. Julian talked to them, explaining what was going on in a very age appropriate manner. Neither of the boys was very happy when they heard they would be getting a few more rounds of chemotherapy, and I couldn't blame them for that.

Julian administered the chemo, and both boys fell into a sound sleep not too long after their treatment was done. After Julian was satisfied that they would be okay, he started packing up his stuff to leave.

When we stepped outside, it was unusually beautiful. It was still hot, but oddly there wasn't any humidity and not a cloud in the sky. I was surprised to see the amount of people out and about. A group of men were working on a hut. Three women gathered around a common area all dressed in traditional African attire. All but one had a baby in what looked to be a papoose on their back. Children everywhere running around playing tag or an unorganized game of soccer, every one of them had a smile, unaware that there was a whole other world out there.

Julian tried to locate Rapula and Tau's mother to give her an update on the boys, stopping dead in his tracks upon seeing a group of children trying to have a wiffle ball game. I looked at him with confusion when he signaled for me to follow him. As we walked over to where the kids were, he began to speak in a language that I clearly didn't understand, but the boy holding that bat did.

An older boy spoke up. "I speak English," he said in a very strong accent. He worked as a translator as Julian asked them if they wanted to have a game. They all began to smile when the boy translated Julian's request to them.

"Okay, tell them, boys versus girls," Julian said.

He turned around to me while the kids began lining up in groups of boys and girls.

"Go ahead, Kat, go with the girls," he said with a cute boyish smile.

"Oh, no, I don't play baseball," I said, laughing.

"It's not baseball, its wiffle ball," he said as if it made a difference. "Come on, the teams will be uneven if you don't play." He sounded like a little kid trying to convince me.

"Fine, but don't get mad when the girls beat the boys," I said, grabbing the bat from his hand.

I hadn't played wiffle ball since grammar school gym class. Aside from dancing and running, I was far from athletic, but I felt compelled to show this group of little girls that they could do anything the boys could do. I gained my confidence in that thought as I handed the bat to the first little girl in line. The boy who had been working as Julian's translator was the pitcher. The little girl swung and missed the first pitch, and all the boys began to cheer. She fouled off the second pitch and pummeled the ball as the third pitch crossed over the plate.

"Run, run!" I screamed as she rounded the bases with a huge smile on her face. The girls began to jump up and down, screaming with excitement as she crossed the makeshift home plate.

It was finally the last inning and the boys were winning 12 to 10. The girls had two runners on base and it was my turn to bat. Julian took the ball from the boy who had been pitching, grinning when I swung and missed his first pitch.

"Come on, Kat, I gave that to you," he yelled.

The second pitch was another swing and a miss. Julian shook his head, finding much delight in my poor batting skills. As I waited for him to throw the third pitch I repeated over and over, *you can do it, keep your eye on the ball.* At least that's what I thought you were supposed to do. As the third pitch came over the plate, I followed my advice and heard the crack of the bat hitting the ball. I stopped to watch it as it flew past everyone's head, giving Julian a great big teasing smile when I finally crossed home plate. Final score: girls 13, boys 12.

"What's the final score, Julian?" I teased.

"That was luck," he said, handing the ball to one of the boys.

I sat with the group of girls while Julian continued with his quest to find Rapula and Tau's mother. The little girls flocked around me, making me feel like royalty.

"What's your name?" I asked the little girl who had sat down next to me.

"Saada," she said with a smile.

"How old are you?" I asked.

"Twelve," she replied. "Are you a doctor?"

"Yup," I answered.

"I want to be a doctor someday too." She looked at me with admiration. "Can I braid your hair?"

"Sure," I answered.

I sat quietly, relaxing and taking in the warm sun until she finished, handing her the elastic ponytail holder when she was done.

"Is he your boyfriend?" Saada giggled as Julian appeared.

"No, just a friend," I answered.

"He's cute," she whispered.

"I know," I whispered back.

"I think he's cute too," Saada said, pointing to a boy who looked to be about her age standing off by himself.

"Well, I think you should go tell him," I said confidently.

She bashfully shrugged her shoulders.

"You'll never know if you don't try," I said.

She looked at me without saying a word and marched over to where the boy was standing. I watched intently, ignoring Julian as he came over to ask if I was ready. He quickly became interested in what was going on as well. I admired the confidence that she displayed as she whispered in the boy's ear, and I actually felt myself getting nervous, wondering how he would respond. I breathed a sigh of relief when I saw him hug her before he went running off with a group of boys. Her smile was a mile wide as she ran back to me. My smile must have been just as big as hers. I couldn't believe how excited I was over watching this first crush unfold.

"I told you he would like you," I said.

"Thank you, pretty lady," she said, giving me a great big hug.

"You're welcome, Saada." I hugged her back.

"You should tell him," she said, pointing to Julian.

"Tell me what?" Julian inquired.

"She thinks you're cute," Saada blurted out as she began giggling.

"No. Well I didn't…" I couldn't get the words out and felt myself turning red.

Julian laughed at my reaction.

"Aww, Kat, you think I'm cute?" he teased.

I finally regained my composure. "Well, actually, Saada said you were cute, and I just went along with it."

"Oh, look at you, blaming it on a little girl." He continued to taunt me.

I shook my head and began to laugh. I knew I was busted and wasn't going to deny it anymore. I actually thought he was more than just cute, but he didn't have to know that. I decided to make an exit, not waiting for Julian's lead. I waved goodbye to Saada, who was still smiling, jumped into the Jeep and angled the rearview mirror to see what she had done to my hair. I was surprisingly impressed with the perfect French braid that she had created. Once Julian was done loading everything in the back, he hopped in, handing me a bottle of water and a protein bar.

"Thanks," I said, taking a sip of the water.

He laughed when I told him that Tricia and I rationed our power bars and how I was in a panic this morning over eating my last one. "Well, I'll share mine with you, since you think I'm cute," he said with a grin. I shook my head smiling back, knowing that he wasn't going to let that go.

We were about twenty minutes into the ride when he pulled over on the side of the narrow dirt road.

"What are you doing?" I asked in confusion as he jumped out of the Jeep.

"Come here," he said as he began walking into a wooded area.

He made me walk ahead of him, following close behind while giving me instructions on which way to go. The forest was filled with lush greenery, providing an immense amount of shade. Up ahead looked to be brighter, and I knew that there must have been some type of clearing. We came out of the forest into what reminded me of a valley, and I was starting to become a little nervous, hoping that I didn't come face-to-face with any wild animals or snakes.

"Eeew," I screeched and grabbed Julian's arm in a state of panic as something small and fast ran past my feet.

He laughed. "It was just a lizard."

"Well, I hate any type of little creatures like that. Can you please tell me where the heck we are going?" Julian was now walking alongside me.

He shook his head. "It's a surprise."

The sound of running water became louder as he grabbed my hand and helped me up a steep hill. When we finally reached the top, I was in absolute awe. There was a beautiful waterfall that didn't even look real. The sheets of water formed a steady pattern of endless rhythm. It wasn't a deafening sound but more of a soft trickle. The cool mist coming off the crystal-clear water was invigorating, and I actually felt tears forming in my eyes—it was the most beautiful sight I had ever seen in my life.

"This is absolutely breathtaking," I said, trying to take it all in. "How on earth did you find this?"

He told me that the last time he was here, he and two other doctors stayed a few extra days. They took up an offer from one of the locals to go backpacking, and this was one of the places they stumbled upon. He said that the falls consisted of five streams, that cascaded from steep cliffs, one being more beautiful than the other. I couldn't imagine anything being more beautiful than this.

We found a grassy area and sat down, and I listened to Julian talk about his backpacking experience, unable to take my eyes off the magnificence in front of me. I found myself so relaxed by the warm sun and the sound of the trickling water, fairly certain that this had to be pretty close to what heaven was like. There was such irony in knowing that something so beautiful existed in a place that seemed more like hell.

"I just had to prove to you that this place isn't all that bad," he said.

"Actually, I was beginning to change my mind about that, after this morning and being with those children."

"How were you so sure that boy was going to be so accepting of that little girl?"

"I just did. I could sense those types of things. I'm very good at reading people just by first impressions," I boasted.

I went on to tell him about my love of old romantic movies. "My favorite thing to do is rate the kisses in movies."

"Really, and how do you do that?"

"Oh, there are lots of things you have to consider. The timing, the setting and the background."

"Wow, that sounds like a lot of work." He laughed.

I shrugged my shoulders. "How's your arm?" I asked as I grabbed it to examine the wound.

I was still holding on to his arm when I felt his lips begin to touch mine, forming the most perfect kiss ever. At first, I was a little shocked, but it only took a second before I began to kiss him back. It was soft and passionate at the same time. We slowly came to a finish, staring into one another's eyes, and my heart was quickly winning the battle with my head.

"How would you rate that?" he asked.

I tried to catch my breath. "Nine point five," I finally answered. He smiled proudly. "Well, you know this beautiful setting was worth nine points alone," I teased.

The sun was beginning to shift, signaling that the afternoon was starting to fade. As we got up to make our way back, I turned around taking in one last glimpse of the beauty surrounding me. Unsure if I would ever return to this majestic place, I quickly etched a photo of the beautiful waterfall in my mind and the most absolute perfect kiss in my heart–wanting to always remember them both.

CHAPTER 8

The weeks were flying by at a rapid pace. My days were jam-packed with seeing patients. By the time my twelve-hour shifts were over I was exhausted. I was still checking on my dad weekly, meticulously gauging the tone of his voice during each conversation to see if I could pick up on any sign of something being wrong, health-wise. If there was, he was hiding it well. He certainly wasn't offering any information to me. He immediately caught on to me when Charles' wife, Claire, paid him a visit.

I was seeing Tricia a lot more since we were working the same schedule, which made me happy. I hadn't seen Julian quite as much. He was spending almost every day at the other village–which I had to confess, made me a little sad. Rapula and Tau still hadn't had their surgeries. Julian didn't feel that it was safe to do so yet. The few times that I did encounter him, he acted normal, as if there was never a kiss exchanged between the two of us, and I was grateful for that. I didn't want to feel uncomfortable around him. He was his usual carefree self, teasing me and joking around like normal.

I was also seeing less of Charles and James, as they too were spending most of their time at the other village with Julian. Julian and James were becoming fast friends and after getting to know Julian, it was apparent why–they both had the same sense of humor and the same strong career drive.

I felt like a robot with the same routine every day. It was very monotonous, but it helped me from over-thinking things too much, which I always had a tendency to do.

Tricia wasn't feeling well and had left early, and I foolishly agreed to take on her patients in addition to mine. It had been a long day and my head was pounding. I was so happy to finally be wrapping up, checking on one of Tricia's last patients. Before I could even look at the chart, I was approached by a very familiar looking young male doctor. I sensed before he even spoke that he was one of those arrogant type doctors that I despised. That was confirmed when he grabbed the chart from my hand abruptly.

I looked at him in disbelief over his rudeness. "Excuse me!" I snapped.

"This is not your patient, it's mine," he said, not lifting his head from the chart.

As soon as I heard him speak in a thick British accent, I was able to place how I knew him. He was the doctor who Julian had been talking to a few weeks ago, along with the two French doctors.

"And why on earth would you prescribe an antibiotic for her when clearly she has a virus?" he asked. "I honestly think some people must sleep through medical school," he mumbled lightly.

The total exhaustion that I felt was now replaced with rage. "First of all, Dr...." I said, waiting for him to fill in his last name.

"Dr. Reeves. I'm a pediatrician at one of London's finest children's hospitals," he answered, never making eye contact.

"Well, Dr. Reeves, I don't know if that's how you treat people over in your fine hospital. But you will not talk to me that way," I snapped. "Oh, and maybe if you had bothered to check the chart when you so rudely ripped it out of my hand, you would have noticed she has a strep infection, so that is why she needs an antibiotic." I was so angry that I didn't even acknowledge Julian, who had just walked in and witnessed my entire wrath. He stood there stunned as I packed up my stuff.

"This is why they shouldn't allow women to be doctors, they are much too emotional," Dr. Reeves chuckled to Julian.

I slammed my bag down on the table, whisking past Julian, who just stood there as if entertained by the whole event. Dr. Reeves backed away when I got right in his face and shouted, "The same could be said about arrogant men like you who think they know everything–go to hell, you little prick!"

He didn't reply, seeming stunned that anyone dare speak to him that way. I grabbed my bag and flung it over my shoulder, slamming the door on the way out. Doctors like him were the one thing that turned me off about this profession. They clearly were in it for the money and the prestige of putting MD after their name, not because they truly cared about people. My head was spinning. I couldn't believe that I had let such an egotistical man like him get to me.

I took double steps once I got outside, just wanting to get some food, get to bed, get anywhere as long as it was far away from Dr. Reeves and the scene I had just made.

"Kat, slow down!" Julian shouted.

"What?" I answered, sounding a little abrupt as I came to a quick halt.

"What's the matter?" he asked.

"Nothing, this was just a very fitting end to a horrible day!"

He stood alongside me with his hands in his pockets. "That was pretty funny—the look on his face." He was unable to control his laughter. He finally removed his hands from his pockets and took my hand in his. "I like a girl who's not afraid to speak her mind." The look in his eyes became more serious. *Oh God, he's going to kiss me again.* I took a deep breath and followed my heart once again when he gently moved my hair out of the way, touching my face softly as his lips tenderly grazed mine. The butterflies in my stomach were unleashed as he began to kiss me with more intensity, and I kissed him back just as eagerly. The stress of the day melted away instantly when he moved his hands up and down my back and through my hair.

"Kat!" James' voice sounded like nails on a chalkboard at that particular moment. I reluctantly released myself from Julian's embrace as we both tried to regain our composure.

"Oh, I'm sorry. Did I interrupt something?" James asked with a sly grin plastered across his face. He had clearly witnessed what had just taken place.

"No, nothing at all, I was just talking to Julian," I answered, playing along with his game. "What's up?" I asked.

"I just heard you laid into Reeves."

"Where did you hear that?" It was amazing how quickly the word had spread.

"Two of the nurses were just reveling in it," he answered.

I was quickly learning that I wasn't the only one who had a problem with this man, making me feel somewhat better about the situation.

"Geez, word travels fast around here," I remarked.

"Wow, who would've thought that quiet little Kat would have the guts to tell him what we were all thinking?" James put out his hand to give me a high-five. I shook my head refusing to give him one back, feeling a little embarrassed now at how I had handled that situation.

"What the heck got into you?" James asked, still in amazement.

"I don't know. I got a lot on my mind." I tried not to look at Julian but couldn't help myself.

"I just went and checked on Tricia, she's feeling much better," James said. He continued giving me an update on her condition, while I half-paid attention. I just wanted him to leave so I could be alone with Julian, but even if he did leave now, we would never get back to that moment.

"Hello? Kat, would you mind?" James waved his hand in front of my face to break me from my daydreaming.

"Huh?" I had no clue what he had just asked.

"Would you mind getting Tricia some soup?" He was looking at me strangely.

"No problem," I answered.

"Thanks, Kat, you're the best," James said, wrapping his arm around me and squeezing my shoulders.

I went from being the best to almost non-existent in just a matter of seconds. James excitedly told Julian that one of the doctors swore that he was able to get game seven of the World Series on his portable TV, and he invited Julian along to watch it.

"Well, you guys have fun," I said, feeling more like an outsider in the conversation now.

James continued rambling, while Julian interrupted him. "I'll talk to you later, Kat." He looked like he was feeling the same way that I had about James right about now. However, it still didn't stop him from walking off with him like two boys headed to a frat party.

I walked up the hill toward the cafeteria. It was now dark and the winds were picking up like it normally would before the rain started. I immediately felt a twinge of happiness as I realized tomorrow was Sunday, my day off.

I wondered if my dad was home watching baseball too. Game seven of the World Series meant my favorite time of the year was fast approaching–late autumn. Although you would never know it being in this dreaded place, that seemed like a perpetual hot humid bowl of soup, but back at home there was just something about fall that always put me in a better frame of mind. There was nothing more therapeutic than bundling up and going for a long walk on the beach late in the afternoon on a brisk November day. The summer tourists were long gone. The water always seemed a little more powerful with the gray sky as the backdrop, adding to its ferocity. The perfect ending, coming home and warming up by the fireplace with a hot cup of tea.

I was daydreaming so much I almost forgot to get Tricia's soup. When I entered the cafeteria, I was surprised to see Tricia at a table all by herself already eating. I grabbed a bowl for myself and sat down beside her. She appeared a little better than earlier, but her normal olive colored skin tone was still very pale.

"Hey, what are you doing here?" I asked.

"I was dying of starvation waiting for James," she said sarcastically.

"Actually, that's just what I was coming in to get for you."

"Are you kidding me? He asked you to get it for me?"

I filled her in on what had happened with her patient and Dr. Reeves, trying my best to defend him by telling her that he must have gotten sidetracked by it.

"Yeah, he was sidetracked by other things, like hanging out with the guys," she said, sounding a bit jealous.

"So, I can't believe that you of all people went off on that little weasel," Tricia said with her light-up-a-room smile reappearing.

"Why is everyone finding that so hard to believe?"

"Because you are usually so quiet," she answered, slurping her soup.

"Yeah, well I didn't plan on it spreading so quickly. It was bad enough that Julian was there to witness the whole thing."

"Oh, Julian was there?" Tricia arched her eyebrows. "What's going on with that?"

"With what?" I played dumb. I had never told Tricia about the kiss, the waterfall, or anything that had to do with Julian. I would have loved to share these things with her, but she had a tendency to overreact, and would probably start planning my wedding, so I kept it all to myself.

"Well, his new buddy James says that he's quite taken with you!" She grinned.

Her comment piqued my curiosity. "What did he say?" I tried to come off as if I really didn't care.

She shrugged. "Just how funny you are and what a nice, caring person you are."

"Oh, well that hardly qualifies for talking about me all the time."

"I'm just telling you what James said. It's pretty obvious how he feels just by how he looks at you."

I shook my head in disbelief, deciding to change the subject. We both began to reminisce about home, and I quickly realized that Tricia was just as homesick as I was. She came from a very close-knit family. She had two older brothers and her mom and dad were divorced, so in addition to her parents, she had a stepmother and stepfather. I was always amazed by how well her parents and their new spouses all got along. They all had the same carefree, bubbly attitude as Tricia. That is what I liked most about her–she provided me with a sense of balance. Every time I would stress out about something, she would be right there to calm me down. She never let anything get to her, taking life at her own pace.

We talked for some time as people entered and exited the cafeteria, laughing uncontrollably over something the other would say like a couple of schoolgirls. Even though I was still a little upset over having my time cut short with Julian, Tricia helped to fill the void perfectly. In a way, it was probably for the best, since I didn't know how far that kiss would have gone. The last thing I wanted was to become Julian's latest conquest because I was unable to control myself.

"So, what do you think James is doing tonight?" she asked.

"Don't know," I answered. "Do you care?" I teased.

She smiled. "Well, maybe I'm kind of seeing him in a new light," she confessed.

"Oh, and have you told him this?"

"No, but tonight was a perfect example, he ditched me to go hang out with the guys."

"Well, Tricia, if he doesn't know how you feel, then he's going to treat you as a friend."

"Meaning?" She seemed puzzled.

"That you hold the same priority as his guy friends. You've got to claim your status as *girlfriend* if you want special treatment," I said, taking a bite out of a rock-hard brownie.

"Yeah, but I don't want it to ruin our friendship," she said, sounding a little disappointed.

"Well, you have to decide if you want to cross that line." I was probably the last person to give advice on love and relationships given my disastrous relationship with Jake. It finally dawned on me that suddenly Jake was starting to fade into the distance. As much as I tried fooling myself, I knew exactly why.

"Well, I guess it's time for us to get some sleep," Tricia said looking down at her watch.

"Are you feeling better?" I asked.

"Much." She smiled.

I knew that she wasn't just talking about her sickness from today. She was feeling better about unloading everything that was on her mind to me, and I was happy that I could be there for her.

"Good." I smiled back. "I really do think you should tell James."

"I think that you should really tell Julian." She raised her eyebrow.

I wasn't even going to defend myself by saying I didn't have feelings for him. I knew that it was too late. Tricia was able to see right through me. Still, I knew that as far as Julian and I were concerned, it was better to keep those feelings inside. It wasn't like we had any type of future beyond this. I would just enjoy the butterflies in my stomach while they lasted. Soon enough I would be home, and he would be a distant memory. My stomach dropped just thinking about that, but I had to be honest with myself. Charles was right, all the pieces were in place for another heartbreak. This time instead of being surprised, I knew it was coming, and as much as I tried to avoid it, I found myself being drawn to it more each day.

CHAPTER 9

I woke up feeling like I had a hangover, only I hadn't been drinking the night before. I was finally coherent enough from my sleep stupor to remember that it was Sunday, which meant I didn't have to jump out of bed. When I rolled over, I realized I couldn't even if I had tried. My head was pounding and my throat was on fire. I looked over to find Tricia already up and gone. I grabbed my watch off the nightstand and was astounded to find that it was 9 a.m. I never slept this late, even on my day off. I had so much to do today. I had slacked off last Sunday and had not done laundry, so now I had a mountain to tackle today. Getting such a late start would now mean a battle over the only two washing machines. I stepped out of bed, sitting back down immediately as a spell of dizziness overcame me. I cannot be getting sick, I just can't, I said to myself, realizing I had no voice. I forced myself out of bed and into the shower, finishing up as fast as I could when I felt like I was going to pass out from the steam. After getting dressed, I gave myself a glance in the mirror while I brushed my teeth, realizing my eyes were unusually puffy with raccoon-like circles around them, and my healthy glow from the sun had faded overnight.

I gathered my clothes at a snail's pace, shoving as much as I could fit into the laundry bag as the sweat poured off me. I headed down the hallway to the laundry area, delighted to find one of the washing machines open. After overstuffing the washer so I could get my clothes all done in one wash, I decided to go to the cafeteria for a cold drink to soothe my throat. My tank top that had been covered in sweat immediately dried up as I walked out into the hot blazing sun. The heat was unbearable, and the short walk to the cafeteria seemed endless, feeling much like I had crossed the finish line of a marathon by the time I reached the door.

I was greeted by Charles, who was just walking out. "Hey,

stranger!" He reached over, putting his hand on my head. "You are burning up!"

"I'm fine," I whispered, forgetting I didn't have a voice.

"You are not fine, you shouldn't be up and walking around, you should be in bed," he scolded.

"Open your mouth and say *ahh*," he demanded.

"Charles, I'm…" I said, straining what little voice I had left.

Charles gave me his fatherly look, and I knew that I had better do what he asked. I opened my mouth, and he pulled a small flashlight out of his pocket looking in the back of my throat.

"You have strep. It's clear just by looking at your throat," he said. "I have to get you some antibiotics and you need to get into bed."

I shook my head, unable to talk, trying to signal that I had no intention of spending the day in bed.

"Hey, Charles." This time James' voice was a welcomed distraction. I waited patiently for Charles to get wrapped up in a conversation with him, so I could sneak away into the cafeteria to get my drink without being sequestered to bed. It was starting to work as Charles began chatting and I moved slowly, almost getting my hand on the door until Charles grabbed my arm, pulling me back.

I sighed in defeat and noticed James checking me out oddly.

"What?" I mouthed, shooting him a dirty look.

"What the heck happened to you?" he asked. "You look horrible!"

"Thanks," I mouthed, not able to get the words out.

"Sorry, but you look really sick," he said, now sounding concerned. "Maybe you lost your voice from all the yelling you did last night," he joked.

"Yelling?" Charles asked.

I shook my head at James as he explained to Charles about how I laid into Dr. Reeves yesterday. Watching Charles' expression, I could tell that he was as surprised as everyone else by my outburst.

"Well good for her, nobody should talk to her that way," Charles said.

"Are you ready? We're running late," James asked.

Charles looked at me and then at James. They began to discuss the situation, as if I wasn't even there. Charles had committed himself to going over to the other village and helping James. Tricia was gone as well, attending a last-minute all-day seminar. Charles seemed to be in a quandary because there was no one here to look after me. I couldn't believe my ears–I didn't need a babysitter.

"Charles, please just…" I started to get out before he put his hand up for me to stop.

I spotted Julian off in the distance talking to a few of the villagers. I was hoping that I was delirious when I heard James yell over to him. Shaking my head in protest at James, knowing exactly what his intentions were, I placed my hands on my temples trying to stop my throbbing head.

"What's up?" Julian asked as he walked over.

"Kat, are you okay?" he asked. "I didn't even realize that was you."

I couldn't answer, my voice wouldn't let me, but I tried my hardest to tell him I was fine.

"She's not fine, Julian," Charles jumped in. "She has strep, she's burning up, and she refuses to get some rest," Charles finished, explaining to Julian that he and James had to go to the other village, and he didn't feel comfortable leaving me here alone.

"Are you going to be around for most of the day?" Charles asked.

"Yes, I just have a few more patients I need to check up on, and I'm free for the rest of the day," he said.

"Would you mind looking in on her for me while I'm gone?" Charles asked.

I felt so foolish, like a little kid needing to be babysat. I tried one last time to express myself. "I don't need a babysitter," I managed to get out in an almost-audible tone.

Charles continued ignoring me, making me strain my voice in vain. I felt another dizzy spell, immediately taking a seat on the wooden bench near where I was standing. James was the closest to where I stood. He rushed over to sit down next to me.

"Kat, are you okay?" he asked, grabbing my arm.

I was still trying to get my bearings before nodding my head yes. Julian immediately came over, bending down to touch my head. He gazed at me intently with his beautiful eyes, making me feel faint again.

"Wow, she is burning up," he said, turning to Charles.

"Yes, I know. I'm afraid I'm going to have to cancel," Charles said to James.

"No, it's okay. I'll take care of her," Julian said all too willingly. "I'll get her some antibiotics and make sure that she doesn't go anywhere." Charles seemed to be content with that.

"James, get her into bed," Charles ordered.

"No problem," James laughed as he immaturely took Charles' comment out of context.

James walked me to my room, grabbing on to my arm a couple of times when I found myself becoming dizzy again. I got into my bed, wanting to close my eyes more than anything. He turned on the fan for me as Charles entered the room with two aspirins, my first dose of antibiotics, and my much-awaited bottle of water. Swallowing the pills was like a piece of hot lava going down my throat. I had treated tons of kids for strep throat, but this was the first time that I could ever remember having it. I was a lot more sympathetic to those poor kids now, experiencing just how painful it was. I motioned to James to bring me my magazine that was on the dresser. I had to try to find something to keep my mind occupied. Being sick and in this depressing room with no television was going to feel like a day of solitary confinement.

"Are you sure you are going to be okay?" Charles asked as they were readying themselves to leave.

"Yes," I mouthed as he reluctantly walked out the door.

I propped my pillows against the back of the bed, taking another torturous sip of water while fumbling through the pages of the magazine until I was unable to fight my heavy eyes.

I awoke feeling somewhat better. My headache was gone, but unfortunately, the pain in my throat was not. I was soaking wet from the fever breaking, so I decided to jump in the shower. I finished up and threw on my last clean tank top and pair of shorts, jogging my memory that I had clothes in the washer.

I hurried out of the room to get to the laundry room, smiling when I saw Julian as I turned the corner. Then I remembered that Charles had put him in charge of babysitting me for the day.

"Kat, what are you doing out of bed?" he asked.

"I had to put my clothes…"

He signaled for me to stop straining my voice. "You're doing laundry? You were just passed out a half hour ago."

I was shocked and at the same time embarrassed. *He had seen me sleeping, drenched in sweat. What if I was snoring?* Not exactly a glamorous moment that you would want anyone to witness. Especially not a drop-dead gorgeous guy who you found yourself compellingly attracted to.

"Are you hungry?" he asked.

I was a little hungry, but the idea of swallowing anything put an end to that thought. I nodded, but then motioned to my throat, letting him know that I would rather live with the hunger than the pain of swallowing.

"I'll get you something you can eat," he said, understanding my poor attempt at sign language perfectly well. "Now get back in bed, I'll bring it back to you."

I went back to my room and fixed the blankets on my bed, positioning myself with my back up against the wall, reading my magazine and trying very hard to not look sick.

"Come in," I said, as loud as I could muster when I heard a knock on the door.

Julian entered the room with a bowl in his hand and a smile on his face. He sat down on the edge of the bed handing me the bowl, and much to my delight, it contained two large scoops of chocolate ice cream.

"I figured I would have you all covered. You have the coldness for your throat and you get your chocolate fix at the same time."

Little did he know, but his beautiful smile was making me feel better already.

I smiled back with gratitude. The cold ice cream was heavenly going down my throat, immediately putting out the fire that had been raging all morning long.

Julian filled me in on what he had been up to the past couple of weeks while he was virtually non-existent. He explained that there had been four more kids diagnosed with cancer in the other village, and it was now becoming clear that it was more than likely that it was something environmental. He also gave me an update on Rapula and Tau, and some hurdles they had encountered as I listened intently. I, too, was very interested in their progress, knowing how much these boys meant to Julian.

"I've been talking so much, I didn't even realize it was time for your next dose of antibiotic," he said as he looked down at his watch. Little did he know, but he was providing the best medicine for me, just by his mere presence.

This was a complete role reversal for us. Normally I was the one who couldn't stop talking. Since I didn't have a voice, I had no choice but to listen, and I really liked it. He stopped his chatter briefly to hand me my bottle of water and an antibiotic, insisting that I take two more aspirin as well.

"What is going to happen to these children once you leave?" I asked.

"They'll have another team of oncologists come over."

"When are you leaving?" I asked as my voice started to sound clearer.

"February."

I was happy, knowing he would be here the whole time I was. He explained to me that once he got done here, he would be going back to the hospital in Chicago for a few months. Then he would be heading to Germany for a year to study under one of the most renowned pediatric oncologists in the world. I was so impressed with his determination. I knew that one day he would surpass that German doctor and he would be the one that other doctors would go to study under. Charles was exactly right with his observation—Julian was not relationship material, as much as I wanted to see it differently, he was just way too absorbed in his career. This was a great thing for him, but not for someone who was finding themselves more attracted to him with each passing day. I sat with my back propped up against the wall hugging my knees as he sat next to me, once again feeling a little more inadequate. The only thing that I was looking forward to in February was going home to see my dad and the ocean, not travel across it to further my career. I painfully realized the stark differences in the two of us, but he still had a way of making that so hard to see. He never acted as if he were better than anyone else, never judging anyone else's life choices. I was beginning to realize that I was dead wrong in my initial assessment of him. After spending time with him, he was slowly breaking down the wall he had up around him, and I was beginning to see a totally different person—he wasn't like Jake at all. I was even able to understand his take on relationships better. He clearly had his heart broken before and didn't want that to happen again, something that I could relate to very well.

"Thank you," I said in a barely audible tone.

"For what?" he asked.

I wanted to tell him, for taking care of me, for keeping me company and preventing me from going completely insane locked up in this depressing room, but I knew that my strained voice wouldn't let me get the words out.

"Thank *you*," he said. I looked at him puzzled. "For making me slow down a little today," he continued. "I have a harrowing week coming up, trying to get Rapula and Tau ready for surgery, along with all of the other recent cases that had been added to my workload. I had planned on taking today to just check in on a few patients here and then taking it easy, but relaxing doesn't come easy for me. If it hadn't been for you getting sick and keeping you company, I'd probably have ended up working another twelve-hour day."

"You're welcome...I guess," I whispered.

"How are you feeling?" He touched my forehead with his cool hand, making sure the fever didn't come back.

"Much better."

"Good." He flashed that beautiful smile once again.

We sat for a few seconds in silence. His beautiful eyes accented by his long dark lashes put me in a trance. I had never felt so at ease with anyone as I did with him right now.

"I just hope you don't get sick, being stuck in a little room with me all day," I whispered, finally breaking the silence.

"I don't get sick," he boasted as I looked at him in disbelief.

"I don't," he defended himself, able to read the look on my face. "Probably has to do with all the chemo and radiation I'm around, it sucks the sickness right out of me," he joked. I began to laugh, thinking maybe there just happened to be some truth to that theory.

My laughter was broken when I heard the doorknob turning and the door flinging open, revealing Tricia holding my laundry bag of clean clothes.

"Oh my goodness, how big was the train that ran you over?" she asked, looking directly at me.

"Thank you," I whispered sarcastically.

Her eyes shifted to Julian. "What happened?" she asked with total concern in her voice.

Julian got up and explained to her that I had strep. He gave her directions as to when I had to take my antibiotics and aspirin again, once more making me feel like a child. I knew what time I had to take my medicine and was quite capable of doing it myself.

"Geez, I leave for the day and you fall apart," Tricia joked.

Julian laughed. "Well, you're in good hands now. I've got to get going and do my final check-in on those patients. Feel better, Kat," he said, heading to the door.

Outside of the day we had spent at the waterfall this had strangely been one of the best days ever, even with a raging fever and a burning throat, I still wouldn't trade it for anything. I was beginning to find that spending time with Julian, getting to know more about him in any capacity, was a great day—sick or not.

"Thanks for taking care of my girl," Tricia said to Julian as she closed the door behind her.

She had a mega-sized grin as she sat down next to me. "You get the gorgeous doctor that makes house calls, and I get the obnoxious one that can't even bring me back soup."

I shook my head and smiled, looking down at my bag of laundry Tricia had brought back, wondering how she knew I had stuff in the dryer, I pointed to it. Tricia knew exactly what I was trying to say without even talking.

"Kat, it's Sunday, which means laundry day, and you always forget your stuff in the dryer! So, I decided to check for you on my way by the laundry room," she explained.

Guilty as charged. That was a terrible habit of mine. I was so thankful that today of all days Tricia was so on cue with that.

"So why was Doctor Handsome taking care of you today?" she asked.

I explained to her in the best voice that I could about what had transpired in the morning.

"Well, he certainly didn't seem like he was forced into doing it. In fact, by the way you two were laughing when I walked in, I'd say he was rather enjoying it," she said, raising her eyebrows.

She touched my forehead as she looked at her watch. "Time for more medicine," she said. "You should be in your pajamas," she demanded. She dug through my laundry bag, handing me a pair. I didn't argue with her as I began undressing and putting them on.

"Is this all you've eaten all day?" she asked as she picked up my empty bowl of ice cream.

I nodded, trying to explain that I hadn't had much of an appetite, but she wasn't having any part of it.

"I'm going to get you some soup and you are going to eat it all," she demanded. "Do you want anything else?"

I shook my head, knowing there would be no arguing with her. I watched her walk out the door, and it suddenly dawned on me that I hadn't made my weekly phone call to my dad. I quickly dismissed the thought, realizing I wouldn't be able to say much anyway without a voice. I decided I would wait until tomorrow, hoping I would be able to talk somewhat better. If I were home right now, my dad would have been doting on me nonstop like he always did when I was sick. As much as Charles annoyed me this morning, I was grateful to have him here filling that role.

I leaned my head back against the wall, laughing to myself, knowing I'd be feeling better in no time, now that Dr. Tricia was on duty. She was a sweetheart, but at the same time, she had toughness to her when it came to her patients. Unfortunately for me, I had now become one of them–like it or not.

Chapter 10

I sat up at the sound of my alarm and immediately began talking to myself. My voice had come back with just a little hoarseness.

"I got my voice back," I said to Tricia as she exited the bathroom.

"I really think you should take one more day to rest up," Tricia advised in her doctor-like tone.

"I'm fine. I'll go crazy if I have to spend any more time in this room," I answered, letting her know that I relinquished myself as her patient.

"Okay, but you're eating something before you take those antibiotics," she said, getting one last order in.

Tricia and I agreed to meet in the cafeteria. I was feeling much better once I showered and dressed. I even looked better compared to yesterday. As I walked out the door to head to the cafeteria, I was pleasantly surprised to see Julian, loading up medical supplies along with James to take to the other village.

"Well you look like a whole new person today," Julian said as he strode over to me.

"I guess that's a good thing, compared to what I looked like yesterday," I joked.

"You looked fine Kat—nwanyi marama," he said as he began to load up more supplies. I knew I had heard that phrase before and then thought back to the first day Julian and I had gone to the other village. It was the same word that the man had said to Julian referring to me. I was amazed that I subconsciously did make a mental note of it.

"What did you just say?" I asked.

"Nwanyi marama," he repeated. "Beautiful woman," he translated.

I was still a little perplexed until he finally clarified, "You are a beautiful woman," this time in a more serious tone.

"Well now that I have my voice back and I can *say* it—thank you for taking such good care of me yesterday and keeping me company."

"No problem. I told you that yesterday, it was fun." He took my hand and gazed into my eyes. My knees were just about going weak, when we were interrupted yet again by James, who was clearing his throat loudly to announce his presence. This time instead of being annoyed by him I just smiled.

"Sorry to interrupt, but we have got to get going, Julian," he said, almost sounding sincere.

"Okay, I'll be right there," he said as James walked over to the Jeep to wait for him.

"I'm gonna be working round the clock, trying to get a handle on these new cases," he informed me. I was happy to hear a little optimism in his voice at the mention of Rapula and Tau's names.

"Good luck," I whispered as he softly but playfully kissed my forehead.

"See ya, Kat, and don't overdo it today," he said.

"I won't," I replied as I watched him walk away.

***

The week flew by, and by the end of it, I was finally feeling one hundred percent myself again. Julian was right about working round the clock—I hadn't seen any sign of him or James all week. Throughout the week, I was paired up with Tricia and, to my disdain, Dr. Reeves. At first, he didn't have much to say to me, but as we worked together on the same patient, we had to brainstorm together for the best course of treatment. Even though he never admitted it, I sensed he now had a newfound respect for women doctors.

I tried reaching my dad several times throughout the week since I had missed our usual Sunday phone call, each time getting the answering machine and leaving several in-depth messages. I found it odd that I wasn't able to get in touch with him, but knew that each time I had called him was on a whim. He could have been out and about doing a number of things.

Tricia and I were just sitting down to some so-called veggie burgers when James appeared, looking thoroughly exhausted. The butterflies were released in my stomach, thinking that maybe there was a chance that Julian was back as well. He took forever to pick out his food, and I began biting my nails and shaking my leg, two very annoying habits of mine when I became anxious about something. I caught myself and stopped immediately when Tricia raised an eyebrow at me.

"Hey, welcome back," Tricia said with a glimmer in her eye when James took a seat with us.

I didn't want to come right out and ask if Julian was back, so I decided to sit and listen hoping that James would give some type of clue.

"I'm actually glad to be back," James said. "It's like a death camp over there." His entire jokester personality had changed in a week.

"That's so sad," Tricia replied, shaking her head.

"Yeah, I don't know how Julian does this," James said.

My ears perked up at the sound of his name.

"I guess you just can't get too attached," Tricia commented.

"Yeah, well that's easier said than done," I chimed in, thinking of how I felt the day that Akin had passed away.

"Yes, it is," James agreed. "Even Julian, who sees this type of situation on a daily basis, wasn't prepared for losing a patient."

"Who?" I asked without hesitation.

"One of the brothers who was supposed to have the surgery done–the older one," he said.

"Rapula," I whispered, starting to get upset, the same way I did when Akin had passed away. I thought of Rapula's bright smile and how much fun we had that day playing UNO. Most of all, I thought of how close Julian had become to both boys. He was so hopeful that they would beat the cancer and go on and live healthy lives. I knew he must have been crushed by not being able to achieve that.

"Kat, are you okay?" Tricia asked, reading the expression on my face.

"Yeah, it's just really sad," I wiped a stray tear that had fallen from my eye. "How's Julian doing?" I asked James.

"He's pretty upset, although he's not admitting it, but he was pretty much quiet the whole ride home."

I had gotten the answer I had been waiting for–Julian was back. But my entire mood had shifted, and the excitement of seeing him that existed just minutes ago was now gone. All I could feel was sadness. I sat listening to Tricia giving James a recap on her week, and I couldn't stop thinking about Julian and how he must've been feeling. I excused myself to allow Tricia and James to have some time alone.

As I entered the main building, I had every intention of going to the left hallway, which was where my room was located, but something was compelling me to go the other way, to go see Julian. I walked down the hallway, second-guessing myself as I stopped at the door. What if he just wants to be alone? James said he was quiet the whole ride home. Maybe he doesn't want to talk. I thought of how Julian was there for me when Akin had died, and how much better I had felt after I had talked to him.

I lightly knocked on the door. The few seconds it took him to answer seemed like hours. My stomach dropped at the sound of the doorknob turning, quickly turning back to butterflies upon seeing him standing in the doorway shirtless. He must have just gotten out of the shower, and his hair was still wet and his bare chest still had water beads on it. He managed a smile, it wasn't the same dimple-flashing smile that he always gave, there was definitely something missing from it. Even his vibrant blue eyes were lacking their luster tonight. I walked in, and he closed the door behind me.

"Hey, Kat, what's up?" He grabbed a towel off the chair and rubbed his hair dry.

"I just heard about Rapula. I'm so sorry, Julian."

"Well, I knew it wasn't a guarantee." He tried his best to play it off coolly.

"Yes, but I know how close you became with those boys."

He sat down on the bed and was quiet for a few seconds, and I felt a little guilty for noticing just how sexy he looked at a time like this.

"I almost wish I didn't get his parents' hopes up by arranging the surgery," he said, breaking the silence.

I sat down beside him. "Well what about Tau? He's still able to have the surgery, right?" I asked, trying to sound optimistic.

He nodded.

"Then how can you second-guess yourself for arranging it?"

He looked at me, not saying a word. The only sound in the room was the rattling of the ceiling fan overhead. I couldn't stand the awkward silence any more or the hurt in his eyes. I took his hand in mine. "You did everything you could for him, and because of you, his time that he did have was a lot more enjoyable."

He stood up, giving me a full view of his flawless body. "How did I make his life more enjoyable? By pumping him full of chemo and radiation, watching him in pain and throwing up every day only to have him die anyway."

"That was part of your job to make him better. You didn't have a crystal ball telling you that it was all in vain. I'm talking about the time you spent with him, the way he lit up when he would see you."

He became quiet once again, raking his hand through his hair and staring into space. I could see that his mind was a million miles away and realized that maybe he did just want to be alone. Not everyone was like me, needing a sounding board when something was bothering them. The last thing I wanted to do was make him more upset, so I decided I would leave, hoping that he would feel a little better about himself in the morning. I stood up next to him and moved closer. "You can't save them all, Julian," I whispered.

There was a look of sadness and desire in his eyes, and my heart began to melt for both. He wrapped his muscular arms tightly around me, and I pressed my face against his firm chest, inhaling the strong scent of soap coming off his skin. My hands moved up his back toward his shoulders as he slightly released his hold and gazed down at me. His eyes had now returned to their natural vitality, the same color I had grown so fond of since the day I had met him. He tilted my chin up and leaned down kissing me with a sense of urgency, and I found myself responding just as vigorously. His hands slid down to the small of my back as he pulled me closer while his lips gently grazed my neck. He effortlessly lifted me off the floor, raising me to his level removing his lips from my neck back to my lips. I ran my fingers through his thick damp hair as we continued kissing. Slowly placing me back down on the floor, he released me as we disengaged from the kiss.

"I want you, Julian. I want to be here for you tonight and *with* you tonight." My hands caressed the side of his face.

He pressed his forehead into mine. "Are you sure?" he asked.

"I've never been more sure about anything in my life." I placed my lips on his chest, moving their way up to his neck.

He let out a pleasurable sigh as my hands began to wander up and down his back. "Are you on–"

"We're good," I whispered, not wanting to ruin the moment. I took his face in my hands and kissed him hard while I slowly unbuttoned his pants. He smoothly lifted my shirt over my head and removed my bra with ease. My bare chest was touching his, and I could feel his heart beating faster. He lifted me up and carried me over to the bed, and I let him take the lead, as he slowly removed my shorts and then removed his own pants at a much faster pace. He was so gentle and caring with every move he made. He kissed me softly throughout my body as I did the same to him. His warm hands tenderly caressed my face, and I was overcome with emotion as he entered me, pulling him closer as he continued to bring butterflies to my stomach with each gentle thrust. I had never wanted anything more and had never felt so fulfilled in my life. We made love for hours, reaching my breaking point several times, each time more pleasurable than the first. I finally felt my body begin to tremble one last time as I let out a soft cry of complete satisfaction. He continued a few minutes more, burying his face into the pillow, letting out a light groan. His heart was beating rapidly as he turned on his side and hugged me tight. I rested my head on his chest as he gently played with my hair.

"You seriously have no clue how long I've wanted you, do you?" he asked.

"Hmm...was it that day that you were undressing me with your eyes in the cafeteria?" I asked grinning on the outside and inside.

"Ah, you're very observant." He smiled. "Actually, it was the moment that you called me stuffy, boring, and full of myself." I raised my head from his chest and kissed him as we both began to laugh. "God, you are so beautiful." His tone was much more serious as he pulled me closer and hugged me tightly.

I fell asleep wrapped in his arms and awoke the next morning with a smile on my face. As I kissed his cheek softly, and stared at him sleeping, I knew I had never felt this way about anyone before, and realized that I had broken another one of Charles' rules–I had completely fallen for Dr. Julian Kiron, and there was no turning back now. He finally opened his eyes, and they were even more beautiful first thing in the morning. "Good morning," he said, lacing his fingers into mine.

"You know this wasn't my intention when I came here last night," I said, laying my head on his chest.

"Oh, you know you came here to seduce me," he laughed.

He grabbed his watch off the nightstand. "I have to get going soon." I sensed regret in his voice. "I need to see how Rapula's mother is doing and check on Tau. I don't want anything to happen to the only child she has left."

I didn't think I could have any more admiration for him than I already did, but listening to him now, made me see that it was possible. He invited me to come along with them but warned me, it was a lot worse than it was when I was last there. I graciously declined, feeling a little selfish. I wanted to savor the happiness I was feeling today, and I knew if I were to go, that happiness would immediately be whisked away. I didn't feel so bad, knowing he'd have James to keep him company for the ride there.

Worries immediately flooded my mind. What if Julian slipped to James about what we had shared? James had a big mouth, and it wouldn't take very long to get back to Charles. "Julian?" I was lying with my head on his chest as he gently traced his finger up and down my face. "You're not going to say anything to James about this, are you?" I continued.

He looked down at me, pushing my hair behind my ear. "Of course not," he replied, sounding very matter-of-fact. I began to scold myself for even thinking such a thing. I knew Julian wasn't the type of guy to kiss and tell—at least I hoped he wasn't.

"I'm sorry, for even asking that. I just know James has no problem telling anyone who will listen about his sex life, however inappropriate." I continued, feeling as if I had to further justify my comment to him. "James has a really big mouth and would end up telling Charles, who then in turn would give me a lecture." I knew that I had probably said too much as soon as the words were out.

Julian looked puzzled. "Why would he give you a lecture?"

I sat up and started dressing, trying to create a diversion from the question that he just asked, but he wasn't forgetting as he asked again. I explained to him the relationship that I had with Charles and how he was like a second dad to me, always looking out for my well-being. How he and his wife Claire were there for me just as much as my dad when Jake and I broke up. They had seen how heartbroken I was, and he just didn't want to see it happen again.

Julian still looked confused. "I still don't get it."

I decided to be as direct as possible. "He didn't want me to fall for you only to never see you again in a few months." I bit down on my lip and waited for his reaction.

"Oh." He looked away as if it was all making sense to him now. "Well, that won't be a problem then," he said with a grin.

Now it was me who had the total look of confusion on my face. "Because clearly you haven't fallen for me."

I was at a loss for words not knowing how to answer that. I knew that I had fallen for him completely, but I didn't want to come out and say it, so I played it off with a nervous laugh.

"So, what happens if I fell for you first? Do you think he would still be mad at you then?" My smile was a mile wide. Was this his way of admitting he was feeling the same way for me as I was for him, or was I just another girl to check off on his list of many?

I finished dressing, and he walked me to the door. I hugged him tightly as he rested his lips on the top of my head. "I'll see you soon," he whispered.

I nodded and looked up at him. "Please don't ever second-guess yourself as a doctor again," I said in a very serious tone.

"As long as you don't ever second-guess your feelings," he responded. I stood on my tippytoes and kissed him softly on the lips before walking out the door. I was unable to wipe the grin from my face. I knew Charles was right–this would probably end with heartache, but I didn't care, I couldn't control the immense feelings that I had for him. Being ecstatic was nice for a change, and I wouldn't trade what I was feeling for anything. For once in my life I wasn't thinking of the future, I was just reveling in the present–and it felt good!

Chapter 11

I was still beaming by the time I got back to my room, not even caring that I would have a lot of explaining to do to Tricia about where I had been all night. Still, I was a tad bit relieved to find an empty room when I arrived. I knew I would have to deal with that later, but I didn't care. I showered and dressed, deciding to take everything at a little slower pace than usual. I tried relaxing without much success, jumping up to the light knock on the door. Those familiar butterflies took over with the absurd thought that maybe it was Julian. I tried hard not to show my disappointment when I saw Charles on the other side of the door, looking somewhat distraught. The only thing that popped into my head was that he knew— somehow James must have found out and told him. I played the scenarios over quickly in my head, still unable to imagine how he could have possibly found out so quickly. I was getting ready to plead my case. When he took me by the hand, signaling for me to sit down on the bed, I knew he was here for another reason, and it was something much more serious—the look on his face said it all.

"What's the matter, Charles?" I asked with apprehension.

"Kat—your dad—he's in the hospital," he faltered.

"What?" The deep pit in my stomach opened wide.

"The last few times Claire had checked on him, he wasn't there. She was finally able to reach him on his cell phone. It was then that he admitted to her what was going on."

"Well, can you please tell me what's going on?" I snapped.

"He's been diagnosed with a rare form of intestinal cancer that's spread to his lungs." He sighed heavily. "I spoke to the doctor taking care of him and he had suggested that you come home right away."

"How long does he have?" My voice cracked.

"About two months."

My whole world had come crashing down in a matter of

seconds. I tried to pull it together, half-paying attention as Charles let me know that he would make all the arrangements for a flight home as soon as possible. I was grateful that he was planning to come home with me, so I didn't have to be alone.

"I'm so sorry, Kat," he said, embracing me tightly. He must have sensed that I wasn't fit for company as he exited the room.

I burst into tears as the door closed behind him. This was so unfair. I had lost my mom at such a young age to cancer, and now my dad. He was all I had left, the one person whom I could always depend on, to whom I could share all my deepest secrets. The one person who mattered most to me. I couldn't imagine my life without him.

I sat on my bed just staring at the cinder block walls in complete shock, hoping this was just a horrible nightmare I would wake from soon. I didn't even acknowledge Tricia's presence as she walked into the room. She sat down on my bed next to me and hugged me tightly. I couldn't even hug her back—I was completely numb.

"Charles was able to get a flight out tonight, so you have to be ready to leave in a few hours." Her voice was calm and gentle. I was unable to respond, still staring at the wall. My head felt like it was about to explode from crying all morning long.

I wanted so much to tell Tricia thank you as she began to clear out my drawers and place everything into my suitcases, but I just couldn't get any words out. I had never felt so helpless in my life. She finished packing my stuff and walked into the bathroom, returning with a cold damp rag that she placed on my forehead, handing me a bottle of water along with two aspirin.

After a while, the aspirin started kicking in and the pounding in my head subsided, just enough to make it somewhat bearable to think. I was so angry at myself for not making an effort to call him last Sunday when I was sick. I realized that it wouldn't have made a difference—he would still be dying. I couldn't believe how quickly the day had changed from the euphoria I was feeling this morning to the pain I was in right now.

Something made me think of Julian. I was leaving in a few hours, we didn't have a few months, and I would probably never see him again, which only added to my sadness.

Tricia looked like she was in shock when she finally heard me talk for the first time in hours. "Tricia, do you have a piece of paper and a pen?"

She fumbled around looking for both, trying to appease my wishes, exiting the room as I began to write. My eyes were almost swollen shut from crying, and I could hardly see as I began to pour out my words.

Dear Julian,

I am so sorry I didn't get to say goodbye to you in person, and I wish I didn't have to leave, especially under these circumstances. I want to thank you for making this place a lot more bearable for me, even if you didn't realize it—you did. I'm so honored to have met you and happy to call you a friend. You're a great doctor and an even greater human being. Please take care of yourself.

Love always,

Kat

There was so much more I wanted to say, but I couldn't. I folded up the letter and walked down the hallway to his room, sliding it under his door.

The taxi arrived at 4 p.m. to take us to the airport. I hugged Tricia goodbye as Charles loaded up the bags in the car.

I wasn't much company for Charles on the long plane ride home, not saying much of anything. As I stepped off the plane in my cut-off denim shorts and flip-flops, it became clear that November at home was a lot different than November in Africa. The only thing I had keeping me somewhat warm was my favorite black hoodie. I was in such a trance as I watched the luggage going around on the conveyor belt, I almost missed mine. Charles grabbed the larger of my two suitcases, looking like a pack rat, carrying my bags and his.

I forced a smile at the sight of Claire, standing by the entrance waiting for us. She was such an attractive woman, at fifty-seven years old, she didn't look or act a day past forty. She took such good care of herself, eating healthy and exercising, and it clearly showed. She had a petite frame, always managing to keep up with the latest trends with her keen sense of fashion. I would sometimes find myself raiding her closet for a last-minute event that I had to attend.

As we got closer to her, I gazed into her warm brown eyes that were always so comforting and threw my arms around her. All the emotion I had bottled up the entire plane ride home was now coming out. She embraced me tightly, trying to console me, handing me a tissue and then greeting Charles with a kiss. She wrapped her arm around me as we walked to the parking lot.

I wanted to go straight to the hospital, but it was only 6 a.m. I sat in the back seat, trying to make conversation the best I could, but I couldn't wait to get home and be alone in my house—the most comforting place in the world.

A temporary flash of happiness overcame me when we pulled into the driveway. Charles and Claire walked me in, and I assured them that I would be fine as they walked out the door. I stood in the kitchen looking around, taking everything in. It seemed strange to me that I had to readjust to my own home after being away for so long. I put on a kettle of water for tea to try and warm up before venturing off to my bedroom to change into warmer clothes. I broke down completely when I walked into the bathroom and flicked on the light to reveal the beautiful terracotta tile. When I could no longer ignore the cries coming from the tea kettle, I ran my hands one last time over the tile and walked out of the bathroom.

My ears got a reprieve when I reached the kitchen and finally turned off the burner. I smiled to myself when I opened the drawer, looking for a spoon and noticed how every piece of silverware was meticulously placed in its spot. It drove my dad crazy when I would unload the dishwasher and throw the silverware haphazardly in the drawer—these were the little things I was going to miss.

After fixing my tea, I ventured out into the living room to watch some TV. Flicking through the channels, I finally decided on the news. I was still freezing, so I lit the gas fireplace and watched the flames dance as I began to recap exactly what had just transpired in these past twenty-four hours. Yesterday at this time, in my world, my dad was not dying of cancer, I had just spent the night with the man of my dreams, and I was turning over a new leaf of not obsessing so much over the future. It amazed me how much things could change in such a short period of time. I thought about Julian and wondered if he had gotten back and got my letter yet, and if it even mattered to him that I was gone. I looked down at my watch that was still set for Nigerian time. It was 1:10 p.m. there while the clock on the mantle displayed 7:10 a.m. here—Julian really was a world away. I grabbed my favorite throw blanket from the back of the couch and closed my eyes. I was finally in my happy place, only I wasn't feeling very happy at all.

The chiming of the mantel clock began to draw me from my sleep, when I was finally awake enough to realize that it was 10 a.m., I jumped from the couch and straight into the shower. Ten o'clock was the start of visiting hours, and I had planned on being there first thing, but my plan was foiled by oversleeping. I tried to shower as fast as possible, but couldn't help but take a few extra minutes. It felt so nice to be showering in my own bathroom with water that didn't smell like sulfur and turn everything brown. I rinsed off quickly, getting ready to just throw my wet hair back into a ponytail, but quickly pulled out the blow dryer, remembering that I wasn't in 90-degree weather anymore. When I was finally satisfied that my hair was dry enough, I slipped it back in a ponytail and quickly dressed. It felt weird putting on jeans for the first time in months. I realized they were a little loose on me from my lack of eating the horrible food over there. It would only be a matter of time before they were fitting back to normal, now that I was back and would be eating real food.

I gave myself one last look in the mirror before heading out the door, grabbing my coat on the way out. There were a lot of things that you had to get re-acclimated with after being away from them for several months–driving was one of them, as I stepped on the gas a little too hard backing out of the driveway and almost crushed my neighbor's garbage can.

The fact that my dad was admitted to the same hospital that I was affiliated with was good and bad. Good because I was able to park in the staff parking lot and didn't have to drive around forever looking for a parking space, that always were few and far between. Bad because there were too many people who worked there who knew I was supposed to be away, and the last thing I felt like doing was taking the time to explain to anyone why I was back.

I hurriedly made my way to the fourth floor going unnoticed. My dad was lying in bed, half asleep, with the television blasting. I startled him as his eyes opened wider, taking a minute to realize it was me. As soon as he did, a huge smile appeared on his face.

"Look who's here!" he said as I bent over to hug and kiss him.

He didn't look sick to me, he had lost a little more weight, but fortunately he looked a lot better than I had been expecting.

"Dad, why didn't you tell me?" I asked, starting to fill up with tears.

"I don't want to talk about that right now," he said in a very dismissing tone. I didn't want to upset him, so I decided to obey his wishes.

"I want to hear all about what's been going on, how was Africa, how is your oncologist friend?" He tapped the chair next to his bed for me to sit down.

"Africa was depressing. You wouldn't believe all of the sickness over there, Dad, it's just devastating."

I decided to tell him about the good parts: the beautiful waterfall, the little kids in the village, and I saved the best for last—Julian.

"He took such good care of me when was sick, Dad. He's such a great guy, unfortunately, I'll probably never see him again."

"Oh, why is that?" he asked.

"Because, he's a workaholic. He doesn't have time for relationships, besides even if he did, it would be long distance at best."

"Well, Kat, if you really care about each other, then you make it work somehow," he said, taking my hand.

I knew he was right, and if that had been the only hurdle in the way, then maybe it would be something we could get past. But the fact that he would never be around and even when he was home, he would be in Chicago and I would be in New Jersey, which was still quite a distance for a relationship to overcome. The biggest red flag was that he didn't want children, and that was just something I wasn't ready to give up for any man. I had always known I wanted children from a very young age, and now facing the loss of my dad it made me want them even more.

"Okay, and even if we were able to make it work. He doesn't want kids."

My dad sighed heavily. "Kat, you are going to make a wonderful mom someday—don't let anyone deny you that chance."

"Yeah, well that's if I ever find a husband to have kids with," I said.

He raised his eyebrows. "You really care for this guy, don't you?"

"I really do," I said, being completely honest with him and myself. "He's just so caring and easy to talk to."

"Don't forget handsome," my dad joked.

"Oh, Dad, he's beyond handsome. He's beautiful," I sighed.

"Well, maybe he'll start to see things differently."

"I doubt it, and besides, I really don't know if he feels the same for me as I do for him."

"How could he not feel the same way, Kat? Everyone who

knows you loves you."

"Well of course you would think that," I teased.

I walked over to the other side of his bed, checking out his IV to see what medications they had him on.

"Are you in a lot of pain?" I asked.

"Not anymore," he said as he pointed to his IV bag containing pain medication.

He had declined any radiation or chemotherapy after being told his chances of it having any effect on the cancer were very slim. He wanted to live what time he had left peacefully.

His doctor walked into the room with his head buried in his chart. "How are you feeling today?" he asked.

My dad introduced me as his daughter, *the doctor*. I always laughed when he did that, as if he had another daughter somewhere else in another profession, but it made him so proud to say it. I knew that he should be equally proud of himself as well, if it weren't for him, he wouldn't have that honor of including that title in his introduction of me.

"Oh, so I finally get to meet Dr. Vallia, whom I have heard so much about," his doctor said, shaking my hand.

I laughed, knowing that he had probably gotten more information than he really cared to hear from my dad, who would just talk endlessly about me, having no regard if the other person wanted to hear it or not.

"Yes, that's me," I replied.

"Well, I want to keep him one more night for observation then after that, I don't see a reason why he can't go home, where he would be comfortable." I cringed knowing that *comfortable* meant living out the rest of his days happily. He confirmed that I would be at ease, administering his pain medications, and I assured him I would. After he finished checking my father's vital signs, I followed him out the door and into the hallway to get a better grasp on my dad's condition. He explained to me that the type of cancer my father had was rare but very aggressive, spreading to other parts of the body quickly.

"Are you sure that the chemo won't touch it?" I asked.

"It's a ten percent chance, and quite frankly I agree with your father to not put him through it," he answered.

I was hoping there would be some miracle and he would tell me something different.

"What about the pain meds? What are you prescribing for him to take at home?" I was relentless questioning every possible thing that I could when it came to my dad's care.

"Well, right now, as you know we have him on a morphine drip. Once he gets home he'll be on a patch. I'll explain everything in detail to you before he's released. Just be there for him, spend as much time as you can with him," he said, placing his hand on my shoulder. "The important thing is keeping the pain tolerable," he added.

I shook my head, the whole conversation seeming so surreal. I never thought I would be going through this with my dad. He was always the strong one, the one who always took away my pain. I had to get used to switching the role; something I knew would be hard for him. He always hated being doted on. The fact that he was dying of cancer wouldn't change that.

I forced the best smile I could manage before re-entering the room, only to find my dad sound asleep. I sat down in the chair next to him, feeling a little disappointed, I had so much more to tell him. At the same time, I was relieved, I was now able to wipe the fake smile off my face and replace it with the tears that were just waiting to fall.

Chapter 12

I spent the entire day with my dad. He was just finishing up with his dinner, and I could tell he was getting tired while trying to be polite by listening to me babble on.

"Are you getting tired?" I asked.

"Just a little," he answered.

"I'm gonna get going so you can get some rest." He must have really been drained because he didn't even try and argue with me about it.

I checked his IV one last time, making sure that he had enough medication in there to get him through most of the night before kissing him lightly on the head and saying goodbye.

The temperature seemed to have dropped immensely from this morning as I walked out into the darkness. I didn't want to go home yet, I didn't feel like being alone. I sat with the car idling, thinking of where to go, finally deciding to pay Charles and Claire a quick visit to try to lift my spirits.

Charles and Claire lived ten minutes from me, in the town of Cape May. It was a quaint little Victorian seashore town with tree-lined streets, consisting of everything from grand Victorian bed-and-breakfasts resembling mansions to adorable little gingerbread-style homes. They were all in an array of colors, looking like they were plucked right out of a fairy tale. I found a parking spot on the street with ease with the summer crowds being long gone, parking wasn't an issue. It was hard for me to pinpoint when my favorite time of year was in this town. I loved the spring because the beautiful gardens were just starting to bloom with tulips and daffodils. Summertime went without saying, this was where I had found myself spending most of my summer days, whenever possible. Autumn was always a little quieter with all the summer crowds gone. They would hold lovely fall festivals as the green leaves on the trees that lined the streets transformed into vibrant shades of orange, yellow, and red. In the winter, the little town would come alive once again with loads of people shopping in the quaint little shops that filled the three-block pedestrian mall all decked out in Christmas lights. The bed-and-breakfasts became spectacular light displays on the outside, while the insides were precisely decorated, true to the Victorian era. The clopping of the horse-drawn carriages in the distance made you feel like you were in a Dickens novel. I had noticed that some Christmas lights were already starting to appear and within the next two weeks the entire town would be lit up to prepare for the Thanksgiving weekend.

Charles and Claire's house, just happened to be one of those adorable gingerbread types. I would normally never just pop in on anyone, but with Charles and Claire, I never felt uncomfortable doing so. Claire opened the front door, seeing me coming before I even made it up the steps of their big front porch.

"What a nice surprise!" she greeted, giving me a hug.

I walked into their cozy little home that felt just as comfortable to me as my own. Their house was just as adorable on the inside as it was on the outside, decorated in blue and yellow schemes which gave it a very beach-like feel, while keeping the Victorian style at the same time. I was envious of Claire's knack for decorating. She missed her calling as an interior decorator. They had the fireplace going in the living room, and the strong smell of apple pie came from the candle that she had lit on the mantle.

"Charles is just getting ready, we were going to get a quick bite to eat," she said, insisting that I come. It didn't take much persuasion–I was starving.

I finished giving Claire an update on my father just as Charles came walking down the stairs.

"Look who's here," he said, walking over to give me a kiss.

"You look happy to be home," I said, just seeing the glimmer in his eye.

They grabbed their coats and we headed outside, taking the short three-minute walk to the casual pub-style restaurant that was right up the street from their house, as I filled Charles in about my dad along the way. We arrived at the restaurant, which was like a ghost town compared to the usual line of people who were normally waiting for seats during the summer. We were seated immediately, much to my appreciation, as my stomach had been growling the whole walk over. I scrutinized the menu several times, wanting to make the right choice. This was my first real meal since coming back. After much indecision, I ended up just going with a burger and fries.

We continued talking about my dad. Charles wanted to make sure that I would be okay taking care of him when he was home. I told him there was no doubt in my mind that I could do it. But still he offered to come over and help if it started to get too much for me. Claire must have sensed my unease over talking about my dad and the cancer, changing the subject completely.

"So, Kat, Charles said you really didn't care for the trip," Claire said.

"It's not that I didn't like it, it's just not my type of thing," I clarified.

"I could imagine that it would be depressing," Claire said.

"Well you certainly wouldn't go there for vacation," Charles added.

"I don't know, that waterfall was pretty spectacular," I said, wanting to take my words back immediately. I forgot I had never told Charles about that day.

"Waterfall?" Charles seemed puzzled.

I began to backpedal, trying to cover my tracks as I downplayed the day to Charles and Claire. "Oh, it was just a little waterfall on the way back from the other village that Julian had quickly stopped off at to show me."

"I never saw a waterfall on the way to the other village," Charles said.

"Oh, I don't know." I shrugged as I took a bite from my burger that had just arrived.

"Who's Julian?" Claire asked. I watched as Charles raised an eyebrow, waiting for my reaction.

"Oh, just some doctor that I met over there," I said, making it so obvious that he was more than just *some doctor*.

"Does he happen to be handsome?" Claire asked.

"Well, kind of," I said as I looked at Charles who was raising his eyebrow once again at me in disbelief. "Yes, he is very handsome," I finally conceded.

"How did I guess that?" Claire laughed.

"And I warned her about someone like him," Charles chimed in.

"Well, I don't get it, if he's young, successful, and good-looking, why on earth would you warn Kat about him?" Claire asked Charles, sounding displeased.

It was as if I were listening to a broken record hearing Charles explain to Claire exactly what he had said to me that night in the cafeteria. He reminded her of how tough it was for the two of them when he had become so wrapped up in his job. Claire listened to Charles, but I could tell she wasn't in agreement, waiting until he had gone into the bathroom to say anything.

"Kat, you do what makes you happy."

"I know, but that's just a lost cause now anyway."

"Why?" She seemed confused.

"Because it just is." I dismissed it, not wanting to talk about it anymore.

She gave me a questionable gaze but ended the topic of conversation there anyway.

We finished eating, and for the first time in a long time, I finished everything on my plate, right down to the last French fry. My lack of sleep was finally catching up to me once we arrived back at Charles and Claire's house after the short walk home. I declined Claire's offer of a cup of coffee, hugging them both and saying my goodbyes.

I walked into the dark house, immediately turning on all the lights, trying to chase away the loneliness I was feeling. I changed into my sweatpants and jumped on the couch, curling up under a warm soft blanket. Flicking through the channels, I settled on reruns of *Seinfeld* to try to lighten my mood, finally starting to relax for the first time since being home. I was just starting to dose off when I heard my phone ringing from inside my purse. My stomach dropped as the first thing that came to mind was my dad. I rummaged through my mess of a purse, finally locating my phone, staring at the strange number that displayed on the caller ID.

"Hello?" I answered.

"Kat?"

My stomach dipped over the familiar voice on the other end.

"Julian!" I could actually hear the happiness coming from my own voice. I quickly calculated the time in my head. There was a six-hour time difference, which meant it was after 3 a.m. there. "What are you still doing up?"

"I just got done working. How are you? How is your dad?"

I told him everything that had happened and what my father's doctor had said. When I told him my dad's chances of survival with the chemo or radiation treatments, he concurred with my dad's doctor that it wasn't worth putting him through it. It didn't make me feel any better, but it put my mind at ease, hearing it confirmed by Julian.

"I'm really sorry, Kat," he said.

"Thanks," I whispered, feeling that familiar lump in my throat. "And thank you so much for calling, you have no idea how much it means to me."

"Not a problem."

"You really should be sleeping," I scolded.

"Sleep is overrated," he joked.

I suddenly felt like I was beginning to enter the land of the living just hearing his voice.

"How's Tau?"

"His surgery is scheduled for next week." He didn't elaborate much more. He seemed to be more interested in what was going on with me than what was going on over there, making me feel a little special. I looked at the clock realizing that we had been talking for almost an hour. I didn't want the phone call to end, but I couldn't ignore the fact that it was almost 4 a.m. his time and instead of sleeping he was on the phone with me.

"Well, you better get going," I said.

"Yeah, I guess," he responded.

"Thank you so much for calling."

"No problem, I wanted to call you sooner, but this is the first chance that I've had."

My heart fluttered over knowing that he had been thinking about me. I wanted so much to be able to just hug him right now, and I wondered if that would ever be conceivable again. Although I knew how I had felt about him, I didn't have a clear read on what his true feelings were for me. I knew that we had shared something special together, but I wasn't sure if it meant the same to him as it did to me. He was a genuinely nice and caring person to everyone. It made me wonder if this phone call was just a natural response that he would have done for just anyone.

"Good night, Kat."

"Good night," I whispered.

I hung up, feeling wide awake, trying to recapture my state of relaxation I had been in prior to my phone call as I plopped back down on the couch. I was anxious over what tomorrow would bring, wondering just how many days I had left with my dad, wondering if this is how lonely I would feel for the rest of my life once he was gone. I had been so happy to hear from Julian. It had been so comforting to talk to him, but he was yet another man who I was beginning to care for so deeply who would soon be exiting my life–if he wasn't gone already.

I couldn't think anymore so I decided I would go into my bedroom and lie in bed, the place that I had been yearning for, for the past five months. My soft satin sheets and pillow top mattress were a welcoming change to the rock-hard bed that I had been sleeping on just 48 hours ago. I fluffed my pillows before getting in, pulling the comforter up to my neck. The rain was just beginning to fall outside when I turned off the light. I closed my eyes, trying to think of happy thoughts, if there were such a thing right now in my life–the only thing I could think of was Julian. I ended up falling into a sound sleep with the rain beating on the roof and the wind singing a fierce melody in perfect unison, creating a flawless lullaby.

Chapter 13

My dad was waiting impatiently for me to finish talking to his doctor as I went over his list of medications. I wanted to make sure that he was going to be as comfortable as possible. He couldn't get out of the hospital fast enough, once I was finally content with his treatment plan. I grabbed his bag and he snatched it back from me, seeming insulted that I would think he wouldn't be able to carry it. I smiled at his stubbornness, glad that he was still exhibiting that trait.

We walked down the hallway, passing the nurses' station, and the two nurses sitting behind the desk stopped what they were doing to walk over and say goodbye to him. They too must have fallen for his impeccable charm that so many people couldn't resist.

"Bye, ladies," he said with a huge smile on his face.

We walked out into the chilly November morning. The sun was just starting to peek through the clouds, trying to warm up the day. The ground was still damp and the grass covered in moisture from the heavy rain the night before. I hated that my dad had to sit in the cold car, waiting for it to warm up. I had planned to get him home, make a nice breakfast and just relax with him for the rest of the day. My plan quickly changed.

"I haven't had a real cup of coffee since I checked into this joint," my dad said.

"Okay, I'll make some coffee when we get home."

"Nah, let's go to the diner for some breakfast."

"Are you sure you're feeling up to that?"

"Sure, why not?"

I quickly obliged as I pulled out of the hospital parking lot and headed in the direction of my dad's favorite diner, which was also a local cop hangout. I knew that part of his reasoning for wanting to go there was to catch up on the latest gossip from his old coworkers. The sun was starting to win the battle over the clouds, making it hard to see with the early morning glare coming in my car window. I haphazardly had one hand on the steering wheel and the other digging through my purse looking for my sunglasses when my dad slapped my hand, cautioning me to pay attention to the road. He stuck his hand in my purse finding my sunglasses with ease, opening them up and handing them to me. It was these little things that made me wonder what I was going to do without him.

As we pulled into the diner parking, there were several police cars scattered throughout. I smiled seeing the look of excitement that came over my dad's face. As we entered, we were greeted by my dad's old partner, Tom. He was a couple years younger than my dad and had been his partner for the past twenty years. He planned on retiring within the next year as well. I wasn't sure who my dad had told about his condition, but I knew immediately after hearing Tom speak in a very quiet tone that he was aware.

"Kat, you're back!" Tom said, finally acknowledging my presence. He stood up and gave me a huge hug.

"Yup, I'm back." I smiled as I hugged him back.

He leaned over, talking to the other police officer who had been sitting next to him. He was much younger than my dad and Tom. I guessed somewhere around my age. He wasn't in-your-face handsome, but there was something about him that made you take an extra look.

"This is Anthony's daughter, Dr. Katrina Vallia," Tom said just as proudly as my dad would have.

He stood up to shake my hand. "Nice to meet you, Dr. Vallia," he said with a crooked boyish smile.

"Please call me Kat."

"I'm Daniel."

Dad and Tom exchanged glances, and I immediately realized what the two of them were thinking. I widened my eyes at my father, signaling for him to remove any preconceived notions he was conjuring.

"Well, let's go get a seat." My dad relented.

We said our goodbyes and headed to a distant booth. The waitress immediately came over and poured us coffee. She must have been new, because she didn't spend the usual ten minutes chatting with my dad like all the others would. I was glad because I wanted to scold him for his latest attempt at playing Cupid.

"Honestly, Dad, you really don't have to feel that every single guy that's my age and has a pulse is a potential husband," I said, sipping my coffee.

"What? He's a really nice guy," my dad said as if he'd done nothing wrong.

"I'm sure he is, but I'm quite capable of finding my own guy. I just don't have an interest in doing so right now." The truth was, I had already found who I wanted to be my own guy. Unfortunately, he was a million miles away and would probably never fill that title.

"Well it doesn't hurt to try. But it seems to me you have found *the one*," he said as if he were reading my thoughts. I smiled thinking of Julian being *the one*. My dad was right, from the first time that I saw Julian, I knew there was something about him. "You see that, you're beaming just thinking about him," he said, again seeing right into my mind.

I laughed at my dad's keen sense of perception. "Even if he is the one, I hope there is another one out there or else I'm doomed," I sighed.

"Stop being so negative," he scolded.

"I'm not being negative, just honest."

"Just remember everything happens for a reason. There's a grandiose plan that we're all unaware of," he said in a serious manner.

I was unable to see any reason for losing the greatest man that I had known, in just a few short months, leaving me all alone. How did that make any sense in this big plan at all? A giant lump formed in my throat and I was beginning to choke up just as the waitress came over. I had time to regain my composure as my dad playfully joked with her while giving his order, something he always did to the waitresses when we would go out to eat. I placed my order and watched her walk away. The conversation changed, which I was grateful for, as Dad asked my opinion of his tile job.

"Oh, it looks great," I said. "Thanks!"

"Well, I knew how much you wanted it," he said.

He had no idea how much that tile job had meant to me. Even when it became old and outdated. I would never ever take it down or change it. To me, that would always be a symbol of my dad's love, one of his very last home improvement projects. We continued to talk, not skipping a beat in the conversation throughout breakfast.

"Ready?" I asked once the waitress brought us the check.

"Yup," he answered, grabbing the check from my hand as we made our exit.

When we arrived home, I could tell that he was getting tired. I gave him one of his pills and forced him to go lie down in his bed. I checked on him a half hour later and he was fast asleep.

I decided to tackle some laundry and was sorting through the clothes when I heard a knock on the front door. Glancing out the window, I saw Jake's car parked in the driveway. I instinctively looked at myself in the mirror hanging in the entryway, took a deep breath, and opened the door. I had to admit that he was looking very handsome dressed in a perfectly tailored suit. His dirty blond hair seemed much shorter than usual while his light hazel eyes had flecks of green shooting through, reflecting the colors in his tie.

"Hi," I greeted, opening the door and letting him in.

He walked in and gave me a hug. "I just heard about your dad."

"How did you hear?" I asked.

"I ran into Charles and Claire at the coffee shop this morning. I was working locally on a case today and just wanted to swing by to see how you were doing." He sounded very sincere.

We walked into the kitchen and I offered him something to drink. He declined, sitting down at the kitchen table to talk. I was hoping Dad wouldn't wake up. I didn't know what his reaction would be seeing Jake here.

"He-he has a very aggressive form of cancer. It's just a matter of keeping him comfortable now." My eyes filled with tears.

"Kat, you know I'm here if you need me."

"Thanks, I appreciate that."

"So, tell me about your trip."

"It was okay," I said, not wanting to elaborate.

"Just okay?" he asked, expecting to hear more.

I knew I wasn't going to get away without telling him more so I gave him more details, making sure to leave some out. He listened with interest, which was unusual for him. Normally his mind was off somewhere else when I spoke. Unlike Julian, who had always seemed so interested in everything I had to say.

"Well, you look great," he said.

"Thanks, too bad I feel awful."

The tears were now flowing down my face. I stood up to grab a paper towel and wipe my eyes, turning around to find Jake standing right next to me. He hugged me as he rubbed my back trying to console me. It strangely felt nice to be embraced in his hug with the familiar smell of his favorite cologne. He pushed my hair behind my ear and kissed me softly on the top of my head. I rested my head on his chest and closed my eyes, feeling oddly at ease. I stared up at him, and I could feel him holding me tighter. His lips skimmed mind and I finally came to my senses and pulled away before it went any further. I immediately removed myself from his embrace, angry for even allowing myself to be comforted by him.

"I'm sorry, Jake. I shouldn't have–"

"No, it's okay. I just really missed you a lot, Kat." I knew I couldn't respond the same way, because it would have been a lie. "I know you got a lot going on right now, but I want you to really consider giving us a second chance," he pleaded.

I couldn't lead him on and make him think that there was even the slightest chance of that happening. I had to make it clear to him now, so I didn't find myself running to him once my dad was gone, just to have someone around.

"It's over," I said trying not to sound too harsh.

"Well, I know you're not thinking clearly right now," he said as if in disbelief.

"No, I am thinking clearly where this is concerned."

He gazed at me questionably. "Jake, I met someone. Someone I really care about a lot."

"Who?" He raised his voice in jealousy.

"It's no one you know." That was all the explaining I was going to do.

"Is it someone you met over there?" My silence must have answered the question. "So, you're willing to throw everything we had away for some guy that you hardly even know, that you'll probably never see again, and sure as hell doesn't care about you the way I do?"

"No, Jake, I didn't throw anything away. You did, the day I caught you in bed with someone else. What I do with my life is no longer a concern of yours."

He stared at me a little bit longer before walking out the front door with more of a wounded ego than a broken heart. I closed the door behind him, feeling bad and relieved at the same time.

"Dad, when did you get up?" I asked as I walked back into the kitchen to find him pouring a drink.

"Just now," he responded.

"I would have gotten that for you."

"Was someone just here?" he asked.

I couldn't lie to him. "It was Jake. He stopped by to see how you were feeling, and how I was doing."

"You tell him we don't need him checking up on us!" He raised his voice in anger.

"Dad, he was just trying to be nice," I said, trying to calm him down.

"No, Kat, don't fall for that. He's circling around here like a vulture, waiting for something to happen to me so he can swoop you away. Guys like him don't change, they just get worse."

"Dad, calm down and give me a little more credit than that. I made it crystal clear to him that there is no hope whatsoever of us getting back together."

My dad looked at me proudly. "Well, Kat, even if things don't pan out with this Julius guy…"

"Juli-an, Dad," I corrected him, laughing at how he could never get a name that was more than one syllable correct.

"Well you know who I mean," he continued, ignoring my laughter. "If things don't work out with him at least it helped you get over that jerk."

I smiled at his logic. He was right. If I hadn't met Julian, would I have so easily let Jake walk out the door and watch him drive away without feeling any emotion at all?

Chapter 14

Time, which I hoped would slow down, was instead quickly flying by. Thanksgiving had come and gone and it was almost Christmas. The weeks faded away, along with my dad's health. His tough-guy façade was gone, much to my sorrow, and he was finally admitting defeat. When I looked at him, I didn't see the man I had known my whole life–my protector, my rock–and it scared me. I wasn't sure how much longer he would be able to make it without checking back into the hospital, but I was determined to keep him home for as long as I possibly could. I had until mid-February before I had to return to work, for which I was very thankful. This allowed me to spend all my time with him. The only thing making me smile as of late were my weekly phone calls from Julian. Even though those conversations were usually brief, it comforted me just to hear his voice and get a very valued second opinion on my dad's care.

I pulled down the Christmas decorations from the attic, getting ready to decorate the tree. If it were up to me, I wouldn't have even bothered with anything this year. I wasn't much in the Christmas spirit, but the situation being what it was, I felt that this year more so than any, it was important to make sure I had one, for my dad's sake.

I had invited Charles and Claire over to help trim the tree, hoping to get in the Christmas spirit. My dad insisted on helping, but quickly retreated to the couch when he began to feel weak. I could see he was in a lot of pain, so I quickly gathered up his medication to give to him. He could no longer keep his eyes open and I helped him off to bed.

"I hate seeing him like this," I blurted out, taking a seat next to Charles on the couch. Claire immediately put down the ornament that was in her hand and sat down on the other side of me. "I can't do any more to take away his pain, and it sucks."

"Have you asked the doctor about prescribing him a different medication or perhaps a higher dose of what he's taking?" Claire asked.

"Oh, trust me, his doctor is sick of hearing from me at this point. I've double-checked with Julian and he concurs that the medication that he is taking now is the strongest there is. The only thing stronger would be intravenously, which means he would have to go back in the hospital."

"You've talked to Julian?" Charles asked.

I nodded and Charles raised an eyebrow as if surprised.

"Well, Kat, I know you're trying to avoid it, but maybe he'd be better off in the hospital," Charles sighed.

"I know, I just want him home until Christmas." I rubbed my temples, knowing if he returned to the hospital, he would never come back home.

I gazed up at the tree covered in white lights, red and green ornaments, and topped off by a big red bow. Even though it looked beautiful it was missing its usual magic this year.

***

Christmas Day had finally arrived and my wish had come true—my dad was still home with me. I shopped as usual, buying him presents like I normally would, ignoring the look of disapproval on his face when he saw the big pile under the tree for him. He always lectured me about spending money on Christmas presents for him, but this year I understood why. I just couldn't bring myself not to do it. In some strange way, this helped me to pretend that this was just another normal Christmas.

I sat and watched him slowly open each present as he tried his best to exhibit the same level of excitement that he would every Christmas for my sake. When he finally finished, he directed me to the small box hidden behind the tree wrapped in white paper with a big red bow that overpowered the box. I knew immediately that it was one of Claire's elaborate wrapping jobs. I sat back down next to him and carefully removed the paper, trying to preserve the bow, removing the box's lid to reveal a beautiful, bezel-set diamond pendant dangling from a long white gold chain. I recognized the diamond immediately as the one from my mother's engagement ring. I had looked down at her finger so often as a child, always in awe of the way that diamond sparkled in the light, wishing someday, when I was grown up, someone would love me enough to give me such a beautiful ring.

I unclasped the necklace and lifted my hair out of the way so my dad could help me put it on. Tears streamed down my face as I looked down at it twinkling around my neck.

"It's beautiful," I whispered.

My dad smiled, seeming to know that this was the best Christmas present I had ever received. "Well, I was holding on to that diamond, planning to do something with it for your wedding day," he said sadly, knowing that he would never see that day. "So just promise me when you do get married that you wear that necklace, your mother and I can be part of your special day."

"I promise, Dad." I hugged him, allowing myself to release the sob I had been holding in. We spent the rest of the morning reminiscing about past Christmases. I smiled, thinking how the best Christmases were when my mother was still here and Santa still existed.

I suddenly realized the time, and quickly got up to get myself together. Claire and Charles would be here soon. Claire was bringing over the turkey that she had already cooked, so all I had to do was stick the lasagna in the oven.

I helped my dad back into bed so he could take a nap before they arrived, and then headed back to the kitchen to preheat the oven. I had my head buried in the refrigerator and carelessly grabbed my phone that was ringing on the counter right next to me.

"Hello?" I answered, cradling the phone between my ear and shoulder while trying to wrestle with the lasagna pan in the fridge.

"Merry Christmas."

I immediately shut the refrigerator door, ignoring my lasagna, at the sound of his voice.

"Merry Christmas, Julian." I was unable to wipe the smile from my face. "I hope you are taking it a little bit easy today."

"Trying to," he laughed.

"So, I guess you're not having a white Christmas there," I joked.

"Nope–feels more like July than December." He sighed.

"Well, here neither," I said, trying to make him feel a little better. "Just cold, gray, and dreary."

"How's your dad doing?"

"Not good." My voice faltered. "I think he's going to need to go back to the hospital. I'm just thankful he was home until Christmas. I just feel so useless. I wish so badly that there was something more I could do. I mean, I'm a doctor, Julian–I shouldn't be just sitting around watching him wilt away, I should be helping him."

"Hey, stop that. You've done everything possible for him, Kat. I'm sure he knows that."

"I just can't bear the thought of him never returning home again." I was finally realizing that my decision to keep him home was just as much for me as it was for him.

Julian was silent for a moment, as if he knew I was gathering my thoughts. "So, what are you doing for Christmas?" he asked, trying to sound more upbeat.

"Nothing very exciting, just a quiet Christmas dinner with Charles, Claire, and my dad. I would ask you your plans, but I think I already know the answer to that." If my dad wasn't sick then I would be right there with him, working in the heat like it was just any other day with no signs of Christmas anywhere.

He let out a slight chuckle before silence loomed between us. "Well, I really have to run," he said as it started to get a little louder in the background.

"Okay," I said, always hating having to hang up with him.

"Merry Christmas, Kat."

"Merry Christmas, Julian," I replied back.

***

It was a very nice Christmas, considering the circumstances. Charles and Claire had arrived, we exchanged presents and had a delicious dinner. My dad was even able to eat a little and seemed in very good spirits. He had gone to bed early and Charles and Claire left shortly thereafter. I sat under the Christmas tree, and looked down at my necklace and smiled. It truly was the best Christmas present ever, followed by the second best present–my phone call from Julian.

I curled up and fell asleep on the couch, only to be woken in the middle of the night by my dad in the bathroom throwing up blood. I knew that what I had been dreading most was finally here, and I quickly dressed to take him to the hospital.

He was all settled in by early morning and heavily sedated, unaware of anything that was going on. His doctor suggested that if there was anyone who wanted to say goodbye to him, then now was a good time to do so. I felt a heaviness in my chest, not wanting it to be real.

I was amazed by my strength as I called Charles and Claire and Dad's old partner, Tom. I made them all aware of what had happened and what the doctor had recommended.

Charles and Claire came immediately. Charles promised my dad that he didn't have to worry, he would always make sure that they looked out for me. I walked out of the room when I felt myself beginning to choke up. When they exited the room I could see the tears rolling down Claire's face.

"We're just going to run down to the cafeteria and grab some coffee, did you want some?" Charles asked.

"No, thanks," I replied.

"Okay, we'll be right back," he assured me. I knew that they had no intention of leaving my side today. I realized how lucky I was to have two such wonderful people in my life.

Just as they were walking away, my dad's old partner, Tom, was walking toward me. He hugged me tightly before he entered the room while I stayed outside in the hallway, wanting to give him privacy. He remained with my dad for some time before exiting. I was amazed to see tears in the eyes of this big burly guy who looked like he would never take any nonsense from anyone. He hugged me again, making me burst into tears as well. I thanked him for coming as he left with his head hanging low.

My dad was basically incoherent from all the medication being pumped through his body when I walked into his room. I knew he wouldn't understand anything I wanted to say, so I just kissed him on the forehead. I sat down in the chair next to his bed, etching his face into my mind so I would never forget it. I held his hand as he opened his eyes briefly and smiled, only to close them again forever, as I whispered, "Goodbye, Daddy."

Chapter 15

The funeral was small and intimate, just as my father had requested. After a small luncheon with a few of his close friends, and Charles and Claire, I was glad to be home. I just wanted some alone time to be able to feel however I wanted without being on display where everyone felt sorry for me.

The late afternoon sunlight was coming through the living room window. I plugged in the Christmas tree and turned on the fireplace. Tomorrow was New Year's Eve and while everyone else would be getting all dressed up and going out looking forward to a fresh new year, I would be sitting here reflecting on this one, wishing I could go back and change it. I thought about previous New Years, when I was younger. My mom and dad would never go out; instead we would always have our own little party with lots of junk food that I wasn't normally allowed to eat. The best part was being able to stay up way past my bedtime to watch the ball drop. I smiled, thinking that all those happy memories occurred right here in this same living room I was sitting in right now, but such a long time ago. Things were definitely a lot different now. I was all that was left of those cherished New Year's Eve parties, and it scared me being all alone. My dad's opened presents under the tree were a blow to my heart, causing me to regret my decision to buy them. I knew it was only going to be harder, deciding what to do with them now.

I looked out of the big picture window at the old oak tree in the backyard. That tree was my favorite play place when I was growing up. It provided shade from the hot summer days. It was perfect for climbing during my tomboy phase and the best thinking spot as I got older. It looked so barren in the winter, stripped of its green leaves of summer or the majestic hues of red and orange that it would unveil every autumn. I felt like that tree–empty. I had no one left. I would never be able to have one of my long insightful talks with my dad again. I sighed heavily and focused my attention on the lone wooden swing that hung from the limb of that tree, remembering how my dad had built it for me the summer after my mother had died. It had withstood the test of time, the harsh winters, the hurricane winds that would blow through—just as our love for one another had survived. I grabbed my coat and made my way into the backyard, allowing the brisk December air to hit me in the face. Taking a seat on the swing, I closed my tear-filled eyes and was transformed back into that little girl once again.

"Push me higher, Daddy."

"Okay, hold on, Katrina—here you go!"

I could hear the laughter and feel the happiness that filled the backyard that day.

"I love you so much, Daddy!"

"I love you too, baby girl."

The tears rolled down my face as I began to sob. I leaned back in the swing and began to pump my legs, swinging as high as I could, just like that eight-year-old girl all those years ago. The cold air filled my lungs as the wind burned my face, but I didn't care. I needed to be in this place now. I needed to be close to my dad. I finally slowed down and came to a stop, closing my eyes and resting my face against the rope.

"What am I going to do without you, Dad?"

I was frozen in my thoughts for quite some time until a seagull squawking overhead broke me from my daydreaming. As I looked up at the sky, the late afternoon sun was just beginning to set. Even the beauty of a winter sunset couldn't break me from my melancholic state. My hands were numbed from the cold, so I reluctantly got up and headed back to the house.

I stood by the fireplace and tried to warm up as best as I could. Claire was stopping by, so I went into the bathroom and washed my face, trying to look a little more presentable. I had just finished changing into my most comfortable sweatpants when I heard her knocking on the front door.

I turned on the front porch light before flinging the front door open. My stomach began to do somersaults, and I wanted to smile so badly but I couldn't, I was just too shocked. I had to do a double take to make sure I was seeing correctly—was it really Julian's beautiful eyes I was staring into?

He was standing on the front porch, looking more handsome than I remembered, if that were even possible. I couldn't help but check him out from head to toe. The black jacket he wore was as dark as his hair, which looked freshly cut. Under his unbuttoned jacket he had on a light blue Oxford-type shirt with a white tee underneath, jeans and black shoes.

I temporarily pulled it together and invited him in.

"Were you expecting someone else?" He grinned.

"Well, yeah, Claire..." I stopped myself midsentence, stood on my tiptoes and gave him the biggest hug ever, no longer able to hide my joy over seeing him.

He hugged me back, sending warmth and contentment throughout my body. It felt as if all the loneliness I was feeling just a short time ago had been sucked out of my body completely. My cheek rubbed against his freshly shaven skin which smelled so good, not like he had drenched himself in cologne but more of a fresh, clean scent.

"What are you doing here?" I asked after finally loosening my hold on him.

"Well, my trip to Germany got pushed up. I thought I'd have a few months back in Chicago, but now I need to head to Germany as soon as I'm done in Africa. I had to fly back to Chicago at the last minute to get all the paperwork straightened out with the hospital. I was planning on paying you a surprise visit, and then Charles got in touch with me and told me about your dad."

I was listening to everything he said, still in absolute amazement. I just couldn't believe that he was standing right beside me. "I'm sorry, I just can't believe you're here," I blurted out, realizing how long I had been staring at him.

He smiled that same beautiful smile that made me melt. I took his coat and hung it up, offering him a drink about a million times until he finally agreed to some water. I grabbed a bottle of water from the refrigerator and led him over to the couch. As I sat down next to him, I caught myself staring at him once again. I began to speak, trying to come out of my surreal state of mind.

"So how did you get here?" I asked.

"Um, let's see, a plane a car, some directions, my GPS." He chuckled.

I began to laugh too, thinking that was a stupid question to ask but I wasn't thinking as literally as he was when I asked it. "So, Charles knew you were coming?" I asked.

He nodded, and I assumed Claire wouldn't be stopping by after all since I was sure she was in on this little surprise with Charles; somehow I believed she may have actually played the bigger role of the two, convincing Charles to contact Julian.

"So how long can you stay?" I asked.

"Two days," he said as the lights from the Christmas tree reflected in his eyes.

My heart dropped a little hearing that I only had two days to spend with him, but I would take whatever I could get. Less than an hour ago I wasn't sure if I would ever even see him again, and now here he was sitting right beside me.

"I have to fly back to Africa and help the other team of doctors transition so they can take over. As soon as I'm done there, I have to jump on a plane to Germany." He sounded a little disappointed, almost as if he was looking forward to having those few months back in Chicago between trips, which I understood. I couldn't imagine traveling as much as he did. Then again, I was such a homebody, most people would find me out of the norm.

"Oh, wow, I really don't know how you do it," I said.

He shrugged. "I'm really sorry about your dad, Kat."

"Thanks," I whispered. "So how is Tau doing?"

"So far, so good. He had the surgery three weeks ago, and I've been keeping in touch with the surgeon. As far as they could tell, he's going to be okay. He has to stay in France for the next six weeks for observation, and if all goes well then he could go back home after that."

"That's great news!"

Julian nodded, but I could still sense some regret in his face over Rapula. I knew that he felt like he had let Rapula and his parents down, but he had done everything that he possibly could.

"Are you hungry?" I asked.

"No, I'm fine, I swear," he joked, knowing that I would probably ask him about another hundred times.

We talked for some time, and I could tell he was getting tired, his skin looked paler than usual and the light color of his eyes just enhanced the dark circles that were beginning to form underneath.

"Are you tired?" I asked.

"A little," he finally admitted.

"But I thought you didn't get tired," I teased as I got up to grab the blanket from the other couch. I turned off the overhead light and glanced out the window to see a light snow falling. I sat back down on the couch, covering us both with the blanket as we watched TV with just the glow of the fireplace and Christmas tree lights. He had his arms wrapped tightly around me as I rested my head on his chest.

"Thank you," I whispered.

"For what?" he asked.

"For being here."

I smiled when he pulled me closer and gently kissed my head. It didn't take long before I heard his breathing begin to change and as I looked up he was sound asleep. I put my head back down on his chest, kissing it softly. Just knowing he was here beside me, listening to his heartbeat and feeling him breathe, put my mind at such ease that it wasn't long before I was fast asleep too.

Chapter 16

The bright sunlight shining through the window woke me from my sleep. I reached over and touched Julian lightly—he was still here, I wasn't dreaming. He was sound asleep as I quietly got off the couch and gently covered him with the blanket. A light dusting of snow covered the ground and flocked the trees, creating a picture-perfect winter scene outside the kitchen window. I put on a pot of coffee, and it seemed like an eternity before it was done brewing. As I peeked into the living room, I noticed Julian just starting to wake. I giggled to myself over the boyish look he had about him as he rubbed his eyes, trying to come out of his sleep stupor.

"Good Morning," I greeted him with a cup for him in my hand.

"Good Morning," he responded.

"You were in a pretty deep sleep there."

"Yeah, well that was the first time that I had more than two hours of sleep in a while."

"Here you go," I said, handing him the coffee.

"Wow, you're good." He still looked like he was half out of it.

"Nothing but five-star service here," I joked.

I went back in the kitchen to get myself a cup of coffee and returned to the couch. "Are you okay?" I asked as I sat down next to him while he continued to stare into space.

"Yeah, I just didn't realize how exhausted I was."

"Well working nonstop will do that to you." I took a deep breath. "I can't begin to tell you how happy I am that you're here." He smiled when I leaned over and kissed him on the cheek.

"I've got to take this," he said with reluctance as he picked up his ringing phone from the coffee table and looked at the number on the caller ID.

"No problem." I smiled, getting up and heading in to the kitchen, allowing him his privacy.

"Well, I'm glad I didn't hold my breath waiting for you to get here," I answered when my phone rang and I saw that it was Claire calling.

She laughed. "Well, I figured you would like that surprise better than my boring company."

"Yes, it was a pretty nice surprise. Thanks, Claire."

"You're welcome. You deserve some happiness after all you've just been through."

"Yeah, even if it is just for a couple of days," I said.

"So, since it's New Year's Eve and since I'm dying to meet this Dr. Handsome of yours...I'd love to have you guys come over for dinner."

"Yeah, sure, that sounds great." I hung up the phone feeling a little selfish for wanting to have him all to myself in the short time he was here, but I couldn't deny Claire the opportunity of meeting him.

***

I spent the entire day showing Julian around. We visited several antique shops as he struck up long-winded conversations with the shop owners over various World War II collectibles. Normally I would never set foot in an antique shop, it just never held my interest, but today being here with him, I didn't seem to mind it at all.

We stopped for lunch along the way, and I found myself doing more laughing than eating as I listened to his stories about his mischievous childhood. I wondered how someone could have it all? Usually everyone had some flaw to them, but with him, I just couldn't find one. He was gorgeous, caring, and funny—the complete package.

It was getting later, the sun would be departing soon, and I wanted him to see one more thing before it did. We walked a short distance down the street, crossing over the main road that led to the beach. Making our way onto the deserted beach, the only sounds were the few seagulls flying overhead and the roaring waves crashing on the shore. The wind immediately began to pick up, and I stopped just where the waves washed up on the shoreline. The sky lit up in an array of muted shades of pink above the water. No matter how many times I had seen those colors in the sky, I always became mesmerized when I looked at it, as if seeing it for the very first time. I looked at

Julian, who seemed equally impressed.

"This is my waterfall," I said.

I stood on my tiptoes and wrapped my arms around him, coming very close to perfecting our first kiss. I ended it with a soft kiss on the lips as he pulled me closer, hugging me tightly.

"Now that was a ten." I grinned.

He laughed and took my hand in his as we walked along the shoreline for a bit longer. We took the short walk back to my car to get ready to head over to Charles and Claire's, his hand never leaving mine.

The parking situation at Charles and Claire's house was always a nightmare–tonight was no exception. There was a small spot in between two cars that I normally would never attempt to fit in–but Julian insisted I could. I followed his step-by-step instructions for parallel parking, and it took me four tries. Three of which involved almost hitting the car behind me. I looked over at him in the passenger seat as he tried not to laugh.

"That was pretty scary," he said, finally releasing the laughter he had been holding in.

"Hey, I warned ya!"

Charles had been standing on the front porch watching the whole parking debacle unfold. He was shaking his head as I came into sight. "Kat, you know you are the worst at parking. What would possess you to try and do that?" he asked in his fatherly tone.

I didn't say a word and just pointed to Julian.

"I didn't know she was that bad," Julian said as Charles reached out to shake his hand.

I walked past Charles giving him a kiss on the cheek. "I am nothing if not entertaining."

I headed to the kitchen to find Claire while Charles immediately began to talk Julian's ear off. The delicious smell of something roasting in the oven permeated the air, making me instantly hungry. Claire was in her element, in the kitchen. Along with her many other talents, cooking was at the top of her list. She was just finishing up with frosting a chocolate cake that looked as if it could be on the cover of a magazine.

"Need some help?" I asked as I placed the bottle of wine that I had brought in the fridge.

"Nope, everything is almost done. Just a few more minutes on the prime rib," she said, wiping some frosting from her hands. "So, where is this Mr. Wonderful?" she asked with a smile.

"In the living room, talking to Charles."

She rolled her eyes knowing how long-winded Charles could be at times. "Oh geez, let's go rescue him."

Julian was sitting on the couch across from Charles, who was doing all the talking. Charles continued his banter, having his back to the door and not seeing us enter. Julian immediately stood up when he saw Claire and me enter the room. *Such a gentleman.* I introduced him to Claire, paying close attention to her reaction. I knew immediately that she was just as captivated as I had been the first day I had met him.

It was the perfect night: delicious food, good conversation, and a little too much wine for me. "Oh, Kat, he is such a nice guy, and not hard to look at either." Claire laughed once we were alone in the kitchen. She took another sip of wine, and we both began to laugh like two schoolgirls.

We headed back into the living room after we were done cleaning up. I was finally coming out of my wine coma. It was almost ten when I looked at the clock, and I knew there was no way we would make it until midnight as I looked at Charles, who looked like he was about to fall asleep at any minute. Claire looked like she wasn't far behind either.

"Are you ready?" I asked Julian, yearning for some alone time with him.

He nodded, and Claire put up a little fight, insisting that we had to stay until midnight. Despite her best effort, I knew she really wanted to be sound asleep when the New Year rang in.

Charles was adamant that Julian do the driving. I wasn't sure if it was because of my parking job or because I had two glasses of wine. I finally gave in to his unyielding request, handing Julian the keys as we said our goodbyes.

"They're really nice people," Julian remarked.

"Yeah, they really are." I smiled

"You're very lucky to have them," he said, taking his eyes off the road to look at me for one split second.

"I know." He had no idea how lucky I was. I would have never been able to get through this whole thing with my dad if it weren't for the two of them.

When we arrived back at my house, he excused himself for a few minutes to answer some work emails from his phone. I opted to turn on the radio instead of watching the annual New Year's Eve special. It was still set to my dad's oldies station that he'd always listened to. I looked over at Julian, who was typing away on his phone, deep in thought. I immediately turned the radio up when *Hold Me, thrill Me, Kiss Me* by Mel Carter began to play through the speakers. This had always been my mom and dad's song, and it gave me goose bumps every time I heard it. Julian looked up from his phone for a brief second, giving me a weird look over my choice in music.

I stood behind where he was sitting and wrapped my arms around him. "Dance with me, please," I whispered.

He looked up at me as if I were crazy. "I don't dance," he said, trying to ignore my request.

"And I don't play baseball," I said, pulling him up from the chair and taking his phone from his hand.

"Wiffle ball," he corrected me.

I led him into the living room and wrapped my arms around him. I could feel that he felt as uncomfortable dancing as I had playing wiffle ball. We swayed slowly back and forth, and I sang the words to the song, which I knew by heart, while staring into his eyes. He laughed at my poor singing ability, and I hugged him tightly. I looked up at him again, and he took my face in his hands and kissed me. It was his best kiss yet. The music ended but our tongues were still engaged in a beautiful dance. "I want you so badly." His voice was low and hoarse.

"I'm all yours," I whispered back. He gazed down at me and my insides awakened as he carried me off to my bedroom, and we rang in the New Year making love all night long.

Chapter 17

The only thing better than waking up in my own bed was waking up wrapped in Julian's arms, but my happiness was fleeting when I thought about him leaving later today. I hadn't a clue where our relationship would go after this. I planted a kiss on his chest, stirring him from his sleep. His eyes peeled open, and he flashed me a cute boyish grin, and my heart ached, knowing I wouldn't be waking up in his arms for a long time–if ever again.

"Wow, that was a happy New Year," he said chuckling. I rested my head on his bare chest as he ran his fingers gently up and down my back. There was nowhere else on earth I wanted to be right now than in his arms. I was so content, so alive, and, most of all, so in love with this perfect man lying beside me. He turned on his side, pulling me closer, gently caressing my breast before I surrendered completely to his every want, making love to him once again. I didn't think it was possible to get any better than what we had shared last night, but it was. He left me feeling so content, but at the same time wanting him more. I was beginning to think that there wasn't anything this man was bad at.

After we finished, I pulled him closer while we both tried catching our breath. He kissed me gently and pulled me on top of him.

"You have no clue what you do to me," he said, pushing my hair out of my face.

"I don't want this moment to end." I ran my fingers gently through his jet-black, tousled hair. He flashed a quick smile, and I was pretty certain he was feeling the same way–at least that's what I had hoped. "I don't want you to leave me." The words were out before I could even stop myself from saying them, and I immediately regretted it.

"Kat, you will be fine," he said, looking down at me through his long dark eyelashes.

I'll be fine. What the heck was that supposed to mean? Okay, obviously he wasn't having the same strong feelings that I had for him. When I abruptly sat up to dress, he grabbed my arm, pulling me back to him.

"Hey, what's the matter?"

"Nothing." I tried playing it off, but he wasn't falling for it.

"Kat, please tell me, what just made you upset?"

I couldn't lie to him, as much as I wanted to *pretend* I didn't have any feelings for him—I did.

"I'm just finding myself having more and more feelings for you."

"Okay, and what's wrong with that? Do you think I'm not feeling the same for you?"

I shrugged, knowing it was so much more than that, even if he did feel the same way about me, I knew we were doomed. He was leaving for another country in less than eight hours and even when he returned, we both wanted different things out of life.

"Do you honestly think I would be here with you right now if I didn't have feelings for you?" he whispered. His words filled me with a bout of mixed emotions. He kissed me on the forehead, and I decided to drop the subject for now, not wanting to spend what little time we had left agonizing over this.

"Are you hungry?" I asked. He smiled and nodded. I kissed him softly on the cheek before jumping out of bed to make him my best omelet ever.

The day flew by much too quickly, and my heart sank when I looked at the clock and it was less than an hour before he had to leave for the airport. All the feelings from earlier surfaced again.

"What's the matter?" he asked.

"I'm just thinking about you leaving." He looked at me with sadness in his eyes and pulled me closer. "You think anyone would miss you if I just kidnapped you and kept you here with me forever?" I joked as I rested my head on his shoulder.

"Come to Germany," he blurted after a long silence. I laughed it off, assuming he was just joking, trying to lighten the mood. "I'm being totally serious."

I was still laughing but quickly stopped when I saw his serious expression. "I can't go to Germany with you."

"Why not?"

"Um...for one, I have a job here. My whole life is here."

"So, take a year off, or you can get a job at the hospital there. It would be a good change of pace for you," he said it as if it were no big deal.

I was shocked, unable to believe he would even consider such a thing. Even if I were to agree to it, I knew he wouldn't have time at all for me, given how hard he would be working—so, I would basically be alone, with no one, in a foreign country. I wanted to be with him more than anything, but I knew in my heart it wasn't the right thing to do.

"So, will you think about it?"

"No," I blurted out quickly. Now it was him who seemed stunned by my brusqueness. "Julian, you're going to be working nonstop while you're there. What type of relationship would that be?"

"Kat, I swear we can make it work." He was adamant.

"Okay, and what if we can make it work. There's another huge obstacle in our way." I didn't want to get too far ahead of myself with this relationship, but I felt as if it was something that needed to be discussed.

He creased his eyebrows in confusion, waiting for a response, so I took a deep breath and finally came out with it.

"I know that we're nowhere near this point, but I need the security of knowing that if I am going to invest so much into a relationship, that someday there would be at least a small chance of getting married to that person and having a family." I was proud of myself for being so straightforward.

The long pause and the look on his face confirmed what I already knew. He finally broke his silence. "I'm sorry, Kat, but I can't give you that guarantee. I know I want to be with *you*, but kids, no matter how far off in the distance, are just something I am really unsure about." His words pained me, and I had to look away. "I don't have the time to commit to a child. I grew up with a dad like that. He was never around for my sister or me because he was always too busy with work. I would never want to do that to my own child."

"You can be two things at once. There's no law against it, just because your dad was that way doesn't—"

He stopped me mid-sentence. "Kat, my career comes first right now." I appreciated his honesty no matter how much it hurt to hear.

125

"As much I would love to go with you, I just can't. We would be living out *your* dream, Julian, not mine. I know I want to have kids someday." There was no one else that I would have loved to have all of that with more than him, but I knew that wasn't possible.

"Okay, so what now?" he asked.

The hardest words I ever had to say were about to come from my mouth, and I hated myself for it, but I knew they had to be said, if I was ever going to get on with my life. "You go to Germany and I stay here, but I don't think that we can continue any type of relationship at all." My eyes began to sting from the buildup of tears.

His eyes widened, but I knew he couldn't possibly be feeling any worse than I was. He looked down and sighed deeply, raking his hand through his hair. "Is that what you want?"

"It's not what I want—not at all, but I know the more I talk to you, the more I'm going to miss you, and want to be with you. I need to be able to move on with my life."

"Why can't we just think about this, give it some time before we just end it?"

"Julian, don't you see we want totally different things from life? I've wasted five years on a guy who I thought wanted the same things as me, and I don't want to do that again."

"Oh, so I'm paying for his mistakes?" he snapped.

"No, you're not. You are nothing like him. You're kind, caring, and most importantly, honest."

"Yeah, maybe *too* honest." He shook his head as if he were disgusted with himself.

"No, don't ever think that, Julian; I appreciate your honesty so much."

He put his head on the back of the couch and looked up at the ceiling as if he were deep in thought. "I have never felt about anyone, the way I feel about you—I don't want to lose you." There was so much sadness in his voice that it tore me up inside. "We can be very happy together just you and me," he said, trying his best to convince me.

"I know, I am very happy when I'm with you. You have been the only person who has made me smile since I lost my dad, but I also know that I want a child someday—ever since I was a little girl I knew that I wanted to me a mom."

"Kat, I wish so badly that I could honestly tell you that someday

I'd be willing to be a father, but I can't right now. The thought of never talking to you again..." He paused briefly, looked away and continued. "The thought of you being with someone else—it kills me, but, I have to be fair to you, even though it's not what I want."

I swallowed hard, trying to hold back the tears. When he wrapped his arms around me, I couldn't hold them back any longer. He held me in his arms until it was time for him to go. "Can you just give me your phone for a second?"

I creased my eyebrows in confusion before handing off my phone to him. "I'm putting my number in here. If you need *anything*, promise me you'll call me." I nodded and choked back a sob.

I had a heaviness in my chest as I walked him to the door. I went to give him a hug but before I could, he pulled me close and kissed me. A million thoughts and even more emotions raced through my mind as our tongues collided. He pressed his forehead into mine, and I sucked in my lip, wanting to taste him forever.

"You be careful." My voice cracked with emotion.

"I will," he reassured me.

"I know that someday I'll be reading about you doing some pretty amazing things, and I'll be able to tell my kids that I was just some girl who was lucky enough to have known you."

"You will never be just be some girl to me, Kat. You were *the girl*." He kissed me gently on the forehead. "I love you," he whispered.

My heart leaped from my chest, hearing those words. I pulled him closer. "Julian, please don't make this harder," I sobbed, not wanting to let him go, but knowing I had to.

He looked down at me and wiped away my tears, and I could tell he was starting to get emotional as well. "Goodbye, Kat." His voice faltered.

I caressed the side of his face one last time before he turned around and walked out the door, barely able to see through my tears, I watched him drive away, and whispered, "I love you too." I closed the door and slid down to the floor, burying my face into my knees and sobbing uncontrollably. This past week had been a roller coaster of emotions. Two of the greatest men I had known left my life—one I had no control over, and the other by choice. I only hoped that the choice I made was the right one.

Chapter 18

It had been seven weeks since Julian had walked out the door. I thought about him constantly and was now second-guessing my decision, and doubting that cutting him out of my life completely was helping me get over him at all. I saw his face in everyone I looked at and every place I went. It was the same as mourning a death, only worse because he was just a phone call away. I knew he was in Germany by now, and I would have loved to have heard about how he was doing there.

I had been keeping myself busy with tying up my dad's affairs, and I was wishing more than anything to be able to go to him for advice. I felt so alone–missing my dad and missing Julian. My only consolations were that Tricia was now back, keeping me occupied, and I would be returning to work next week. I was hoping that it would be a welcome distraction to help to take my mind off everything.

I was on my way to the mall to meet Tricia for lunch and some retail therapy. Tricia and shopping were just what I needed to lighten my mood. Over the years, I had found that there was no better medicine than a new pair of shoes or a cute new top, but something told me it was going to take a lot more than that to snap me out of my melancholic state I was in. I smiled upon seeing Tricia already seated at the table when I entered the restaurant. She had a presence that made you happy, no matter how you were feeling. I bent down and gave her a kiss before sitting down as the waitress came right over to take our drink orders. Since this was our usual lunch spot, we already knew what we wanted, so we placed our orders immediately. I had only seen Tricia once very briefly since she had returned, and I was dying to get caught up on all the latest news in her life, but to my dismay, there was nothing to tell.

"Well, what about you and James?"

"What about us?" She smirked.

"I don't know. Is there anything I should know about?" She quickly shook her head. "Not even a kiss?" She shook her head again, this time trying to hold back her laughter. "You're lying." I laughed—something I hadn't done in a long while.

Tricia was a terrible secret keeper, so it was only a matter of seconds before she spilled her guts about the awkward first kiss she and James shared. We both began giggling like two giddy schoolgirls.

She told me they planned to take things slowly, and I knew right away that Tricia was the one who wanted it that way. It was so apparent that James was head over heels for her. He played a good game, acting like he lived this playboy lifestyle, but he would probably propose to her tomorrow if that's what he thought she wanted.

"So, what's going on with you?" she asked.

"Nothing much, just finishing up with the last of my dad's things."

"Oh, Kat, you've been handling all this so well, I don't think I would have been able to have held it together like you have."

I forced a smile. I was hardly holding it all together. I practically cried myself to sleep every single night, and I had to force myself to eat most days—but on the outside I was putting on a strong front.

"So, no phone calls from Dr. Gorgeous?" she asked.

"No, he's not going to call. I told him not to. If there's one thing about Julian, he keeps his word." I sighed.

"Kat, why are you doing this to yourself? You are absolutely miserable without him."

"I know," I admitted.

"Can I ask you a personal question?" She smirked. "Is he as good at sex as he is as a doctor?"

I nodded. Just thinking about being with Julian gave me goose bumps. "Better," I managed to get out.

We both began to laugh even though I was hurting on the inside. "Oh, Kat, you foolish girl, you have to call him," she said before taking a sip of her iced tea.

"I just feel like I've connected with him on so many levels," I said.

"I bet you have!" She giggled.

"Seriously, it's not just about sex, I see more to him than just this gorgeous, intelligent guy. I can be myself around him, and I never felt that way around any man. I feel like I can talk to him about anything, the same way you and I talk."

"Ah, Kat, you found your Prince Charming and told him to never call you again. What's wrong with you?" she scolded.

"He doesn't want kids, he made that clear. Maybe our relationship wouldn't even get that far, but on the off chance that it did, I know I want children someday," I said sadly.

"Ugh, well, at least call him and see if he's as miserable as you. Maybe that will make you feel better." She laughed.

"I've been thinking about it–I don't know. Can we focus on something happier for now, like shopping?"

I was exhausted by the time I got home from our power shopping trip. When I checked my voicemail, I was reminded of my doctor's appointment in the morning. I so badly wanted to cancel it so I could just sleep in, but I had to keep it if I planned on returning to work next week. I needed to go over my blood work to make sure I didn't bring back any communicable disease and to also receive a series of shots. I was so exhausted from all the shopping, I decided to make myself a bowl of cereal and call it an early night.

I woke up early the next morning feeling unusually rested and relaxed. Julian was again my first thought the moment my eyes peeled open. I just wished that I could get to a point where I didn't think about him every single second of the day. Even when I would wake up in the middle of the night, he would be the first thing on my mind.

As I sat drinking my coffee, I began to think—what if I threw everything away with him for nothing? There was no guarantee I'd ever find Mr. Right and settle down and have children, just as he couldn't guarantee me that he would ever want to have children. So, should I have just taken my chances with the person I wanted to be with most in the world, in hopes that he would change his mind? I played it over in my head several times before grabbing my phone from my purse, scrolling down my contact list until I got to his name. I came close, but couldn't bring myself to hit the call button. When I looked at the clock, I realized I couldn't call him even if I had wanted to. I had just enough time to get to my appointment. I threw my phone back into my purse, hoping I would work up the nerve after my appointment.

I hurriedly got myself together, taking one last sip of my coffee and heading out the door. Luckily there was no traffic on the highway, allowing me to pull into the parking lot exactly three minutes ahead of schedule. It was unusually warm for mid-February, and I was hopeful that was a sign of an early spring. January and February were always depressing months for me— Christmas was over with nothing to look forward to except the dreary days of winter. I began to wonder what the weather was like in Germany right now, then immediately tried to change my thoughts to something else.

I walked into Dr. Ember's office and signed the clipboard, scanning the waiting room to find only one other person, I was hopeful I would be in and out in no time. I took a seat and looked through the latest *Better Homes and Gardens* magazine at some of the latest recipes. I was thoroughly absorbed in a double chocolate fudge pie recipe, barely hearing the nurse call my name.

"He'll be right in," she said as she led me into Dr. Ember's office, closing the door behind her.

I looked around his office, taking in the beautiful landscape pictures of local beaches hanging on his wall. His bookcase was filled with medical journals, along with photos of his family. I began to wonder what Julian's office had looked like. What type of pictures did he have around? I scolded myself for once again relating everything to him, making my urge to call him even greater. I thought of what I would say to him. Should I just casually call him just to say hello and see how he was doing or should I tell him the truth–I couldn't stop thinking about him and was ready to give up everything to be with him? The knot in my stomach pulled tighter from overthinking it all. I decided that the right words would come to me once I heard his voice. I just wished that Dr. Ember would come in soon, so I could get out of here before I chickened out.

I breathed a sigh of relief as I heard Dr. Ember's voice just outside the door. He entered the office and greeted me with a hug. He had been my family's doctor since I was eight years old and was almost as proud as my dad when I became a doctor.

He sat down at his desk and opened my chart, adjusting his glasses as he looked over my results. "Well, Kat, let's see, we just got your blood work in late yesterday, so I still haven't had a chance to look over your results," he said, flipping through the pages. "How are you feeling?"

"Fine," I answered as I shook my leg anxiously. I was half-paying attention to what he was saying. My impatience was getting the best of me, and my mind was a million miles away—I needed to hear Julian's voice.

He started getting up from the desk before something he had been reading on the page made him sit back down. "One thing here, Kat," he said looking at the page intently.

"What's that?"

He looked over the paper at me. "Did you know you're pregnant?"

As if the look on my face didn't show my answer, I was in complete shock. "What?" I asked with a nervous laugh.

"Have you not had any symptoms?"

"I...I don't know..." I answered with doubt in my voice. I knew that I was battling with occasional bouts of nausea, but I thought that was due to the stress of losing my dad and with everything else going on with Julian. I thought back to when I last had my period and could only remember that it was a few weeks before my dad passed away. There were a few times that I had forgotten to take my pill, but I always doubled up the following day.

"Do you have any idea how far along you may be?" he asked.

"Seven weeks," I replied, still in a daze.

Dr. Ember looked at me, surprised. "Are you certain of that, Kat?"

"Yes," I answered with sadness in my voice, remembering one of the best nights followed by the best morning of my life.

He explained that it was routine to run a pregnancy test on all female patients who were scheduled to have these types of shots, just to make sure that there is no chance of pregnancy before they administer them. He finished fumbling through the rest of the test results as I sat there silently, too shocked to say anything.

"All of your tests are fine. I am not going to give you the shots today due to the circumstances. Since everything came back normal there is really no need for them anyway, it's just a precaution."

I was still speechless just staring into space, feeling like this was a dream I'd wake up from soon.

He looked at me compassionately. "Kat, I know you are under a tremendous amount of stress with your dad's passing. I know how close the two of you were, but please take care of yourself and this

baby. You know he would want the same if he were here right now."
I nodded, willing myself not to cry until I made it out to my car.

We finished up, and I headed out of the office, almost running through the waiting room. I couldn't get into the parking lot quickly enough. My head was spinning. I sat in the car trying to stop myself from shaking. I had no clue what I was going to do. I imagined the look on Julian's face if I were to call him now and tell him this. This was the whole reason I had been tormenting myself for the past seven weeks by not talking to him, because he *didn't* want to have children. How in the world was I going to tell him that he now had no choice in the matter?

I heard his words so clearly in my head as if he were sitting in the seat right next to me. *"I know that I want to be with you, but kids, no matter how far off in the distance, is just something I am really unsure about."* If he wasn't sure about having them in the far-off distance, he sure as heck wouldn't be able to handle it happening now. I wanted to tell him more than anything. Knowing the type of guy he was, he would have rushed back just to do the right thing, and end up hating me for it or worse yet, resent this baby, which was the last thing I wanted. I didn't want him to feel as if I trapped him into something. I wanted him to want to be with me and our baby. I looked down at my belly that was showing no signs of pregnancy, and a wave of emotions hit me—this was a part of Julian that I would have forever. He had given me part of my dream, which included falling in love and having a baby. There was no doubt in my mind that I had fallen in love with him completely, and now I was going to have his baby. The only thing missing would be him. I grabbed my phone from my purse, finding his name in my list of contacts, but instead of hitting the call button, I instinctively hit the delete button, removing him from my phone and my life forever.

Chapter 19

I looked down, rubbing my belly that was fully popped. Being eight-and-a-half months pregnant and still working full time was now taking its toll on me.

I knew that I had nothing to complain about, I had a very smooth pregnancy, not even really beginning to show until a month ago, and of course I knew it would get a little harder toward the end. I happened to be one of those rare people who loved being pregnant, but now I was at the point where I just wanted to get it over with. It was now the very end of August and my due date was mid-September. I found that I was beginning to nest. I was up until late at night cleaning with an exuberant amount of energy, and I wondered if that was a sign that this baby would be coming soon.

Claire and Tricia had become my devout caretakers, catering to my every whim whether I wanted them to or not. At least one of them had gone to every doctor's appointment with me, nearly beating down the ultrasound tech to find out the sex of the baby. I sensed disappointment from Tricia when we found out it was a boy, but she quickly recovered seeing the little outline of the baby on the monitor. Claire was just happy over the thought of a baby, regardless of the sex. My baby wouldn't miss out on the great joy of having grandparents as long as she and Charles were around. I didn't care either way, but all along something was telling me it was a boy. The day of that first ultrasound had been so emotional for me, seeing my baby moving around, making out different parts of his body, seeing his heartbeat—I wondered how you couldn't believe in miracles after seeing that.

Tricia was to be my Lamaze coach. She had attended weekly classes with me, and I wasn't quite sure how much we had gotten out of it. We behaved more like Ethel and Lucy, a few times I felt like I was going to give birth right then and there from laughing so hard. I was happy once again; this baby growing inside made me feel complete. Every kick, turn, and flutter he made let me know that I wasn't alone.

My dad's old bedroom had been transformed into the nursery. It had been meticulously decorated into a nautical theme done in shades of navy blue and red with a beautiful mural of a sailboat on one of the walls; all done by Claire. I would find myself coming into this room more often just sitting in the rocking chair and thinking. It somehow made me feel like I was closer to my dad being there in his bedroom. I had been thinking about him often these days and wished he could be here to meet his grandson. I knew that he would have been angry at first with his old-fashion way of thinking–getting pregnant out of wedlock was just something that should never happen according to him. But I also knew that once he had gotten over it he would have been overjoyed.

I had come so far from that day at Dr. Ember's office, never turning back or second-guessing my decision. It really helped to have the support of everyone around me. Charles and Claire both understood why I had to make the choice that I did and never once tried to persuade me to do anything else. Tricia was a little hesitant at accepting it, she was a romantic at heart and thought things would work out if I had let them. She quickly grew to respect my decision, seeing how adamant I was about my choice. Even James, who I thought would be a problem, was supportive. I wasn't sure if he had kept in touch with Julian, and I didn't want to know.

I sat in the rocking chair, closing my eyes. My world was finally calming down. I would soon be a working single mom with a newborn baby, who would be keeping me up half the night. I wasn't scared, I wasn't nervous–instead I was overjoyed to take on this new role. It was what I wanted more than anything now.

I smiled as I felt a kick, which were few and far between now that he was getting bigger and running out of room to move around.

"There you are." Claire poked her head into the nursey. I hadn't even heard her and Charles come in. "Oh, Kat, you can't continue this any longer, you look worn out."

"Two more weeks," I said, trying to hoist myself from the chair. I had planned on taking off three months after the baby was born, and Claire had graciously agreed to babysit for me once I went back to work. This put my mind at ease knowing he would be well cared for by someone who loved him.

I followed her out to the kitchen, smelling her homemade lasagna that she had brought over for dinner all the way down the hallway.

"Claire, you know I do have plates." I laughed at the paper plates that she had also brought over as she began to set the table.

"Well, that way we don't have to wash dishes," she replied.

After eating way too much I was starting to feel uncomfortable. Even when I wasn't pregnant I could never resist her lasagna. "I think he likes your cooking too. That was one huge kick!" I said as I stood up. Claire jumped up from the seat, putting her hand on my belly trying to feel him move. I started to gather the silverware off the paper plates to load into the dishwasher when I began to feel a light trickle that turned into a huge gush of water. Claire had just walked into the living room to tell Charles to turn down the television as I stood still, trying to stay calm.

"I swear, I'm going to get that man a hearing aid," Claire rambled on when she walked back in, gasping when she saw the look on my face and the puddle that surrounding me. She screamed for Charles, who immediately got up to see what was the matter.

Ironically it was I who was trying to keep the two of them calm the whole way to the hospital. I knew that I still had quite a while to go, my contractions were too far apart, so I didn't get myself in a panic.

I settled into my room while the nurse came in and hooked up my IV. Charles had finally gotten a hold of Tricia, and I felt much better once she had gotten there and was sitting by my bedside.

"Are you scared?" Tricia asked.

"Nope," I answered without hesitation.

She smiled and grabbed my hand. "I'm so proud of you for doing this all by yourself. I don't think I would have been brave enough."

"You'd be surprised what you're able to do when you're faced with it," I said.

Sleepiness was taking over. I tried very hard to keep my eyes open, responding to Tricia, knowing that I was making absolutely no sense at all. It wasn't too long before I finally gave in to my heavy eyelids.

Julian was there, right beside me as I held our beautiful baby in my arms.

He was so happy–we were a family. "I love you, Kat. Thank you for giving me this baby," he whispered as he kissed me softly on the top of my head.

"I love you too, Julian." The words came to me so easily. The same way I wished they had that day I watched him walk out that door.

I was so overjoyed that I must have had a smile on my face when the nurse woke me up as she came to check on my IV. My dream had been so real that I felt a flash of sadness as I looked down still seeing my big belly.

"How are you feeling, honey?" the older gray-haired nurse that had been checking my IV asked as she walked closer to my bed. "Are you in a little more pain?" She must've been able to read the expression on my face before I could get the words out. I nodded, still feeling very groggy. "The doctor is here now, she will be coming in shortly to check on you." She handed me a cup of ice chips as if she sensed my extreme thirst.

I temporarily forgot about the pain when I heard Tricia and Claire cackling outside my door "Sleepy head is up," Tricia said as she entered the room. Claire sat down on the bed next to me, rubbing my back as the pain was starting to become worse. I breathed a sigh of relief when I saw my doctor enter the room.

"I think you're ready to have this baby," she advised after a quick exam.

For the first time during this pregnancy, I was becoming a little apprehensive in not knowing what to expect as the contractions became unbearable. I looked to see Tricia and Claire standing on each side of me and began to calm down a bit. The strong desire to push took over as I bore down, pushing as hard as I could. "Just one more push, Kat," Dr. Hartford coached. I closed my eyes and gave it my all, and it wasn't long until Matthew "Matty" Anthony Vallia came into this world. Listening to him cry was music to my ears as I waited patiently for him to be cleaned up and given to me. The nurse placed him in my arms, swaddled up in a blanket with a little blue cap. He immediately stopped crying as he wrapped his tiny little fingers around my finger. I knew that there was no one on earth that I loved more than this little human being who I had just met only a few seconds ago. He was just perfect in every way as he opened his eyes wider, revealing the brightest shade of blue that I recognized immediately–I was looking into Julian's eyes.

Chapter 20

Five years later

"**M**ake a wish, Matty," I said as he blew out the candles on his birthday cake.

I smiled as he took a deep breath, making sure he got every single one out in one shot.

I had a hard time believing he was actually five years old today. Time was going by much too fast and as exhausting as those diaper and bottle days were, I missed having a baby around. I didn't want to miss out on anything, so I tried to savor each and every minute of his childhood. He seemed to be more mature than most kids his age, and never lacked in the popularity department, having a different play date or attending a birthday party every weekend. I could tell that he was destined to be a leader just by the way other kids had looked up to him at such an early age. He had a caring sensitive side that I had hoped he would take with him into adulthood.

I watched as he ran around and played soccer with the other boys at the party, many of whom were patients of mine. He made sure he was giving all his guests equal attention. I couldn't help but smile when I saw a little girl run up to him and hug him innocently. I knew that in the years to come he would be beating the girls off with a stick. He was Julian's clone in every way, with the same jet-black hair and the way he carried himself with confidence. He only had one dimple compared to Julian's two, but the thing that was undeniable was his eyes. I had never seen eyes the color of Julian's before, and I didn't think eyes that striking could ever exist on someone else, until Matty came along. This made Julian very hard to forget—I saw him every time I looked at Matty.

I had forgotten him the best I could, and realized that I must not have really meant that much to him as I never heard from him again. I was willing to reroute my whole life for him before I found out I was pregnant, and even though I knew he had just obeyed my wishes, I was still a little angry that he did. I felt a little twinge of jealousy when James had returned from a conference in Chicago several years ago and ran into him. Being *James* and not having a filter on anything that came out of his mouth, he couldn't wait to tell Tricia and me all about Julian's bachelor lifestyle. I cringed, hearing how on both nights when James saw Julian, he had a different *hot chick* on his arm. It was silly of me to still be carrying a torch for him after all these years, what we once had was ancient history, but he'd always hold a special place in my heart, and he'd always be my child's father. I had moved on with my life the best I could. Working full time and raising a young child, didn't leave time for much else. I had gone out on several dates with different guys, all of whom were nice, but the longest relationship I had since Matty was born lasted for about five months. I knew it would be nice to meet someone and settle down, but it just wasn't at the top of my priorities.

Tricia was more concerned with my dating life than I was. She had been pestering me for some time about going on a date with Dr. Patrick McGinn, one of the doctors in James' practice. He was a nice guy and great with Matty. We spent a lot of time together over the summer going to the beach, but it was always in a group, which usually consisted of James, Tricia, and Matty. I had never been on an official one-on-one date with him. The extent of our relationship was texts and emails, and an occasional phone call, but whenever we did get together for our group outings, I found he could always make me laugh. Every time we planned on getting together for a drink, something would always come up on either end. The problem was, I viewed him as a friend. I just didn't feel that same spark that I had with Julian. I knew I would probably never feel that again with anyone, but I remained hopeful. Another big part of the problem was, I wasn't ready to let anyone else into mine or Matty's world just yet. Matty surely wasn't lacking in the father figure department— Charles, who he referred to as *Pop*, was always around. Charles had decided to retire a year after Matty was born, so he could spend more time with him. They were inseparable. He loved teaching Matty how to fish, taking him to baseball games, and even golfing–which surprisingly, Matty loved. I was happy knowing that he was the same type of grandfather to him that my dad would have been.

Another unlikely male figure in Matty's life was James. He had been coming around a lot more since he and Tricia had become exclusive and now engaged. He and Matty were like best buds, and I sometimes wondered if it was because they were at the same level of maturity.

Claire and Tricia had been my rock since Matty was born. Claire was the perfect grandma and Tricia the perfect aunt. I realized over these past five years that family is not all about blood. Family is who is there for you the most, and this group of people in my life had proven that they would be there time and time again.

The last of Matty's guests were leaving as we walked them to the door. Matty ran back to the couch, sitting in between Charles and James looking like he was coming down from a sugar high.

"Don't you think you should set a date first?" I teased as Tricia sat at the kitchen table, skimming through bridal magazines while Claire and I cleaned up. She and James had been engaged for a year now with no sign of a wedding date. She claimed she wanted to take things slowly. She was so set in her ways and wasn't a big fan of change.

She looked at me and rolled her eyes. "Come on, Kat, I'm trying to break a record—don't you want to be the world's oldest maid of honor?" She laughed and I smacked her lightly with the dishtowel.

Matty walked into the kitchen and grabbed a bottle of beer from the fridge. "Where are you going with that?" I asked.

"Uncle James wanted it," he said in his gruff little voice, as he ran off to the other room.

"He's such a good role model, and you wonder why I haven't set the date yet," Tricia said sarcastically as Claire and I laughed.

Matty made his way back into the kitchen once again and looked up at me. "Mommy, can Gracie sleep over?" He batted his long eyelashes, which always seemed to help him get his way.

Gracie was a golden retriever who Charles and Claire had adopted last year when Matty had become relentless about wanting a dog. I was adamant about not having pets, because I knew I didn't have the time that was required to take care of one. Charles and Claire, who were unable to see Matty heartbroken, went to the shelter and picked out Gracie. She was Matty's dog but lived at their house. To my dismay, I was slowly getting joint custody of her as she was beginning to have more overnight visits than I cared for. I looked down at his adorable face, unable to say no to him.

"Okay, since tomorrow is Sunday and today is your birthday," I said, trying to let him know this wasn't going to become a habit.

"Yes!" he exclaimed as he ran off to tell Charles and James the news.

After everyone had left, Matty fell asleep on the couch with Gracie lying on his feet, so I decided to use this quiet time to fill out the barrage of school paperwork that had come in the mail weeks ago, and I had been ignoring. I was having a hard time believing that in a week Matty would be in kindergarten. Once I got started, I zipped through the forms, feeling a heaviness in my chest when I got to the line asking for father's contact info. One day Matty would want to know about his dad, but I wasn't prepared for that just yet, for now he was content that his dad was some great doctor who was traveling around the world saving people.

I filled out so many papers that my hand was going numb by the time I put my final signature on the last one. I looked at the clock, realizing it was after eleven. Tomorrow was the last Sunday in August, and the summer days were dwindling, so I had planned to spend the entire day at the beach with Matty.

I walked over to the couch and picked Matty up to take him into his bedroom. I hadn't realized just how heavy he had gotten in the past few months. As I tucked him in his bed, he mumbled something in his sleep. Gracie was right under foot, jumping up on his bed assuming the same position that she had on the couch. I kissed him good night and turned on his night light, closing his door half shut behind me.

***

I could tell that it was going to be a beautiful day as I awoke to the sun streaming in through my window. I hurried out of bed to see what mess awaited me when I heard Matty in the kitchen banging dishes together. He greeted me at my bedroom door, carrying an oversized bowl of cereal.

"Here you go, Mommy." He smiled proudly.

"Is this for me?" I acted surprised.

He nodded, unable to wipe the smile from his face.

"Wow, this looks delicious!" I took the bowl from him and placed it on the nightstand. Taking a seat on my bed, I tapped on the mattress, signaling for him to climb up. He effortlessly made his way up on the bed, and I pulled him closer, squeezing him tightly, and kissing him on his strawberry-shampoo-scented head.

"I love you so much." I rested my lips on the top of his head.

"I love you more," he said in a silly voice.

"Nope, I love you more." I tickled him, and he let out a deep belly laugh.

"Are you ready for the beach?" I asked.

"Yup!" He jumped off the bed, and I followed him out of the room, taking my monstrous-sized cereal bowl with me.

It was a perfect beach day—not a cloud in the sky, with a comfortable breeze coming from the ocean. We spent the day looking for seashells and playing in the sand. I was so happy that Matty loved the beach as much as I did. This had become our Sunday tradition in the summer.

"How many fish are in that ocean?" Matty asked as he stared out into the water.

"Lots." I smiled over his inquisitiveness.

"When I get bigger I'm going to build a great big house for me and you right on the beach," he said, squinting to keep the sun out of his eyes.

"That would be wonderful." My heart melted at how much I loved this sweet little boy.

The breeze picked up and the position of the sun was beginning to change, as well as the tide. I knew that it was getting later. I grabbed my phone from my beach bag to check the time and it was close to five. We were both hungry, and I could tell the sun had worn Matty out. We packed up our belongings, and Matty, always trying to be the gentleman, carried both chairs. I allowed him to carry them for a bit before taking them from him as I watched him struggle up the sand dune.

We stopped off at what had been my dad's favorite diner to grab dinner, both having burgers, with Matty eating more fries than anything else. He claimed he was full, but somehow managed to find room for an ice cream sundae.

Our waitress had been working here for years and had known my father very well. She had a soft spot in her heart for Matty, knowing that he was my dad's grandson.

"Oh my goodness, Matty, are you going to be able to eat all of that?" she asked, placing his sundae in front of him. He nodded, grinning from ear to ear, flashing his dimple and batting his long dark eyelashes at her. "Well, he certainly is going to make the girls melt when he gets older," she said, smiling back at him.

I watched as he prepared to eat his ice cream, removing the cherry right away, sticking his spoon past the whipped cream and going right for the hot fudge, getting more of it on his face than in his mouth. I shook my head at him and laughed, amazed at how something as simple as watching him eat ice cream gave me such great joy.

We arrived home and I immediately got Matty's bath ready. He liked to prove that he was a big kid by giving himself baths, which I always heavily supervised, usually going over him again with soap and a washcloth. But tonight, even though he protested, I was giving him one, wanting to wash his hair thoroughly since he had half the sand from the beach in it. I shampooed his hair twice, scrubbing until I couldn't feel any more grittiness while he played with his action figures, making them swim about in the water. I interrupted him from his play, making him stand up so I could wash his body down thoroughly. As I washed his face he stuck out his tongue and I grabbed it with the washcloth, making him giggle.

"Let me get that dirty old neck," I said, getting every crack and crevice. As I moved the washcloth back and forth, I felt a large lump on his left gland. I took the washcloth away and touched it with my fingers. I examined around the rest of his neck, not feeling anything else before concentrating back on the lump.

"What are you doing, silly head?" he asked.

I shook my head, trying to hide my unease, quickly rinsing him off and wrapping him in a towel.

After getting him in his pajamas, he lay on my bed, watching cartoons while I jumped in the shower, washing the beach away. My thoughts diverted back to Matty's neck. I was more than likely worrying needlessly, it was probably just a swollen gland, and would be gone in the morning.

Matty's cartoons were blasting on my TV while he was sound asleep in my bed when I walked back into my room. I turned off the television and crawled under the covers, cuddling with him as I listened to him breathe. This was my reason for existing. What I wanted my whole life—to have someone whom I loved more than anything in this world, and who loved me back unconditionally. My most important role in life was being Matty's mom.

Chapter 21

As much as I tried, I was unable to sleep in, I couldn't. In fact, I woke up earlier than usual. Matty was still fast asleep next to me, so I quietly got out of bed, making sure that I didn't disturb him. I used the time to relax with a cup of coffee and catch up on work emails that I had received over the weekend. I couldn't believe how much my patient load had grown over the past year. We were now down to three doctors in our group. Two of the doctors had just retired a couple of months ago, and we were eagerly trying to find suitable replacements. I loved my job, and I didn't mind taking on the extra patient load. The only negative was the time it took away from Matty. The increase in patients meant I was spending a lot more time doing rounds in the hospital before and after hours. Even though I was thoroughly exhausted by the end of the day, it was a rewarding kind of exhaustion, and I couldn't imagine having any other career. I also made sure that I had my priorities straight, making Matty my number one at all times. I hit send on my very last email with a sense of relief.

It was almost seven and Matty was still asleep. Since his summer camp was over for the season, he didn't have to be up at his usual early time, so I figured I would let him take advantage and sleep a little later. I was just pouring my second cup of coffee when he appeared in the kitchen rubbing his eyes still looking half-asleep.

"Good morning, sleepy head," I said.

He just waved as if he were too tired to speak. He shuffled his feet over to the fridge to get some apple juice then moved the kitchen chair over to the cabinets to stand on so he could reach the cups. I admired how he always wanted to do things on his own, but I drew the line with his independence once he started trying to pour the juice into the cup, quickly getting up to help him. The last thing I felt like doing was cleaning up a sticky mess of apple juice first thing in the morning.

He climbed up on the stool next to me, and I ran my fingers through his messy hair. "What's going on?" I asked.

He shrugged. "Pop and I are going fishing today." His gruff little voice sounded a bit raspier first thing in the morning.

"I think Uncle James is coming with us too!"

"Well, that sounds like fun—wish I didn't have to work, so I could go too." I made a sad face.

Matty leaned in closer, rubbing his nose against mine. "Eww, apple juice breath," I teased as he blew his breath in my face. He bellowed a deep belly laugh when I laid my head down on the counter, pretending to have passed out from the smell. It was moments like these that I wanted to bottle up, wishing he could stay this sweet and innocent forever.

As I arrived at Charles and Claire's house, Charles was getting the fishing poles together. Matty eagerly ran to help, but not before being greeted by Gracie who jumped on him and covered him in kisses. I went inside to say hello to Claire, finding her in the kitchen making sandwiches to take along, carefully cutting the crusts off Matty's. Claire always went that extra step. I always made him eat around the crust, which he despised—she took the time to cut it off.

"Are you going too?" I asked, seeing her dressed casually in her pedal pushers and sleeveless T-shirt.

"No." She shook her head as if I were crazy. As much as she tried not to, she always got seasick on the boat. "It's a boys' day out," she said. I looked out the window spotting James, who had just arrived. I gave her a quick itinerary of my workday, so she could gauge what time I would be coming back to get Matty.

"No problem. I'll save you dinner so don't eat," she said.

"Thanks, Claire! I'll see ya later." I gave her a quick peck on the cheek and was on my way.

"We're going on the boat!" Matty exclaimed when I walked outside.

"I know." I smiled and gave him a huge hug and kiss goodbye before he anxiously ran off to James and Charles.

I headed off to work to start my day, returning all my calls on the way there. I looked at my schedule when I arrived, and it was packed solid. With my first two patients already in the rooms waiting for me.

The one good thing about being crazy busy all day is that time goes by superfast. I had finished with my last patient and just had to run to the hospital and check on some patients there. I was starving, and not having time to eat all day, I was tempted to hit a fast food drive-thru. I persevered through the hunger, remembering Claire had said she was saving me dinner.

I arrived at the hospital and took the elevator to the fifth floor. "Hi, Dr. V," one of the nurses greeted.

"Hey there!" I replied.

I always managed to have a good rapport with the nursing staff. I knew that many doctors didn't, instead they looked down on them, and that always made me angry. They, in turn, always made sure to tell me how much they appreciated my laidback attitude.

I went in to see my first patient, a sixteen-year-old girl who was being hospitalized and observed after a weeklong fever that wouldn't go away which turned out to be a result of a tick bite.

"How are you feeling?" I asked as I walked in her room.

"Okay," she said, trying to smile.

I looked at her chart and was happy to see that she had been responding well to the medication.

"Well, you will be happy to know, I'm lifting your liquid diet."

Her smile deepened a little bit more after hearing that.

"Is anything bothering you?" I asked.

"No, I'm okay," she said shyly.

"Well, if you keep responding the way you are to the meds, you should be out of here in a few days," I said. "Just in time for the first day of school," I added as she had expressed her concern about that previously.

"Awesome!" she replied now with a full-face grin.

Her mother came in just as I finished updating her chart. I brought her up to date on her daughter, and the worry that was plastered all over her face when she entered began to instantly melt away. I loved being able to tell parents good news, it was the times that I had to deliver the bad news that I dreaded most. Since I had Matty it had become even harder, knowing the strong love that a parent has for a child. I couldn't imagine how I would feel if something were to happen to him.

I was on my way to see my next patient when I ran into Dr. Fowler, one of the pediatric oncologists to whom I would refer my patients. I decided to pick his brain about the lump I had discovered on Matty's neck.

"Dr. Fowler," I said, getting his attention.

"Dr. Vallia, how are you?"

"I'm well, thank you. Do you have a minute?"

"Sure." He put his clipboard down on the table.

"Last night when I was giving my son a bath, I felt a lump on his neck."

"Has he been sick lately?"

"He's been congested all summer long, running fevers on and off, but I just chalked it up as one of those summer viruses going around."

"Well to put your mind at ease, call my office in the morning, make an appointment, and I'll take a look at it. I'll let my staff know that you'll be calling and have them try and get him in tomorrow."

"Thanks," I said gratefully. I knew that it was probably nothing, but I felt much better having him look at it to confirm it.

My day was officially over, and I was happy to finally be heading up the stairs of Charles and Claire's picture-perfect front porch. As soon as I opened that front door and the heavenly aroma of Claire's post roast hit me in the face, I was happy with my choice of skipping the drive-thru. I peeked into the living room where Matty was passed out on the couch. Charles and James were watching the baseball game and looked like they weren't far behind him.

"Rough day fishing?" I asked. They both looked at me as if neither one had the energy to even answer.

I made my way into the kitchen, to the pot roast, roasted potatoes, and sautéed green beans. Claire sat down at the table with me while I ate, telling me about her spa day. It had been a birthday present from Matty and me, that she had finally gotten around to doing. The rest of the conversation was all about Matty. Claire could talk about him for twenty-four hours straight if you let her.

James came into the kitchen to let us know he was leaving and to thank Claire for dinner. She insisted that he take some leftovers home, and went into the hallway closet to get more containers for the food.

"What do you think of Dr. Fowler?" I asked James once Claire was out of earshot.

"The oncologist?" he seemed a little perplexed.

I nodded as I took a bite of my potato.

"Little old for you, don't you think?" he joked, and I rolled my eyes at him. "I don't really know much about him. Why?"

"I found a lump on Matty's neck, and he suggested I bring him in and have it checked out."

"How long has he had it?"

"I just noticed it last night. You know, he's been sick on and off all summer, so it could be just a swollen lymph node from that." I was trying to reassure myself more than him. "Please don't say anything. I don't want to alarm everyone over nothing."

Claire finally returned with containers and piled the food in them while James excused himself to say goodbye to Matty, signaling for me to follow him in the living room. Charles had gone upstairs to take a shower, and Matty was just waking up. He was sitting up on the couch, half-asleep and half-awake. James sat down next to him and gave him a high-five. Matty was so out of it, he didn't even realize James feeling around his neck. I knew that it was still there when his fingers stopped right in the same location that mine had last night. He pressed around and just like last night, it didn't seem to bother Matty at all.

"When is his appointment?" he asked. The look on his face worried me.

"Dr. Fowler said to call the office tomorrow, and he would get me in right away."

"Did you want me to go with you?"

"No, don't be silly. I'm sure I'm just overreacting," I said, trying to brush off the concerned look on his face and tone in his voice.

"Okay, but please call me as soon as you're done," he said, looking down at Matty.

I nodded in response, just as Claire walked in with a bagful of food. "Since I know you are a bachelor living on your own, this should get you through a few nights worth of dinner," she said, handing him the bag.

"Even if he and Tricia were married already, he'd still be fending for himself," I said. Claire and I laughed, knowing Tricia was a horrible cook. He thanked Claire again and gave us both a kiss goodbye, stopping as he walked past Matty, messing up his hair and giving him a kiss on the head.

I sighed deeply, wanting tomorrow to get here already, so I could put my mind at ease and my worries to rest.

Chapter 22

I watched the clock waiting for 9 a.m. so I could get someone in Dr. Fowler's office to answer the phone. As much as I told myself that I was overreacting and it was nothing, I was finding myself more and more anxious to get this appointment. I had already been to the hospital to do my rounds, and was sitting patiently in my office waiting for my first patient to arrive in hopes of occupying my mind. To top it off, Matty had woken up with a low-grade fever and a cough. I had Samantha, a college student who lived down the street from me, babysitting. She had been babysitting Matty since she was in high school and was very responsible. When I had left they were both cuddled up on the couch watching cartoons, where they would probably be most of the day. It was rainy and miserable as the tail end of what was once a hurricane was passing us by.

As soon as the digital clock on my desk flashed to nine, I dialed the number, relieved to hear that I had reached the actual office and not his answering service. I told the lady my name and she immediately knew who I was, offering me an appointment at four thirty, which I instantly accepted. My last scheduled patient was at three o'clock, so I quickly went to the front desk to let the girls know not to schedule any appointments beyond that.

"Do we have a date?" Tricia asked when she walked up just as I was talking to the girls.

I didn't want to worry her, but at the same time, I felt guilty not telling her. We shared everything about our lives with each other. I knew I couldn't keep this from her so I called her in my office and told her about the appointment.

"Tricia, how many kids do we see with lumps that turn out to be nothing?" I asked when I saw the look on her face. "I'm sure it's nothing," I continued.

"Yeah, I know," she said, sounding a little unsure. "But this is

Matty," she added.

She told me that she would check in on my few patients when she went to the hospital this afternoon, alleviating my worry about how I was going to swing that if Matty's appointment ran late. I hugged and thanked her, feeling much better that I had told her.

I finished up as scheduled, with just enough time to run home and pick up Matty. The rain had finally stopped, and it was now just a very dreary and damp late summer day.

I arrived home to find Matty sitting at the kitchen table coloring with Samantha. He looked a little better, but still very pale with tiny dark circles under his eyes. His usual ruby red lips had lost their coloring as well. He smiled as I entered the kitchen, lifting his coloring book to show me the masterpiece he had been working on.

"That's beautiful," I said, making a big deal out of it.

Samantha filled me in on the day's events. I thanked her for her help, grabbed money from my wallet to pay her and then went over the days that I would need her for the rest of the week. She gave Matty a hug and a kiss before walking out the door.

Matty was not happy when I told him we had to leave to go to the doctor. "But why? I'm okay," he protested. "Plus, you're a doctor, silly head."

"This is a different kind of doctor than Mommy is," I tried explaining to him, but

he ignored me, never taking his eyes from his coloring book.

"Matthew Anthony, let's go," I said in a stern voice. He got up immediately, knowing he was never called by his full name unless he was in trouble for something. He gave me a hard time when I made him put on his windbreaker, moaning and groaning as I put the hood up as we walked out the door.

We arrived at Dr. Fowler's office a few minutes late. I didn't sweat it when I saw two other patients still in the waiting room waiting to be seen. His office was located in a new, modern office building, everything there seemed to be top of the line. Matty was immediately drawn to the huge play area. I didn't want him spreading his germs to these children who already had their immune systems compromised, so I took off his jacket and signaled for him to sit in the seat next to me. He leaned up against me, listening closely as I read from one of the storybooks on the table next to us. I glanced over at the hairless little boy who looked to be about eleven, sitting across from us, and my heart ached. He was playing his handheld video game as if unfazed by anything, while his mother read a magazine.

I lifted Matty up and placed him on my lap, when he nodded off during the story. He slept for some time while we waited for our turn, and had just woken up, seeming to be in a little better mood when the nurse called us back to the exam room. She took Matty's weight, height, and temperature and was just finishing when Dr. Fowler came in.

"You must be Matty," Dr. Fowler said in a very friendly tone.

Matty nodded as he sat on the exam table nervously swinging his legs. Dr. Fowler listened to his heart and lungs with the stethoscope, before thoroughly examining his neck. He began pressing around where the lump was located, asking Matty if it caused him any pain.

Matty shook his head, still swinging his legs.

He thoroughly examined the rest of his body then informed me he was going to do some blood work. Matty's ears perked up at the thought of a needle.

"I don't want a shot," he said as his eyes filled with tears.

Dr. Fowler explained to him that it wasn't a shot like he was used to. He described it as a little pinch, assuring him that his nurse was the best at it, and he wouldn't feel a thing.

"Okay, Matty, you're just going to feel a tiny little pinch, and then it will be all over," the nurse said. Her tone was soft and gentle, immediately putting Matty's mind at ease. She quickly found his vein and effortlessly stuck the needle in, without him feeling a thing. I tried to get him to look away, but he was mesmerized by the blood being sucked out of his vein. Once she was done, she removed the needle from his arm and placed a Sponge Bob bandage on him.

"I have to say, you were by far one of my bravest patients," she praised Matty, and he flashed his dimpled little smile. "Can our brave guy come with me to get a lollipop, Mom?" she asked. I smiled and nodded as she and Matty walked out of the room.

Dr. Fowler was writing in Matty's chart as he reentered. "Let's see…today is Tuesday, so I should have the results no later than Friday. I will be in touch as soon as I get them."

"Okay." My voice faltered. As much as I wanted to know the results to put my mind at ease, I couldn't stop obsessing over the alternative.

"Dr. Vallia," Dr. Fowler started.

"Please, call me Kat."

He nodded and continued. "I know you're nervous, but try not to get consumed with the *what ifs*. I like to err on the side of caution and test all my patients who are presenting the same symptoms as Matty, just to rule out any possibility of it being something more serious." He placed his hand on my shoulder. "It's going to be okay," he reassured me before walking out of the room and to his next patient.

Matty ran back in the room with three lollipops and covered in stickers as the nurse who had drawn his blood followed behind him, laughing. "All of the girls in the office are in love with your son and those beautiful eyes of his," she remarked. I smiled, amazed by how Matty had the same effect on everyone he encountered.

I left feeling a little defeated over not getting the answer I had immediately hoped for, instead I now had to wait a few more days for it.

***

The next few days were grueling. I tried to get my mind off it as best I could, but every time my phone rang, my heart would leap from my chest. Tricia and James were relentless with calling to see if I heard anything. I assured them that they would be the first to know when I did, especially since they were the *only ones* who knew.

Matty was still running an on-and-off fever that I was hoping that he would shake off before his first day of kindergarten, which was only a few days away. I was so happy tomorrow was Friday. I had taken a few days off so I could spend the entire Labor Day weekend with Matty.

I had just finished up with a patient and hurried back into my office to grab some lunch when I noticed a missed call and a voicemail. My stomach dropped when I dialed my voicemail and heard Dr. Fowler's voice.

"Kat, I just got Matty's blood work back. I'd like for you to schedule an appointment to come in and speak with me immediately."

My heart was beating out of my chest, knowing that *immediately* wasn't a good sign. My hands shook as I dialed his number, hoping I could get a hold of him.

"Hi, this is Dr. Vallia," I introduced myself to the girl who answered the phone. "Dr. Fowler called and left me a message regarding my son. Is it possible to speak with him?

"Oh, Doctor, you just missed him, but he did leave us a message, letting us know to get you in right away when you called back. Does tomorrow at noon work for you?"

"Yes," I responded flatly, hanging up and feeling like I could vomit.

"Dr. V, your next patient is here," Melanie, one the nurses, knocked on my office door, breaking me from my inner-turmoil.

"Okay, I'll be right there," I said as I threw my sandwich in the trash, not having much of an appetite anymore.

The day muddled on at a snail's pace, and I was happy when it finally ended. I called Samantha and arranged to have her watch Matty for a few hours while I was at Doctor Fowler's. She happily agreed, making me feel like I had tackled at least one problem. My mind was a million miles away as I sat in my office, trying to finish up paperwork.

"Hello, madam." Tricia startled me when she entered my office.

"Oh, hey," I responded, trying a little too hard to sound upbeat.

"What's the matter?" she asked as she took a seat.

I sighed heavily and looked down at my desk. "Dr. Fowler wants to see me *immediately* regarding Matty's blood work."

"I want to go with you," she responded.

I knew that wasn't possible. She was booked solid for tomorrow. Besides, I knew if it was bad news, Tricia would be just as big of a mess as me.

"Tricia, I appreciate that offer so much, but you have to work, and if it is bad news..." I couldn't finish. Just the thought of something being wrong with Matty was too much to bear.

"Well, James is off, and he's going–I don't want you going alone," she demanded.

Normally, I could tackle things on my own, but this was going to be a tough one for me. I didn't put up a fight and took her up on that offer.

I was immediately greeted by Gracie as I walked through my front door, and I knew I'd probably be having an overnight guest again. When I was finally able to get past Gracie's overwhelming welcome, I noticed that the house was nice and quiet.

"I'm out here, Kat," Claire called. I walked out to the backyard where Claire was sitting on the patio reading a magazine.

"Where's Matty?" I asked, not seeing any sign of him.

"Oh, he and Charles took a quick walk up to the bay." It was a beautiful day for a walk, the storm that had passed through a couple of days ago had taken all the humidity with it, leaving just a nice breeze and abundant sunshine.

I pulled up a chair and sat next to her as she put down her magazine. "Are you okay?" she asked.

"I'm fine," I answered quickly.

"You just look drained."

I shrugged.

"Well, it will do you good to have a few days off," she added.

"Yes, I'm looking forward to it."

"I got some burgers to throw on the grill," Claire said.

"That sounds perfect," I said, forcing a smile, trying to chase away the dreadful thoughts of this appointment in less than twenty-four hours, and replace them with happy thoughts. Closing my eyes and soaking in the warm sunshine helped a lot. Hearing Matty's voice saying, "Mommy's home," as he and Charles entered the backyard was even better!

Chapter 23

James arrived well ahead of schedule–in fact, an hour ahead. I didn't mind because it gave me time to get ready while Matty had someone to keep him occupied. I finished dressing and came out to the kitchen to find them both eating a giant bowl of ice cream covered in hot fudge.

"Seriously, isn't it kind of early for that?" I asked James.

"It's almost eleven," he said defending his actions. Matty looked up at him smiling, with his face covered in chocolate. I shook my head and dampened a paper towel to wipe down Matty's face and hands. Matty had been out of sorts all week, so I was happy to see that James was able to lift his spirits.

Matty and James were just finishing their ice cream when Samantha arrived, and Matty's eyes filled up with crocodile tears.

"I don't want James to go," he cried.

James bent down to Matty's level and placed his hand on his shoulder. "I'll stop back in to see you when we're done, but only if you promise to stop crying. Deal?" He held out his hand for Matty to shake on it.

"Deal," Matty sheepishly replied, shaking James' hand back.

***

We arrived at Dr. Fowler's and were led back to his office right away. I took a seat while James looked around, reading all of Dr. Fowler's degrees and awards that he had hanging on the wall.

"So, this is how the other half lives," James said, taking in the size of Dr. Fowler's office.

My stomach dropped when Dr. Fowler entered. I introduced him to James, and he took a seat at his desk as he rummaged through Matty's chart, pulling out the blood work.

"Well, the test results weren't what I had hoped for," Dr. Fowler advised. My heart sunk down to my knees. James grabbed my hand

and we prepared for what was to come.

"The blood work shows that Matty has leukemia."

I couldn't believe what I was hearing. Leukemia was a word that no parent wanted to hear.

"I'm going to have to run more tests, but based on his results, it's a very aggressive type, and we're going to have to treat it just as aggressively. I'm recommending very high doses of chemotherapy and radiation in hopes of sending it into remission, but I have to warn you, as a result his bone marrow may become damaged or destroyed, requiring him to need a transplant."

I was in a fog, staring blankly at the family portrait on Dr. Fowler's bookshelf. James listened closely, making sure that he asked the important questions that I was unable to.

I finally pulled it together as best as I could. "When do you recommend that he start the treatments?"

"Well, I want to see the results of the other tests I want to do, but I would say three weeks at the latest."

"He's supposed to be starting kindergarten." My voice cracked with emotion.

"I don't see that happening right now," he said sympathetically. "He's going to have a long road ahead of him and his immune system will be compromised."

I looked away, hoping that this was all a bad dream, and my little boy was going to be okay. "I'm so very sorry," he said. "Please know this is not a death sentence. I've treated many patients who have had this same type of cancer, and they have gone on to live healthy, happy lives."

Cancer. My little boy had cancer. How I hated that ugly vile word that had claimed everyone in my life who mattered most.

"In the meantime, I encourage you to get a second opinion. Also, keep in mind that Matty may need a bone marrow donor. Does he have any brothers or sisters who we could test for a match?" Dr. Fowler asked.

I shook my head.

"Well, ideally a sibling is the best chance for a match, but if that's not an option, then the parents are the next best chance. If he has any aunts or uncles it would be worth a shot to have them tested as well, but anything beyond that would be the same as finding a random donor. I'll also put his information into the national registry in hopes of possibly finding a match there as well."

"What happens if you don't find a match?" I asked, knowing I was his only shot.

"Well, then we will just have to take it a little slower with the treatments." He sounded as if this wasn't his prime choice. "I'll have Matty's records available if you want to get a second opinion." He handed me a card of another oncologist with whom he worked very closely. "Just take it one day at a time, Kat," Dr. Fowler said as he stood up. "I'm going to schedule him for next week for those other tests." I nodded and wiped a tear away. "Take your time and get yourself together before you leave." He placed his hand on my shoulder in support before exiting his office.

I looked over at James, who seemed just as shocked as I was, his normal goofy persona completely gone. "I just can't believe this is happening," I said, grabbing a tissue to wipe my tears. James remained silent. "I don't even know where to begin, I guess I'll give this other doctor a call and see what he has to say."

James' silence was finally broken. "Kat, you can't be serious!" I creased my eyebrows, confused by his reaction. "Matty's father is one of the best oncologists out there and you're going to take him to someone else just because you were given his business card?"

"I trust Dr. Fowler's opinion. I'm comfortable with whoever he would recommend." I defended my actions.

"Okay, and even if this doctor does concur with Dr. Fowler, and you are comfortable with that, Matty *may need* a bone marrow transplant," he painfully reminded me. I tried not to think about that. I was hoping I'd be a match and that would settle everything. "Kat, I promised you I would keep your secret about Matty, even though I didn't agree with it, but if you don't tell him about this, I will."

"What am I supposed to do, James, just barge into his life after all these years and tell him, 'oh by the way, you have a son who has cancer'?" I sobbed.

"It's his son, he deserves to know, and Matty deserves the best care possible."

I knew he was right–Matty did deserve the best care. I also knew that besides me, Julian was his only hope for a possible donor.

"I'm just scared," I finally admitted. "What if he doesn't want to be bothered with all of this?"

"Really, Kat, you're talking about Julian–you of all people should know better than to think that way."

"He's going to hate me for this," I said, staring into space.

James shrugged. "I don't know how he'll react, but you can't worry about that, you have to do this for Matty. If you'd like, I'll call him for you."

I quickly shook my head. If I was going to do this, I was going to be the one to tell him, and not over the phone. This was going to be one of the hardest things I ever had to do, but when I saw Matty's face flashing before me in my mind, I knew that I had no choice.

James drove home, with the entire car ride being silent. I had so much on my mind. How was I going to break this to Charles and Claire, and most of all, Matty? He was so excited about starting kindergarten. We had just gone shopping last week to buy him new clothes, a big boy backpack and a lunch box. How was I going to tell him that he wouldn't be going now? Instead, he would be suffering through grueling months of treatments. I felt sick to my stomach thinking of him going through the chemo and radiation, losing his hair, being sick all the time and being scared–and not understanding why he was enduring all that pain.

We pulled in the driveway, and I gave myself a glance in the rearview mirror, trying to wipe the last traces of mascara from my face.

As I walked in the house, I tried my best to put on a strong face. Samantha must have noticed I had been crying as she hurriedly made her way out the door before I could even pay her. James came in as promised to say hello to Matty, but his crazy playful personality that he had prior to the appointment was now gone. He seemed to be just as drained from the news as I was. I looked at Matty, who had climbed up on the couch next to him, all smiles and happy–so unaware of what was going on, and my heart sank.

James sat with Matty for a while watching cartoons before leaving.

"Thanks so much for coming with me today," I said as I walked him to the door.

"No problem, Kat. You know I'm here if you need anything."

I nodded in appreciation "Just one more thing–can you please tell Tricia about the appointment? I just don't have it in me right now, and I know she's waiting to hear."

"I will–as long as you promise to tell Julian?"

"I promise," I whispered. A deep knot formed in my stomach just thinking about it.

***

After James left, Matty and I took a walk down to the bay. We sat quietly in the sand, trying to spot some dolphins, and it wasn't long before Matty was up and chasing the seagulls. He was so full of life–looking at him, no one would ever know he was sick.

"We should've brought food for them," he said, taking a seat once again.

"No, you don't feed the seagulls, silly."

"Uncle James and I always feed them," he giggled.

"Matty, I need to talk to you." I took a deep breath, trying to put together the right words. I didn't want to scare him, but I needed to explain to him what was going on in the best way that I could explain it to a five-year-old.

"Remember all the colds and fevers you had gotten over the summer?"

He nodded.

"Well, the doctors have to give you lots of extra medicine to make sure they don't come back. So, because they need to give you a lot of medicine, they want you to wait for a while before you start kindergarten to make sure you're all better."

"So, I'm not gonna be able to go on the big boy bus?" His bright blue eyes teared up, and my heart was being torn into a million little pieces.

"Not right away."

"When I'm done getting the medicine...then can I go to the big school?"

"Yes, but it may take a while."

"Okay." He shrugged as he got up to chase another seagull. He was much too young to understand what was going on, and I was unsure if that was a good or bad thing.

We stopped at Charles and Claire's just after dinner, so I could break the dreaded news to them. Matty played with Gracie in the backyard, allowing me to sit the two of them down and inform them of the events of the past week. Claire immediately began to tear up while I tried to hold it together.

163

"Dr. Fowler encouraged me to get a second opinion. He recommended Dr. Auburn. Do you know who he is?" I asked Charles.

"I've heard of him, but Kat—"

"I know." I stopped him before he could get the words out.

I sighed heavily. "I have the next few days off. Would you guys mind watching Matty, so I could do this?"

"You don't even need to ask, Kat," Claire replied without hesitation.

"Thanks," I whispered, closing my eyes and warding off the tears.

"You're doing the right thing," Charles reassured me.

"I sure hope so," I said with doubt in my voice.

"Who wants to go for ice cream?" Charles asked when Matty came running back inside.

"Me, me!" Matty exclaimed.

"Are you coming?" Clarie asked as she slipped on her flip-flops.

"No, but do you mind if I use your computer while you're gone?" I asked.

"Go right ahead, you know where it's at." She placed her hand on my shoulder and gave me a comforting smile before they were on their way to get their ice cream.

I walked into their office and painstakingly began looking up airfare to Chicago. I was able to find a flight leaving in less than twenty-four hours, so I pulled my credit card from my purse and instinctively began to enter my information. Before I knew it, I had my airfare, rental car, and hotel booked. I took a deep breath ready to face my biggest secret, telling myself, I had no other choice—I was doing the right thing.

Chapter 24

Matty and I made an early morning run to the grocery store before my flight was to leave. We arrived home and Tricia's car was in my driveway, since she wasn't sitting in it, I knew she must have let herself in with the key I had given her.

"Hey!" I shouted when Matty and I walked through the front door.

"I'm in here!" she shouted from the kitchen.

I entered the kitchen to find her emptying the dishwasher as I staggered over to the counter to put the grocery bags down and take the weight off my overburdened arms. Tricia picked up Matty and gave him a big hug and kiss before he went running off to his bedroom to play with his latest action figure we had picked up on our shopping trip.

Tricia waited until he was out of the room before looking at me with tear-filled eyes. I had been up half the night, promising myself I was going to remain positive about this whole situation, so, I didn't want to cry now. She gave me a hug and much to my surprise, I didn't shed a tear.

"What time are you leaving?" Tricia asked. I had texted earlier, letting her know about my big travel plans.

"In about an hour."

She dug through her purse that was hanging on the kitchen chair and pulled out a folded piece of paper.

"James wanted me to give this to you," she informed, slipping the piece of paper in my hand.

"What's this?" I asked, taking it from her hand.

"It's Julian's phone number as well as his home address and hospital address." I shoved it in my pocket, not wanting to look at it at the moment.

"Are you going to be okay, going by yourself?" Tricia asked.

"I'll be fine," I said, trying to reassure her and myself at the same time. I had no clue what Julian's reaction would be. Nor did I know if I was even going to be able to get in touch with him while I was there. A phone call would have been much simpler, but I couldn't bring myself to break this to him over the phone.

Tricia yammered on while I put the groceries away. Her endless chatter was a welcomed distraction from my thoughts. As she continued to talk, I went over a mental checklist of what I still had to do. I had already made up the guest bedroom for Charles and Claire, and my one only bag that I was bringing was already packed and ready to go for my two-night stay.

"Hello!" Claire exclaimed as she entered the kitchen with her arms bogged down with grocery bags.

"Claire, why on earth did you bring over food? I just stocked the fridge."

"It's just a few things." She waved her hand, dismissing my comment.

I felt a twinge of jealousy when Claire invited Tricia and James over for barbeque later. How I wished I could be there to join them, instead of going to some strange city to face my biggest fear.

As the time was drawing near, my stomach tossed and turned. I sat down on the couch to spend my last few minutes with Matty, who thought I was going away for work. Unable to ignore the time on the clock any longer, I gave Matty a huge hug and about a thousand kisses before grabbing my bag and walking out the door to confront my past about my present.

***

It was an easy flight with no delays. I arrived at my hotel, feeling tired and at the same time restless. I sent Claire a quick text, letting her know I arrived, and to check on Matty.

I planned on going to Julian's hospital first thing in the morning to try and get in touch with him. Having no clue of what his schedule was, I was just hoping that by some stroke of luck I would be able to connect with him. After replying to a few emails, I put my phone down, too anxious to concentrate on anything at that moment. My stomach was in knots over facing Julian for the first time after all these years, and even more so because of the news that I had to break to him. After turning on the television and nervously flicking through channels, I worked up the courage to examine the piece of paper containing Julian's information. I looked it over for what seemed like an eternity, and my inner-turmoil began. I couldn't do this over the phone. I had to do it face-to-face—I owed that much to him. I summoned up the courage, and before I could talk myself out of it, I threw the piece of paper back into my purse and walked out of my hotel room.

My GPS indicated I should arrive at my destination in approximately forty minutes. Traffic was a nightmare, and when I finally turned down his street, my heart was beating faster. His home was located in a very upscale townhouse complex, surrounded by mature trees and lush landscaping with most of the cars in the parking lot looking like they belonged on the showroom floor of a high-end car dealer. I pulled into an out-of-the-way spot, turning off my car while I sat there deep in thought.

What the hell am I doing? This was not my plan of action.

I was beginning to feel somewhat like a crazed stalker as I watched people pulling in and out. Each time someone would exit a vehicle, I got butterflies, waiting to see if it was him. I had to do this—this was my whole reason for coming here. I knew it wasn't going to be easy, but I needed to toughen up for Matty. I inhaled deeply and took the piece of paper from my purse, memorizing his house number.

You're doing this for Matty. Matty needs him.

I had my hand on the car door handle, preparing to exit when I caught a glimpse of him walking over to the black BMW parked on the edge of the parking lot opposite me. I froze as my heart began to race seeing him again, looking just as handsome as the last time. He was loading a suitcase in the back of the trunk, and I knew that it was now or never. I took a deep breath, opening the car door, when I spotted a beautiful, tall, slender woman with long silky dark hair and a little girl following behind him. The woman was very well-dressed and looked as if she could have been a runway model. Julian picked up the little girl, who looked to be about two, and gave her a kiss on the cheek as she laughed. My stomach clenched, and a million thoughts raced through my head.

Why didn't James tell me he had a family? Maybe he didn't keep in touch with Julian like I had thought, or maybe he didn't want me to be scared off from doing what had to be done.

167

I sat in the car for quite some time after watching them pull away. I couldn't help but think to myself, that could have been Matty and me—we could have been his family. My heart was aching as I came face-to-face with the effects of the choice I had made so long ago.

I went back to my hotel room feeling defeated as I replayed the vision of Julian and his family over again in my mind. I was in such a catatonic state that I didn't even call to check on Matty again. I didn't want to take a chance of him hearing the sadness in my voice, and I didn't feel like tormenting myself by explaining it to Charles and Claire. I knew this was going to make it even more difficult than I had originally thought. My sadness was now turning into anger—he walked away so easily that day, telling me he didn't want children, only to find out that now he had one. I had been raising our son on my own for the past five years, so he could go and have his career because he *didn't* want kids. Everything I thought we had back then was a lie. I was becoming more infuriated by the minute, now feeling as if I did the right thing by keeping this secret from him. He didn't deserve to have a child as wonderful as Matty in his life. I had half a mind to just book a flight on the next plane home. I knew Dr. Fowler was probably just as qualified as Julian to provide Matty with the treatment he needed, but then I remembered the bone marrow transplant. I needed him to at least be tested to see if he was a possible match for Matty's sake. I began to wonder how his wife would feel, knowing he had a child out there with some stupid girl who fell for his good looks and charm. I was so mad at myself for being so foolish when it came to him. I quickly removed those thoughts and remembered—if it weren't for me falling for him so deeply, Matty wouldn't be here.

I took a shower to clear my head. The warm water immediately aided in organizing my thoughts. I would go to the hospital in the morning and leave a message for him, and *hope* that he called me back. This trip was an absolute waste of time. I could be home spending this time with Matty instead. Now that I was content with my plan, I decided, I would try to see if I could change my flight to tomorrow, so I could spend at least one of my days off as planned. I finished showering, quickly blew dry my hair, and crawled into bed. As I lay in bed exhausted, I was still unable to get what I had uncovered today out of my mind. I tossed and turned for a while longer and then, much to my surprise, I drifted off into a deep relaxing sleep–something I hadn't done in a long while.

I woke up trying to put yesterday behind me and salvage something from this trip as I readied myself to go to the hospital. I slipped on my printed maxi halter dress and flip-flops and gave myself one last look in the mirror. I ran my fingers through my hair, trying to give a little life to my waves as I pulled the top back loosely into a clip. My nerves were a lot calmer now, knowing that there was no chance of running into him, since I saw him leaving for what looked to be a nice family getaway. I would have to deal with that *if* he called me back. My worries now drifted to how I'd even be able to get a message to him. I knew that he was a very sought-after physician who worked on a referral basis only.

When I called to check on Matty, they were out to breakfast–again, making me wish I was there with them instead of here. I was a little alarmed when Claire told me Matty had been running a fever again last night, but she assured me Charles had it under control.

"Hi, Mommy!" Matty's voice was like music to my ears when he got on the phone.

"Hey, Matty, what are you eating for breakfast?"

"Pancakes and maybe some ice cream after," he said, whispering the second part.

"Ice cream! It's too early in the morning for that and why are you whispering?"

"Because Pop and Mom-Mom told me not to tell you."

"I miss you," I choked up.

"I miss you too," he said, sounding as if he were getting distracted, which was normal. He had a very limited attention span when talking on the phone.

"I love you," I said.

"I love you more." He giggled.

"I'll be seeing you soon!" I blew a kiss into the phone and hung up, feeling a little better after hearing Matty's voice. I just couldn't wait to get home, I missed Matty so much.

I packed my bag, so it would be ready to go when I got back. All I would have to do was change my flight and check out, and I'd be home in time to tuck Matty into bed. I smiled at the thought of that as I closed my hotel room door behind me.

Chapter 25

I was overwhelmed by the size of the hospital when I pulled into the parking lot, twice the size of the one where I worked, and this hospital only dealt with pediatrics. I stopped at the reception area to find out exactly where Julian's office was located then took the elevator up to the fourth floor, prepping myself to make sure that I was successful in getting a message to him. I took a deep breath and headed to the nurses' station, putting on my best business persona. I was immediately met by an older nurse who acted as if she ran the whole hospital as she fumbled through papers and barked orders to a much younger nurse.

Great, out of all the nurses, I have to deal with the Gestapo.

I instinctively gave the younger nurse a smile as she smiled back in appreciation. "Can I help you?" the older nurse asked in an unfriendly tone.

"Yes, I wanted to get a message to Dr. Kiron." I handed her my business card.

"Is this regarding a patient?" she asked, giving my business card and me the once-over.

"Actually, it's not. It's personal, and I just ask that you please give him the message." I was growing more irritated by the moment.

"The doctor has a very tight schedule, and I can't make any guarantees if it's not regarding a particular patient," she said, brushing me off.

My temper flared as I thought of Matty and my urgent need to get in touch with Julian. "Well, I don't think that is up to you to decide who Dr. Kiron responds to and who he doesn't. Your job is to just make sure that he gets his messages." My face was burning up in rage.

Her eyes widened as the younger nurse stood behind her with a slight smile on her face. I knew that after my snide remark to her, she would probably just rip my card up and not give him the message, leaving me to have to call him after all, but I felt some satisfaction in putting her in her place.

I turned around to exit, feeling totally defeated and wanting to cry, until–I saw him, walking out of the elevator, talking to another doctor. I pushed a loose piece of hair that had fallen from my clip out of my face and bit my lower lip, frozen for a moment, not knowing what to do. I took a deep breath, knowing this might be the only chance I was going to get.

"Julian!" I shouted as my heart beat out of my chest.

He stopped mid-sentence and his eyes met mine. He looked as if he had seen a ghost, and I immediately got butterflies in my stomach when he flashed that familiar smile that I had loved so much.

"Dr. Kiron, are you okay?" the female doctor he was with asked.

"I'm fine, I'll have the report for you later," he said in a dismissing tone.

I was unable to move as he approached me. "How are you, Kat?" he gently placed his hand on my arm.

"I'm well, thank you," I answered, as my knees began to shake.

He was even more handsome than I had remembered. His hair was cut much shorter, and his eyes were just as beautiful as ever–just like Matty's.

"What are you doing here–are you here on business?"

"No, not really." My voice shook. "Julian, I need to talk to you, somewhere private." I looked around, knowing that this was not the place to do it.

"Okay, I should be done here in an hour." He seemed somewhat confused. "There's a coffee shop right at the end of the street." He glanced at his watch. "Do you want to meet me there at noon?"

"Okay," I replied in a very flat tone. He gave the address to where we'd be meeting, I made a mental note of it.

"I'll see you then." I nodded as I watched him walk away.

I finally made my way to the elevator, trembling the whole time. I took the short drive to the coffee shop and sat out on the bench just outside, still trying to pull it together. Just seeing him again after all these years had stirred so many emotions inside of me–emotions I didn't even know I had. Now, I was going to be stirring up even more emotions after I broke the news to him, and I only hoped he wouldn't hate me forever because of it. I pulled out my phone and began to check my email, enjoying the sunshine when Julian pulled up in a black BMW. The shock of seeing him at the hospital had worn off, allowing me to examine him a little better. He looked stunningly handsome in blue jeans and a white button-up shirt. Nothing had changed about him over the years. I threw my phone into my purse and stood up to greet him.

"I really appreciate you taking the time to meet me," I said, sounding very business-like.

"No problem, Kat–actually it was a really nice surprise seeing you. You want to go in?" he said, opening the door for me.

We walked into the coffee shop and the smell of freshly brewed coffee and delicious desserts hit me in the face. Normally I'd want to dive into one of those desserts, but at that moment my stomach wouldn't allow it. We sat at a small table, which was thankfully out of the way.

"Sorry for making you wait. I just had some catching up to do. I had just taken a few days off to spend with my sister and niece who were here visiting."

His sister and his niece. He didn't have a family after all.

"So, what have you been up to?" His gaze was intense.

Let's see–working, and raising our son for the past five years.

"Nothing special," was all I could muster.

"Married?" he asked, getting right to the point. I shook my head and gave him an uneasy smile.

"What about you?" I asked, making sure that I had been wrong in my callous assumption that I had made about him last night.

"I barely have time to sleep, let alone maintain a relationship." He leaned back in his chair with his hands intertwined behind his head, assessing me up and down, so much like that first day I had met him. "You look great, Kat."

"Thanks," I whispered.

I was too uptight to make conversation with him, and I was certain that he sensed my edginess. I was always able to talk his ear off, but today, given the circumstances, I felt like I couldn't get any words out, even though there were a lot that had to be said.

"So, how's work?" he asked, trying to make small talk.

"Fine."

He nodded as if running out of things to say as I sat nervously twirling my hair around my finger, finally catching myself and stopping.

"How's James doing?" he asked.

"He's doing well. He and Tricia are engaged now."

"Yes, I knew that. I haven't talked to him in a while. I owe him a phone call."

"So, you're chief of oncology now?"

He nodded.

"Well, congratulations. I always knew you were destined for great things."

He gave me a warm smile. "So, what did you need to talk to me about?"

"Bone marrow transplants."

He seemed to be caught off-guard by my brusqueness. "What?" he chuckled.

"What do you know about bone marrow transplants?"

Stupid—what are you saying? He's an oncologist, of course he knows a lot about bone marrow transplants.

He explained to me what I already knew, but I sat listening as if I were clueless. "This is pretty common knowledge that you learn in medical school," he said once he was finished. Clearly, he wasn't buying into my naïve act.

"Yes, I know, I just wanted to get your advice, since you are one of the top doctors in your field."

"So, you came all this way just to ask me that? I'm sure you have doctors who are just as versed as me and a lot closer. That must be some special patient."

I froze, trying my best to find my voice. "It is." There was a brief moment of silence before I continued. "It's my son." I paused for a moment.

"Oh man, Kat, I'm sor—"

"It's *our* son, Julian." I could feel the blood rushing out of my face with those words.

"What?" His eyes widened. "Why didn't you tell me?" His voice was sharp.

"Because you made it clear to me what you wanted out of life, and that didn't include a child." I couldn't get the words out quickly enough.

"Not now!" he snapped as the waitress came over to take our order.

He stared into space, and I was wishing that he would say something so I could gauge how he was feeling. I pulled my wallet from my purse and took out Matty's pre-school picture, placing it down in front of him in case there was any doubt in his mind.

"His name is Matty, he's five years old, he's a great kid, and he has leukemia." My voice cracked with emotion as I had just basically summed up everything I wanted to tell him. He picked up the picture and stared at it intently. "Almost like looking in the mirror, isn't it?" I asked, breaking the silence. When he finally lifted his head, his eyes were a mixture of anger, sadness and regret. "I know I was wrong to have kept this from you, but what would you have done if I told you back then?"

"I would have taken responsibility for my son," he answered without hesitation.

"I'm sorry, but I did the wrong thing for the right reasons." My voice quivered.

"What were those reasons? Can you please tell me what your reasons were for keeping my son from me for the past five years?" he shouted.

I wasn't sure what was worse—the anger in his voice or the sadness in his eyes. I looked around to see a few people noticing what was transpiring. "You left and we never spoke again because you didn't want kids, do you remember that?" I lowered my voice.

"Really? So, you felt that gave you the right to do this?" He raised his eyebrow at me. "What, were you trying to punish me for not wanting what you wanted?"

"No, that's not at all what I was trying to do!" I snapped.

He shook his head as he looked away. "I can't believe you just assumed I wouldn't want to be in his life."

"I'm sorry, I didn't want you to feel trapped into something you didn't want."

"I missed out on five years of my son's life because you actually thought that's what I wanted?" The fury in his voice was unrecognizable. "Why didn't it ever occur to you to ask me what I wanted? Would I have ever known if he hadn't gotten sick?"

I looked away, knowing that he was right—I wouldn't be here now if Matty weren't sick. He shook his head in disbelief, making me feel as if I had to defend my actions.

"Right before I found out I was pregnant, I was planning on

calling you to tell you that I would go to Germany. I was willing to uproot my whole life, forgo everything I wanted just to be with you. Once I found out that I was pregnant, that changed everything. There were days I had wished you would have called to tell me that you would be willing to rethink your plan for me, but you didn't." I searched for some softness in his eyes—but there was none.

"You told me not to!"

"Exactly. I thought I knew what you wanted, and you thought you knew what I wanted," I said, a little more calmly.

"You had no right to just assume what I wanted!" The tone in his voice didn't match my calmness in any way.

"I know I was wrong, and you can hate me if you want to." The tears were streaming down my face. "But Matty needs you now. Please, Julian, I'm begging you."

He didn't reply and just stared at me coldly, which upset me even more. "I came here to ask you if you would be willing to be tested to see if you're a match and to oversee his medical treatment." I grabbed a napkin from the table and wiped my eyes. "I want you to be part of his life. I want you to be his father. I want you to fall in love with him the same way I have." He was unresponsive, unable to look at me.

I pulled out Dr. Fowler's business card, which had my cell phone number written on the back, and handed it to him. He snatched it from my hand and glared at me with an unfamiliar look in his eyes. Getting up from the table without saying a word, he abruptly walked out the door.

I was unsure of what to do. Part of me wanted to go running after him and beg him. I sat there for a few moments, trying to get myself together, wishing he'd come back through the door to tell me he forgave me. Since I knew that wasn't going to happen, I composed myself as best I could. The secret I had harbored for all these years was finally out—and it was bittersweet.

Chapter 26

I arrived home just in time to tuck Matty into bed. The look on his face as I walked through the door was priceless.

We spent my last day off together, walking up to the bay to have a picnic lunch. I tried not to think that tomorrow would have been his first day of school. I had emailed the principal, making her aware of the circumstances. I was very appreciative of her email back, telling me if there was anything that the school community could do to help out to please let her know.

We went back to the house to have some burgers on the grill for dinner, and I was surprisingly able to relax a little, taking in the sun and watching Matty play with his dump trucks in the backyard.

Before I knew it, Tuesday was here, and I was back to the same old routine of working. I was feeling guilty for putting a heavier burden on Charles and Claire. With Matty no longer attending pre-school and Samantha back at college full time, I had no one else to watch him. I knew they didn't mind, it was only for another few weeks. Soon Matty would be spending most of his days in the hospital.

I stopped at the hospital to do my rounds before heading into the office, trying to stay focused as best as I could. I couldn't stop thinking of Julian. I was hoping that I would have heard from him once he had cooled down, but I didn't. I had no clue if he had any intention of even calling Dr. Fowler or seeing if he was a match for Matty. As I replayed that day at the coffee shop over and over in my head, trying to think of how I could have done things differently, I came to the realization that there wasn't any good way to have broken that news to him. I had no choice but to just go forward with Dr. Fowler's recommendations for Matty and hope that I or some random stranger would be a match for the marrow transplant.

"Well if this isn't a coincidence," Dr. Fowler said as I literally walked right into him coming off the elevator. "I was going to call you as soon as I was done here. Do you have a minute now?" he asked.

I nodded, and we went into one of the empty rooms. He sat down on the bed with a serious look in his eyes, while I remained standing, hoping there wasn't more bad news from Matty's test results.

"I received a message yesterday from Dr. Kiron regarding Matty."

"You did?" I asked, sounding somewhat surprised and relieved. "I had no idea that the two of you even knew one another."

"Jul–I mean, Dr. Kiron and I know one another from years ago, when we were in Nigeria together."

"I understand you wanting to get a second opinion, but there are other doctors who are much closer."

"I know." I walked away and stared out the window.

"Well then why would you make Dr. Kiron travel out here to see Matty?" he asked. "I mean, don't get me wrong, he's probably one of the most brilliant oncologists in the country, but I can assure you of what he is going to tell you."

"Because that's not the only reason I contacted him." I turned my attention from the window and back to Dr. Fowler.

"Oh, then I don't understand." He arched his eyebrows.

"He's Matty's father."

"Oh." He paused briefly. "I'm sorry. I didn't mean to pry."

"No, it's okay, you would have found out soon enough."

"Well Matty has another good shot at finding a match then–this is great news." He stood up, and we walked out of the room together, putting my mind at ease when he informed me that he'd let me know the outcome after he had spoken with Julian.

***

I was finally finishing up for the day, returning phone calls and catching up on some paperwork. I was deep in thought and nearly jumped out of my skin when my cell phone rang, displaying a number on the caller ID that I didn't' recognize.

"Hello?" I answered.

"Kat, it's Julian."

His voice brought butterflies to my stomach.

"Hi," I responded sheepishly.

"I'll have Matty's records tomorrow to review." He was short and emotionless. "I'll be flying out there on Thursday–are you free on Thursday afternoon to meet with Dr. Fowler?"

"Of course," I answered.

"Okay. Be at his office at two o'clock."

I could feel the ice coming through the phone when he didn't even say goodbye as he hung up. I knew I deserved everything I was getting, but a small part of me hoped that someday he'd forgive me.

***

I tried to remain focused for the next couple of days. I had gone for my blood test and was anxiously awaiting the results to see if I was a match for Matty. Matty had begun to run his low-grade fevers on and off again over the past few days, making me want to get everything underway even more.

"Damn," I shouted by the time I had hit the third red light. I was running behind with my last appointment and in turn was now running late to Dr. Fowler's office.

I pulled into the parking lot and hurriedly made my way in. The front desk receptionist took me back to Dr. Fowler's conference room where Dr. Fowler, Julian, and another younger doctor were already seated and deep in conversation. Both Dr. Fowler and the younger doctor stood up as I entered. Julian remained seated, not even acknowledging my presence.

"I'm sorry I'm late."

"Dr. Vallia, this is Dr. Devin," Dr. Fowler introduced me to the younger doctor.

I shook his hand and took the only available seat, which happened to be next to Julian, who was purposely going out of his way to ignore me.

Dr. Devin began to speak, giving us a rundown of his credentials and medical training, sounding like he was on a job interview.

"I just returned from Switzerland, and they're coming leaps and bounds with curing the type of cancer your son has," Dr. Devin went on to inform us. I glanced at Julian, and he didn't seem impressed. Dr. Devin was talking to Julian as if he were just an average clueless parent of a child with cancer. As I listened to him speak, I noticed, he did have many of the same traits Julian had when I had first met him. He was young and very driven. The only other feature he exhibited that Julian didn't, was a very strong characteristic of self-importance.

"We've been using a great experimental drug—"

"That's not happening," Julian interrupted.

"Dr. Kiron, I've read many articles and journal write-ups about you, and you are always welcoming of new and innovative treatments," Dr. Devin continued.

"Not experimental drugs," Julian answered sharply.

"These children have been spared the physical and emotional hardship of a bone marrow transplant thanks to this drug." Dr. Devin kept at it.

"And what side effects are these children going to have years from now because of this so-called miracle drug?" Julian asked, clearly already knowing the answer to his question.

"None that they can tell," Dr. Devin replied.

"Well, I was in Germany and was introduced to these so-called types of drugs. The children who took them are far worse off now than if they had just gone ahead with the bone marrow transplant." Julian's voice grew louder.

"They have come a long way in six years," Dr. Devin responded.

"I have recommended Matty's course of treatment, and that is what we're going with. It's not up for discussion anymore," Julian snapped.

"What are the drugs you're referring to, Dr. Devin?" I chimed in, trying to ignore the intense glare Julian's had cast upon me.

"Kat, it doesn't matter, it's not an option," Julian interrupted, finally acknowledging my presence.

"Well, maybe I would like to know what they are, *Julian*," I replied.

"You know nothing about these drugs and the side effects they will have on him for years to come!" he snapped.

"You're right, I don't know, so that's why I want Dr. Devin to explain," I challenged him.

"Oh, imagine that…you're actually getting all the facts before making assumptions."

My face heated and my anger grew over his callousness. I shook my head in disgust at him as I looked across the table at Dr. Fowler and Dr. Devin, who were clearly growing uncomfortable with the heated exchange between me and Julian.

"Would you mind if I spoke to Dr. Kiron alone for a few minutes?" I asked.

They both gladly obliged and left the room.

The smug look on Julian's face was making me even angrier. "How dare you sit here and insult me in front of them!"

"I don't think I was insulting you. If you've got a guilty conscience, that's not my fault," he said, avoiding eye contact.

"You're right—I do have a guilty conscience. I can apologize to you a million times, and I know it will never give you back what I took from you." My voice softened. "I understand if you hate me for it, but can we please come to some common ground and at least be civil to one another where Matty's concerned?"

He let out a deep sigh, and raked his hand through his hair as we sat in silence until Dr. Fowler re-entered the room.

"I just got Kat's test results—she isn't a match for Matty," Dr. Fowler said as he took a seat.

I sighed deeply, trying not to cry. Julian was Matty's only hope now. I quickly glanced Julian's way, sensing disappointment from him as well. I listened to him and Dr. Fowler going over Matty's plan of treatment, this time remaining quiet and letting Julian take over. I signed off on everything Julian had recommended—never having any intention of doing otherwise, feeling defeated, not knowing what would happen to Matty if Julian wasn't a match.

Dr. Fowler left the room once again to get more paperwork. "What happens if he doesn't find a match?" I asked Julian.

"He will," he said confidently, as if he didn't want to think of any other alternative. "I want to meet him," he blurted out, finally making eye contact with me.

"Sure—of course," I quickly obliged.

He began to open up to me a bit, informing me that he had been tested back in Chicago and would have the results any day now. He was staying with James and would be here until Sunday and then had to fly back to Chicago for another week, assuring me he would be back in time for Matty to start his treatments.

"When did you want to meet him?" I asked.

"Today."

I nodded in agreement and started to feel a little anxious and at the same time a twinge of excitement for both Matty and Julian.

Chapter 27

We finished with the paperwork and Julian followed me to my house. I called Claire on the way to make sure they were there. She informed me that Charles and Matty were up at the bay fishing.

"He's up at the bay fishing," I said to Julian as we arrived at my house. "Did you want to take a walk up there?"

He nodded and we began the short walk. I sensed his anxiety as he walked with his hands in his pockets the entire time, jingling loose change.

"Why are you so nervous?" I asked.

He shrugged. "I don't know, Kat…why do you think?"

"You're great with kids, you deal with them for a living," I replied, ignoring his sarcasm.

"Yes, but they're *other* people's kids," he reminded me.

"You are successful at everything you do. I'm sure that this will be no different. Besides, Matty is the most easy-going kid you will ever meet."

We walked onto the beach, and it took me a couple seconds to locate Charles and Matty with there being more people than normal on the usually deserted beach. I finally spotted them when I saw Gracie running amuck. Charles turned around and immediately came striding toward us while Matty was oblivious, running around with Gracie, chasing the seagulls.

"Julian, how are you?" Charles greeted him with a handshake.

"I'm well, thank you," Julian responded.

"Well, I'm going to head home now that you're here." Charles directed his attention to me while Julian stared straight ahead, never taking his eyes off Matty.

"Good luck." Charles placed his hand on Julian's shoulder just before waking off the beach.

"Matty," I called, using my hand to shield the sun that was

slowly sinking into the water.

"Mommy," he said as he picked himself up from the sand, running over as fast as he could with Gracie right behind him. I bent down to give him a hug, getting covered in sand in the process.

"Did you see Gracie and me, chasing all those bad seagulls away?" he asked while trying to catch his breath.

I shook my head and smiled. "Matty, I have someone very special that I would like you to meet." Matty finally took notice of Julian standing there. "Matty, this is your dad," I said as I stood up.

Matty looked up at Julian in awe, giving him the same bashful little smile he always gave when meeting someone for the first time.

Julian bent down, taking in everything about him. He was becoming more emotional as he laid eyes on his little boy for the very first time. "Hey, Matty, how are you?" My eyes burned as I tried to swallow the baseball-sized lump stuck in the back of my throat.

Matty's smile was a mile wide now. "My mommy said that you were far away."

"I was, but not anymore," Julian said, still unable to take his eyes off Matty.

"We have the same color eyes," Matty said, looking at Julian and then at me. "My mommy told me that only really special people have this color eyes." It amazed me how astute he could be at only five years old. Julian looked up at me, and I looked away, unable to meet his gaze.

Gracie finally greeted Julian in the usual Gracie way. "She likes you," Matty giggled as Gracie gave Julian a kiss on the cheek.

"Did you catch anything?" Julian stood up and looked at Charles' and Matty's fishing poles, sticking up in the sand.

Matty gasped as if he had forgotten all about the fishing poles. "Oh no, not yet, but I'm gonna catch a shark," he said. "Come on, you want to help?" He grabbed Julian's hand to take him over to the poles.

"I'll be back at the house. Okay?" I said, wanting to give the two of them some time alone.

He nodded as Matty whisked him away.

I walked off the beach, taking Gracie with me. I turned around as I reached the top of the sand dune, beaming inside and out as I watched Julian and Matty fishing together, just as the sun was beginning to set—it was the most beautiful picture ever. So perfect that I couldn't resist, taking out my phone and snapping a picture of the two of them as they sat together side by side with their backs to me, so much alike it was scary.

***

They were gone for some time before I finally heard Matty's gruff little voice, coming through the front door covered in sand.

"Did you catch any sharks?" I asked

"No, but we saw dolphins," Matty said, seeming just as satisfied.

"Have a seat," I said to Julian.

Matty sat down next to him and whispered in his ear, "Tell her you want ice cream." What Matty didn't realize was that his whispering was loud enough to be heard in the next room. Julian began to laugh as I just shook my head.

"I'm hungry," Matty said, getting up from the chair.

"I have homemade macaroni and cheese in the oven. It will be all done by the time you get out of the bath," I said, trying to get him to get a move on.

"Will you have some macaroni and cheese with me too?" he pleaded with Julian.

"Sure," he answered.

"Yay," Matty exclaimed as he went skipping off to take a bath.

After giving him a quick bath, Matty couldn't wait to get back in the kitchen to Julian. "I'm back!" he giggled. "You want to see my room?" He grabbed Julian's hand before he could even answer.

"Dinner is just about done," I said. Matty ignored me as he led Julian down the hallway and into his room.

I removed the macaroni and cheese from the oven and set the table, listening to Matty talk Julian's ear off. When I went into Matty's room, they were sitting on Matty's bed amongst all the action figures as he explained who each one was to Julian.

"Dinner's ready." I smiled at the mess.

"Yum!" Matty exclaimed, running down the hall ahead of us.

"I guess I should have warned you, he's a chatter box," I said to Julian.

"Can't imagine where he gets that from," he joked, and for one brief second, the old Julian was back–the one who wasn't angry at me.

185

We came out to the kitchen where Matty had proudly poured two cups of apple juice for him and Julian. "Do you even like apple juice?" I asked Julian.

"It's fine," he said.

"Sit here." Matty pointed to the chair next to him for Julian to sit.

"Geez, Matty, you're awfully bossy tonight." I raised an eyebrow at him.

"Sit here, *please.*" He batted his long lashes at Julian, and neither Julian nor I could resist, spewing with laughter.

After cleaning up from dinner, I joined Matty and Julian who were watching cartoons in the living room. Matty's energy was fading fast, and I knew it wouldn't be too long before he was fast asleep.

Julian also must have noticed how sleepy Matty was getting. "Well, I should get going," Julian announced.

"No," Matty cried. "Why are you leaving?"

"Because it's getting late, and you're tired," Julian explained.

"But you're the daddy, and the daddy and mommy live together with the kids."

Julian looked at him sadly, as if he didn't know how to answer.

"Not all mommies and daddies live together," I explained, giving him the example of his friend Brandon, who lived here with his mom while his dad lived in California.

"I don't like that at all!" Matty cried.

"I promise, I'll be back tomorrow to spend time with you," Julian reassured him. "How about if I stay here until you fall asleep?"

Matty nodded as he grabbed the blanket off the back of the couch. He covered himself and moved closer to Julian, resting his head against his chest. I knew it wouldn't be long before he would be out like a light, so I quickly went into his bedroom and cleared his toys from his bed. Just as suspected when I walked back out, he was fast asleep as Julian softly felt around his neck, concentrating on the lump.

"What are you thinking?" I asked, concerned by the look on his face.

"It's consistent with what the tests show," he said calmly.

"I guess I should get him into bed so you could get going," I said.

I walked over to pick him up, but Julian stopped me. "It's all right," he said, wanting to be with Matty for a little longer. He gently pulled Matty closer to him and wrapped his arm around him. He watched him as he slept, taking in his every breath. Matty looked so peaceful in his arms, like it was right where he belonged. Julian gently kissed him on the top of his head and I was on emotion overload, watching this whole interaction. I felt like such a horrible person for keeping this caring, loving man from his son for so long. We sat watching TV a little longer while Matty slept. I could tell that Julian was getting tired as well. He finally carried Matty into his room, tucking him into bed, and laughing as Matty did his usual incoherent sleep talking.

"Do you mind if I spend some time with him tomorrow?" he asked as I walked him to the door.

"Of course not," I quickly answered. "I'm working a half-day tomorrow."

"I'll come over in the afternoon."

"Sounds good." I smiled.

He nodded and took a step out the door before turning around. "He's a great kid, thank you."

"For what?" I asked.

"For helping to make that so easy."

"I didn't do anything. You were a big hit all on your own."

"I'll see you tomorrow." His tone was gentler now. His anger seemed to be dissipating a bit.

I stood in the doorway as he walked to his car and drove out of sight. The only sound I could hear were the crickets singing their familiar yearly tune. It was an unusually cool September night, the kind that made you long for the cool crisp days of autumn. As I watched the leaves on the big oak tree on my front lawn blow in the light breeze, I felt a sense of calmness overcome me. For just a brief moment, it was as if none of my problems existed. I took in one last breath of the cool night air before closing the door behind me.

Chapter 28

"**W**e're in the kitchen," Claire called as I entered her house to pick up Matty.

"Hi, Mommy." Matty smiled up at me with his face smeared with chocolate, as I walked into the kitchen to find him and Claire, making chocolate chip cookies. "We made cookies," Matty beamed as I leaned down and gave him a kiss.

"I can see that." I smiled.

Claire put some cookies on a plate and poured two glasses of milk, bringing them outside on the patio where Charles was. I watched out the window as Matty followed close behind, pulling a chair next to Charles and wasting no time sampling his cookies.

"Yes, he did eat lunch first," Claire said as she came back into the house, as if she knew exactly what I was thinking. I couldn't resist taking a cookie off the cooling rack as she began to clean up their baking mess. "So it sounds like Julian and Matty hit it off well. Matty hasn't stopped talking about him all day."

"Yes, things went really smoothly yesterday with the two of them," I agreed.

"I'm glad." She sat down and took a cookie, and I changed the subject, to their big anniversary trip that she and Charles were taking to New York City this weekend.

I waited for Matty to finish his cookies, stopping him when he came in for seconds. We said our goodbyes to Charles and Claire, took Gracie along with us, and headed home.

I arrived home and straightened up a bit while Matty was in his bedroom playing. I heard a knock on the door and wasn't surprised when I opened it up and saw Julian.

"Hi," I greeted, opening the door further and letting him in.

Matty came running down the hall, beaming when he saw Julian. "You came back!" he exclaimed.

"I told you I was going to," Julian replied, laughing at his reaction.

It was a beautiful day, so Matty and Julian headed into the backyard while I decided to use this valuable time to answer emails and return phone calls. I logged on to my email, ready to tackle the twenty-plus messages I had gotten since I left my office only two hours ago when I noticed an email from Patrick, the doctor from James' practice who Tricia was always trying to fix me up with.

Dear Kat,

Sorry I haven't called, I had been in Ireland visiting my family for the past two weeks. I just heard about Matty, and I wanted to let you know if there is anything I can do, please do not hesitate to let me know. I will try and give you a call soon so we can catch up. Until then, please take care.

Patrick

I smiled at his email, knowing James must have told him what was going on with Matty. How I wished I could see him as more than just a friend—but I couldn't. There was just something missing. Maybe once this was all over with Matty, we could go out on an official date and I would perhaps view him differently.

Dear Patrick,

Thank you so much. I really appreciate your kind words, it means a lot, look forward to catching up soon.

~ Kat

I hit the send button and worked my way through the rest of my emails. I was just returning the last of my phone calls, trying to convince a new mom that it was perfectly normal for her baby to run a low-grade fever while teething, when Julian and Matty came inside. I looked up at the clock, amazed to see it was already 5 p.m. As I hung up, I noticed Matty whispering into Julian's ear, this time low enough so I couldn't hear.

Julian laughed. "How about if I take you and your mom out to dinner first, and then you get ice cream?"

"P-l-e-a-s-e, Mommy!" Matty begged.

"Okay," I agreed, laughing at how pathetic he looked. Gracie came running over to Matty upon seeing his excitement, jumping on him and covering him in kisses. Matty giggled as she licked his face.

I couldn't help but laugh myself as I listened to Matty's deep belly laughs. Julian, however, didn't look amused.

"I hope you're going to wash his face after that," he said in disgust.

"Will you relax–of course I'm going to wash his face."

"You do realize that once he starts the treatments, his immune system is going to be compromised?"

I didn't appreciate his condescending tone. "Really, Doctor Kiron? I didn't know that, but leave it to a worldly doctor such as yourself to remind a lowly pediatrician like me of that fact."

He rolled his eyes at me. "It's not a joke. You really have to start getting in the habit of doing things differently to prepare him for the treatments. He shouldn't be eating all this garbage," he said as he picked up a bag of cookies from the counter. "And you certainly shouldn't allow a dog to lick his face."

"Well, he hasn't started the treatments yet, and until he does, he will continue to live his life the same way he always has, like a normal happy little boy. If he wants a cookie, he can have a cookie, and if he gets happiness over a dog kissing his face then I'm not going to stop it." My voice grew louder.

Matty looked at Julian and me, clearly sensing the tension. "Come on, Matty, let's go wash your face…we wouldn't want you getting any germs." I glared at Julian while I took Matty's hand and led him into the bathroom.

Matty chose our usual spot to eat–my dad's favorite diner. He crawled up into the booth making sure that Julian sat next to him. My dad's favorite waitress came over to take our order.

"Hey, handsome," she greeted Matty.

"This is my daddy," Matty said proudly, leaning his head on Julian's arm.

"Well there's certainly no denying that," she said, no doubt seeing the resemblance between the two of them.

Matty chattered nonstop through dinner. I was grateful for that– I was still annoyed at Julian for making me feel incompetent and didn't feel like engaging in conversation with him. I was surprised to see that Matty had eaten everything on his plate and was ready to work on his hot fudge sundae.

I excused myself to use the ladies' room and returned to my cell phone vibrating away on the table. I sent it to voicemail right away when I saw it was Patrick. Matty, who was only able to read a few words, was easily able to recognize the name *Patrick*, thanks in part to being a *Sponge Bob* junkie.

"Mommy, aren't you going to answer? It's Patrick."

"No, not right now."

"Who's Patrick?" Julian asked.

"Dr. McGinn. He's friends with Mommy. He's really nice, but he talks funny," Matty giggled, referring to Patrick's Irish accent. My eyes met Julian's gaze, and I was beginning to feel a little uncomfortable.

We arrived back at my house and Julian stayed outside to return some phone calls. His phone had been beeping with messages the entire time we were at dinner, but he never once looked to see who it was. I was impressed with how devoted to Matty he was when he was with him.

Julian finished his calls and came back in as Matty and I were playing with his dragons—he was the knight and I was the princess.

"I saved the beautiful princess," Matty said proudly, giving me a kiss. "Don't you think my mommy is a beautiful princess?" he asked Julian, making me feel a little uncomfortable.

Julian stood silently, just staring at me, and I was thankful to whoever was calling me at the moment to help break up the awkwardness of the moment.

"Hey, where have you been all day?" I answered upon seeing it was Tricia.

"I'm in Maryland. My dad had to go in for emergency surgery."

"Oh no, is everything okay?" I asked.

"Yeah, it was his gall bladder, but I wanted to see if you could take my rounds tomorrow at the hospital, so I could spend the night here."

"Sure, no problem," I responded, remembering after I hung up the phone that Charles and Claire were away, and I had no one to watch Matty.

"Darn it!" I said as I threw my phone back in my purse.

"What's the matter?" Julian asked.

"I just told Tricia I would cover for her at the hospital tomorrow, totally forgetting that Charles and Claire are away."

Julian looked at me, confused.

"I need someone to watch Matty," I clarified.

"Well, I'm here," he said as if it were a no-brainer.

I was just so used to doing this on my own, it didn't even dawn on me that Julian would be around tomorrow to help out.

After Matty had fallen asleep, I walked Julian to the door. "So, if you could be here my seven tomorrow morning that would be great," I instructed.

"Not a problem," he responded with his hand on the doorknob before turning around and taking me a little off guard when he asked, "So do you introduce Matty to all of your boyfriends?"

"What? Patrick isn't my boyfriend—he's a friend," I clarified.

He rolled his eyes in disbelief. "Look, Kat, I really don't care who you date, but do you think it's a good idea to get Matty involved?"

My anger grew—how dare he judge my parenting and to whom I chose to introduce my son? "Julian, I'm not dating him. He's just a friend," I clarified, not knowing why I even felt the need to justify this to him. "I think I know what's appropriate and inappropriate where Matty's concerned. I don't need you to lecture me like you're my father."

"Whatever. If you think that's appropriate." He was smug with his reply.

"So, it's perfectly fine for you to be sleeping with every woman in Chicago, but because I'm friends with a male, who I happened to introduce to Matty, I'm wrong?"

"I didn't say that, but Matty shouldn't be getting attached to someone who may not be in his life permanently."

"Well then, I guess the same could be said for you," I snapped.

"What's that supposed to mean?" he asked.

"How do I know you'll be in his life permanently? Remember, you don't want children." I knew that I had probably crossed the line with that statement, and that was confirmed by the look on his face.

"You are unbelievable!" he shouted. "Why do you have to get so damn defensive whenever someone tries to offer you any advice?"

"Okay then, thank you for that insightful advice, but I have been raising him on my own for the past five years, and I think I've done a pretty good job so far—is that better?"

"Oh please, Kat, don't play the martyr. You chose to raise him on your own—remember? I wasn't ever given that option."

"Look, Julian, don't tell me who—"

"I'm done with this conversation. I'll see you tomorrow," he said calmly, turning around and walking out the door.

I was infuriated and wasn't done with the conversation by any means, but I had no choice as I watched him drive away.

***

One patient ended up turning into four more emergencies. I found myself not leaving the hospital until late in the afternoon. With all of the excitement of the day, I found that my anger over Julian and our disagreement dissipating ever so slightly. When I walked outside, I realized the beautiful sunshine from the morning had turned into a torrential downpour. The temperature had dropped about twenty degrees as well. I threw my jacket over my head and ran to my car, taking my time driving home in the pouring rain.

I couldn't wait to get out of my wet clothes when I walked through the front door, surprised when I didn't get my usual Matty greeting—just Gracie coming up to sniff me. I followed the sound of the television blasting from the living room and couldn't contain my smile at the sight of Matty and Julian sound asleep on the couch. Julian was sitting up with Matty wrapped in his arms. They were so alike, even when they slept. The anger I was feeling for Julian from last night was now completely gone. From that moment on, I knew that Julian had fallen in love with Matty as quickly as I had. I also knew Matty had seen the same qualities in Julian that made me fall in love with him, so long ago. I reached for the blanket, covering them both up, still unable to take my eyes off the two of them.

Chapter 29

Julian was back in Chicago, and I was back to work, trying to act as if my life were normal like the days before Matty had gotten sick. The only silver lining, if there was such a thing, was the day I had gotten the phone call from Julian, letting me know he was a match for Matty. I was overjoyed at first, and then slowly became painfully aware of what lay ahead for Matty. He had gone for all of the additional testing that was required and was now himself becoming aware that something was happening, as much as I tried to downplay it.

Julian was to arrive in the morning at which time Matty's first treatment would begin. He was going to receive three rounds of chemo over several months and then the bone marrow transplant would follow after. I tried to mentally prepare myself for this as best I could, but realized that there was no way to prepare yourself to see your child suffering.

Julian called Matty every night before he went to bed to tell him good night. Matty truly did miss him, asking about him every day. We had finally hired a new doctor and nurse practitioner, allowing me to cut my hours extensively at work. I knew that there was no way possible for me to keep up with my workload while caring for Matty.

All of Matty's stuff was packed and ready to go for the hospital. He would be in the hospital for at least a week after each round and then home for about three weeks in between to let his counts recover. I tried to explain to him as best I could, without scaring him, but it was just too much to expect a five-year-old to comprehend.

I had invited Charles, Claire, Tricia, and James over for pizza, trying to make it a little special for Matty, knowing it was going to be the last night in a long while that we would all be getting together like this. I had barely heard the doorbell ringing through all of the chattering in the house and apparently no one else had either as they all continued to talk while I went to answer the door.

"Julian!" I exclaimed as I opened the door. "I thought you weren't coming until tomorrow?"

"I was able to get out of work a little earlier than planned and was able to catch a flight out instead." I walked him into the living room where Matty was deep in thought playing with his action figures with James.

"Hey, Matty," I shouted, causing him to look up.

His smile brought tears to my eyes.

"Daddy!" he exclaimed, running past everyone to give him a hug and a kiss as Julian swept him up in his arms. "My mommy said you weren't coming to see me until tomorrow." Matty pressed his forehead up against Julian's, still unable to wipe the smile from his face.

"I was, but I wanted to surprise you," Julian replied as Matty kissed him on the cheek and rested his head on his shoulder, still smiling, creating another perfect picture.

Matty didn't leave Julian's side the entire night. It made my heart happy, knowing he was surrounded by the people he loved the most—especially tonight.

It was getting later, and I was hoping that the night wouldn't end. "Are you ready to go?" James asked Tricia as he came into the kitchen.

"What's the matter? Matty's got a new friend and doesn't want to play with you anymore?" Tricia teased as she got up and grabbed her purse.

"Julian, I'm leaving. I'll see you later on at my house," James shouted into the living room. Matty began to cry, hearing that Julian was planning on going to James' house. This time it was actual sobbing, not his normal tired whiny cry. Claire tried consoling him by telling him that Gracie could sleep over, to no avail.

"Please, will you stay with me tonight?" Matty asked between his sobs, with huge crocodile tears pouring out of his eyes.

Julian gazed at me, not knowing how to answer. I mouthed the words to him letting him know that it was up to him. "It's okay, Matty. I'll stay with you," Julian said. Matty hugged him and his sobs began to subside.

Matty finally calmed down once everyone had left, and he was sure Julian wasn't going anywhere. "Sorry," I said to Julian.

"For what?" he asked.

"For Matty putting you on the spot."

"It's not a big deal."

Matty went into his bedroom to get something, and I used that time to fill Julian in about how overly emotional Matty had been all day. Almost as if he knew something was going to happen, even if he didn't understand it.

Matty finally appeared with his pillow, blanket, and an array of stuffed animals. "You can sleep with him," he said to Julian, handing him his favorite teddy bear that he slept with every night. Julian thanked him and smiled as he put the bear down on the couch.

"Matty, you're not sleeping on the couch," I said.

He looked at me, bursting out in tears once again. "She's mean!" he screamed and pointed at me.

"Perfect example," I said to Julian, who was finding it all amusing.

Matty was fighting sleep as hard as he could. I caught him looking up a few times, making sure that Julian hadn't left before finally giving in and closing his eyes. Julian carried Matty into his bed while I went into my bedroom to change into my pajamas. I was just about to exit when the photo box containing Matty's baby pictures caught my eye.

"What's this?" Julian asked as I took a seat next to him on the couch and placed the box on his lap.

"Matty, from birth to present," I replied.

He smiled as he took the lid off. I had them all organized in date order. He grabbed the first half, and I immediately remembered that I had some pregnancy pictures of my belly that Tricia had taken against my wishes.

"Oh, those aren't Matty," I said, trying to grab them. He tightened his grip and raised his hand higher so they were out of my reach. I lost my balance as I stood up, trying to take them from his grasp and fell onto his lap. He placed his hand on my back while gazing at me intently. Suddenly, the playful mood from just a few seconds ago was much more intense. It was strangely comfortable, but I quickly got up, putting enough distance between us.

A huge grin spread across his face as he studied the picture. "Wow, I was having a hard time imagining what you looked like pregnant." As if that weren't bad enough, there was the whole gamut of pictures Claire and Tricia had taken right after I had given birth.

"I guess I really should have gone through these pictures before I let you see them," I said.

"What's wrong with them?"

"I look like death."

"You just had a baby," he said sweetly, giving me another glimpse of the old Julian. I noticed that he paid particular attention to the pictures that represented various milestones in Matty's life–his birth, his christening, and his birthdays. I guess in some strange way, he was hoping he could relive those times through these photographs.

He was just about to close the lid on the box when he noticed another small package of photos shoved in the back. I watched as he took them out. I was just as curious, having no clue what the envelope contained. I leaned over to see which picture of Matty he was staring at so closely. Only, it wasn't a picture of Matty, it was a picture I had forgotten all about. One that was buried in the back of that box because it had hurt too much to look at it. It was of Julian and me, taken on that New Year's Eve at Charles and Claire's house. I was flooded with memories of that perfect night, wishing I could change how I had dealt with the outcome. If I could go back in time, Julian would have been there with his son from the day he was born, instead of looking at the first five years of his life through photographs. My heart ached just thinking about all the years I had robbed from him, and all of the time he could never get back.

He put the pictures back in the box and closed the lid. "So, how come you never got married?" he asked, taking me a little off guard.

I shrugged. "Well that would be a little difficult when according to you, I shouldn't be introducing any male friends to Matty." I couldn't resist getting one last dig in. He rolled his eyes at my sarcasm. "Guess I just never found the right guy." The truth was, I found myself comparing every guy I dated to him. "Why didn't you?" I asked, turning the tables, knowing that was a ridiculous question to be asking him, of all people.

"Because marriage isn't for me." He was complacent.

"Oh, but one-night stands are?" I asked before I could even register what I was saying.

"It's a lot less work," he said, looking away.

"So these girls are okay with it too?"

"I really don't care if they aren't." He was smug with his reply, sounding so heartless.

"That's a little harsh, don't you think?"

"No. I don't make promises I don't intend to keep. If they're not okay with it—it's nobody's fault but their own."

I couldn't help but wonder if he was including me in with that statement. "Kind of like how you didn't make any promises to me, right?"

He looked away and was silent for a brief moment. "No, it's not the same thing," he finally responded.

"Don't you want something beyond physical?" I pried deeper.

"Nope. I did the emotional thing already—it doesn't work." He cast a strong gaze upon me, and I was starting to feel a little uncomfortable with the direction the conversation was going, clearly understanding that he was now referring to our relationship.

"Well I'm going to bed. The guest room is all ready for you."

"Okay, I've just got to return some emails," he said as he checked his phone.

I got up and headed to my bedroom before turning around. "Thanks," I blurted out.

"For what?" he asked.

"For surprising Matty tonight, it meant a lot to him."

He nodded and gave me a warm smile.

I had caught a small glimpse of the old Julian tonight. The one I got along with, laughed with, and had such strong feelings for—how I wished that old Julian would stick around a little longer or even forever.

Chapter 30

The weather outside was fitting for the day that lay ahead, damp and dreary. I was already feeling sick just looking at Matty in the hospital bed. As the nurse came in to get his IV set up, he began to cry at the sight of the needle. I held his hand, and she gently explained to him what was happening in a five-year-old vocabulary. Both she and I told him not to look, but as much as he hated getting needles of any kind, he couldn't stop himself from watching. She managed to get the IV into him fairly easily with just a few tears on his end.

"It's okay, Matty," I said as I sat down on his bed and he clung to me.

As the nurse returned with the IV bags, one containing fluids and the other containing the chemo, I took a deep breath. It all seemed too real now. Matty managed a smile when Julian entered the room with Dr. Fowler.

"Good morning, Matty." Dr. Fowler greeted Matty with handshake and explained to him what was going to happen over the next week.

I was glad Julian was sitting back and overseeing Matty's care, allowing Dr. Fowler to do all the hands-on work. I didn't want Matty associating any pain or trauma during this whole process with Julian. As far as Matty knew, Julian had nothing to do with any of this–he was just here as his dad.

The first drip slowly made its way down the tube and into his body, and I couldn't watch anymore. "Did you want to watch a movie?" I asked Matty as I reached in my bag and pulled out my iPad.

"Can you sit with me and watch a movie?" Matty asked Julian.

"Sure." He sat down on the bed next to him.

"Which movie do you want to watch?" Matty asked, taking control of my iPad.

"You decide?" Julian smiled as Matty scrolled through the choices, finally choosing, his usual, *Toy Story*. He moved closer to Julian and nuzzled up against him as the movie began to play.

Julian had explained to me earlier that Matty may show some effects within the first few days or he may not. Everyone was different in the way their body reacted. I was hoping that he would handle it well with very few side effects. I knew that might be asking for too much, but I was trying to stay positive.

Before I knew it, they were coming around to take Matty's lunch order, and to my surprise, he ordered a grilled cheese. When his lunch arrived, true to Matty's style, he took two small bites from his sandwich and went right for the ice cream that was on his tray. After devouring the ice cream, he announced that he was full.

We had gotten through his first day without any major hurdles. We stayed with him well past visiting hours. Julian assured me that he would be asleep the rest of the night from the medicine, which put my mind at ease a bit. I didn't want him to wake up in a strange place in the middle of the night, scared and alone.

I was dreading the next two days because I had to go into work briefly on each one. I was riddled with guilt for not being there for Matty, but I took comfort in knowing that Julian would be there. After I got through these next two days, I would be off for some time to devote myself fully to Matty, while Julian flew back to Chicago for a few days. I was fortunate that the hospital was close enough to both my house and work, allowing me to go back and forth between the two with ease. It was Julian who was going to have it rough, flying back and forth, working sixteen-hour days on the days that he was home to try to catch up, but something told me he wouldn't have it any other way.

I woke up early from a horrible night's sleep, immediately calling the hospital to check on Matty. The nurse informed me that he had had a very good night and was still sleeping. I wanted more than anything to be there with him today. I just had to get through a few hours of work until I could be by his side. I was happy when I received a text from Julian letting me know he was there, and I was even happier to hear that Matty was eating his breakfast.

I made it through my very short workday, wasting no time getting to the hospital. The smile on my face quickly disappeared when I entered Matty's room to find him vomiting uncontrollably.

My heart sank to my knees, seeing him this way and wanting desperately to help him. Julian remained completely composed, rubbing his back, trying to calm him down. I couln't get over how pale and fragile Matty seemed from just twenty-four hours ago. He began to cry even harder upon seeing me in the doorway, and it took every ounce of energy I had not to cry myself. I knew I had to stay strong for him, so I ignored the lump in my throat and the burning in my eyes and pulled it together.

"I'm all dirty," he sobbed.

"That's okay, sweetie, we'll have you cleaned up in no time," the nurse said.

Julian wiped off Matty's face with a damp cloth as the tears streamed from Matty's eyes. "Now my favorite pajamas are ruined," Matty managed to get out in between sobs.

It amazed me how the mind of a child worked. With everything going on, his worst fear was that his pajamas were dirty. "No, they're not. I'll take them home and wash them right away for you," I reassured him.

"Matty, how about if you take a nice shower to get cleaned up?" the nurse asked.

"I don't know how to take a shower. I take baths." He was sheepish in his reply.

"Oh, well, then how about if I help you?" the nurse offered very sweetly.

He looked at me for approval. I nodded and helped him out of bed, and into the bathroom, maneuvering his IV pole along the way. "If you can get him started, I'll take over. I just want to grab his clothes," I said to the nurse.

"No problem." She smiled and turned on the water.

I walked out of the bathroom and grabbed some clean clothes from Matty's bag. "Hopefully he'll calm down a little after a nice hot shower," I said to Julian who was staring out the window, deep in thought.

"It's going to happen," he replied, turning his attention back to me. "That's one of the biggest side effects."

"I know," I whispered.

"You're a doctor—you should be used to this," he said nonchalantly.

"Yes, I am a doctor, but I'm Matty's mother first, and it takes on a whole different perspective when it's your own child that you're watching suffer. Maybe you would realize that if you stopped treating him as one of your cases and more like your son."

"What the hell are you talking about?" he snapped.

"Don't you see? This isn't one of your patients—this is your child. Perhaps you should stop thinking a little less like a doctor and more like a father." I suddenly realized I was sounding a little harsher than I intended.

"Well forgive me, Kat, if I don't have this whole parenting thing down as well as you. I've only had a few weeks' experience as opposed to your five years."

"Are you going to hold that over my head for the rest of my life?" I asked.

"I don't know—are you going to stop acting like it's my fault that you've been raising him alone for the past five years?"

"Well, isn't it, in a way?" I snapped back.

"Okay, Kat—I can't wait to hear this one. How the hell is it my fault?"

"Oh, don't you remember? Your career came first. You left me no choice, Julian."

He shook his head and moved closer to me. His voice becoming harsher. "You always had a choice. You could have picked up the phone at any time and told me, and I would have been there for him in a minute. Don't blame me because you wanted to play the victim. I don't walk away from my responsibilities—when I know they exist."

"I wanted to play the victim? Are you kidding me? You have no idea what I went through or how I felt. You think that I actually wanted to raise my son alone without his father?" I realized my voice was growing louder, and I was hoping Matty didn't hear.

"Then why didn't you tell me?" he demanded.

I looked away, suddenly my strong demeanor was melting away. "Because I wanted you to *want* to be with us, not because you felt like you *had* to." I met his gaze once again.

He was silent as his eyes pierced into me. Shaking his head, he let out an agitated breath before exiting the room.

I sighed deeply. The last thing I wanted to do was to strike up a fight with him. I just wanted him to see things differently instead of his black-and-white way of thinking. But this was his livelihood, what he had trained for most of his life—to cure cancer. He didn't have any experience with being a father. Just a few weeks ago, he didn't even know he had a son. Deep down inside, I knew he was right, I had to try to pull it together a little better for Matty's sake, but I would never be able to see Matty as just another patient—he was my reason for living, my whole world, and for feeling that way, I would never feel guilty.

***

Thankfully, the week was over and so was the first round of treatments. Julian had gone back to Chicago, and it had been just Matty and me for the past few days. I was impressed with myself in dealing with his bouts of nausea, which made me realize, I was a lot stronger than I had thought, where Matty was concerned.

We checked out of the hospital and headed home. Claire was over, stocking up my freezer. She had cooked enough dinners to get me through the next week, and had also bought a couple boxes of ice pops to help with Matty's mouth sores that he had contracted—another side effect from the chemo.

"Welcome home!" Claire hugged him and handed him a bag containing one of the new action figures he had wanted.

"Thank you." He smiled.

"You are very welcome."

He slowly made his way into his bedroom to add it to his collection while Claire and I sat down for a cup of coffee. I was finally able to decompress a bit as I filled her in on the last few days.

I went into Matty's room to check on him and he was fast asleep on his bed. I covered him up, placing his teddy bear next to him, and planting a kiss on his cheek.

"He's sound asleep," I said to Claire as she prepared to leave.

"Well maybe you should take a nap too. You look exhausted," she suggested as I walked her to the door and we said our goodbyes. As I returned to the kitchen, the ringing from inside my purse startled me.

"Hey," I answered right away upon seeing it was Julian.

"How's Matty?" He got right to the point.

"He's fine. He's sleeping now. He's dealing with some mouth sores, but he's toughing it out."

"Just make sure you keep on him about washing his hands, and don't let that dog around him."

Here we go again.

"Yes—I know."

"Is he still vomiting?"

"Yes, but not as much."

"Well, just have him eat smaller, more frequent meals with more protein and fats, not all of that junk that you allow him to eat."

I wanted to scream, but I tried my best to stay calm. "Okay, Julian."

I heard a woman's voice in the background. *"Julian, are you ready?"*

"I'll be right there," he responded. "Kat, I have to run, are you going to be okay with everything?"

"Yes, I'm fine. I'm a doctor. Remember? Go lecture your girlfriend there with your medical advice." I knew I was sounding catty, but I was beyond annoyed with him at this point.

"What?" he laughed. "That's not my girlfriend, she's—"

I cut him off and did my best to mimic him. "Look, Julian, I really don't care who she is, just as long as you don't introduce her to Matty. You wouldn't want him to become attached to someone who's not going to be in his life permanently."

"You are incorrigible," he said.

"I'm incorrigible! Oh, so it's okay for you to make assumptions but—"

"Goodbye, Kat," he chuckled, enjoying the rise that he had gotten out of me.

"Ugh!" I screamed as I tossed my phone back into my purse. I hated when he did that. Every time he would get my blood boiling, he would just walk away or hang up the phone calmly.

I knew I was probably just being overly sensitive because I was so tired. Maybe Claire was right, maybe I should try to take a nap. I had no idea what kind of night Matty would have on his first night home, so I should be prepared with at least a little rest. I went into my bedroom to lie down, tossing and turning, unable to relax. After about twenty minutes and a million thoughts running through my mind, I finally gave up, opting for plan B instead—more coffee. As I walked past Matty's room, I peeked in on him, lured in by his peaceful state. As I lay down on his bed and curled up with him, a wave of calmness overcame me. I rubbed his back, measuring every breath he took. I loved that Julian was in his life now, and I loved how much Matty had taken to him, but the selfish side of me missed my one-on-one time with my little boy. I closed my eyes, hugging him tightly, finally able to relax a bit.

Chapter 31

Matty had finished his third round of treatments, and it had finally taken its toll on him. He looked like a cancer patient now. His already thin body was emaciated, his extra pale skin emphasized the dark circles that took residence around his eyes, and his hair was completely gone. I had been working one day a week, but decided to take a complete leave of absence. There was just no possible way that I could mentally have my mind at work. He had a few infections in between treatments that scared me a great deal, and I knew that the worst was yet to come with the bone marrow transplant, scheduled in three days.

His immune system was at its weakest and they wanted to prevent him from contracting any germs, so his contact with people was limited. Julian was flying in later and had taken some time off as well. He was going in for the donation process the day before Matty would receive the transplant. This was the step in this whole scary journey that terrified me most. I knew everything that could go wrong with a bone marrow transplant and the pain that the recipient goes through.

It was Christmas Eve, and I was trying to make it just as special as Christmases past. It was upsetting for Matty to not have the usual people around as in previous years, but having Julian here and spending their first Christmas together would also mean a lot to him as well. I had to do most of my shopping online. I hadn't been able to get out much due to the circumstances, making sure Santa left the same amount of toys he did every year. I got Julian a watch from Matty, which he excitedly picked out on his own as we shopped online.

Matty was in his pajamas, anxiously awaiting Santa and Julian. We were watching TV and sipping hot chocolate when Julian arrived, with a bagful of presents.

"Wow!" Matty responded as he greeted him at the door seeing all of the presents.

"Santa came to Chicago already and told me to make sure these got to you." Julian smiled.

"Mommy, look!" Matty exclaimed.

"You must have been a really good boy this year." I smiled over Matty's enthusiasm.

"Is it raining out?" I asked Julian, noticing his hair and coat were wet.

"It's snowing," he replied.

I walked over to the window and looked up at the full moon. There was a blanket of snow already on the ground as the snow continued to fall. I imagined what a picture-perfect Christmas Eve this would have been, if only Matty weren't sick.

"Snow!" Matty exclaimed, running over to the window.

"Tomorrow can we build a snowman, please?" he asked Julian.

Julian looked at him sadly. "You know what, that isn't very good snow for a snowman, why don't you open up your presents?"

He slowly opened the presents, so unlike the way he normally would on previous Christmases. This year he just seemed to be missing the whole magic of Christmas. He had finally gotten through the last gift and was trying to figure out which toy to play with first.

"Hey, Matty, I think Santa dropped off a present for your mom too," Julian said as he pointed to a smaller wrapped box under the tree.

Matty jumped up to retrieve the box and handed it to me. I was totally shocked, not at all expecting a gift from Julian.

"It's beautiful," I whispered as I opened it to find a beautiful gold bracelet. I immediately put in on my wrist—it was a perfect fit.

"Thank you." I smiled.

"Mommy, why are you thanking him? Santa brought it, silly," Matty reminded me.

"Oh, that's right, thank you to Santa." I looked at Julian as he chuckled.

Matty was so excited, he whispered in my ear, asking if he could give Julian his present. I told him where it was and he ran off to get it.

I waited until he was out of earshot. "Thank you. It's really beautiful, you didn't have to—"

"This is from me," Matty interrupted. "I picked it out all by myself, but Mommy had to pay for it because I don't have money."

Julian and I both laughed.

"Wow, this is cool." Julian smiled as he opened up his watch.

Matty's grin was a mile wide. "Mommy says its *waterprood...*"

"Waterproof," I corrected him.

He continued on, not missing a beat, "...so next time we go fishing, you can wear it and get it wet."

"This is the best present ever, Matty." Julian picked him up and put him on his lap, giving him a hug and kiss. I grabbed my phone and took a picture of the two of them. As I stared at the image on my screen, I hardly even recognized that little boy siting on Julian's lap. The only thing that remained the same were his beautiful blue eyes— that was the one thing that these treatments couldn't take away from him. He looked truly happy in the picture, and I took comfort in that.

"Since we're giving presents tonight..." I reached under the Christmas tree and grabbed the gift bag underneath, handing it to Julian. His eyes widened in surprise. "It's just a little something." I bit my lip and managed a smile.

His eyes filled with emotion when he pulled out the framed photo I had taken of him and Matty fishing on that very first day they met. He didn't need to speak, the expression on his face told me exactly how much that picture meant to him. He was finally able to peel his eyes away from it and looked up at me with tear-filled eyes.

Matty gasped, breaking up the solemn moment. "We have really good cookies that my mommy made. I'll get you some!" He jumped off the couch, and headed off to the kitchen to grab some.

"Thank you," Julian finally managed to get out.

"You're welcome," I whispered.

Matty came back into the living room with a plateful of cookies. "These are the same kind we're giving Santa tonight when he comes." He took a seat back on the couch and grabbed a chocolate chip cookie.

"Are you hungry?" I asked Julian, realizing I didn't even offer him anything to eat with all the excitement.

"No, not at all," he said, running his hand through his hair. He looked like he was exhausted–all of the traveling and long workdays were finally catching up to him.

After polishing off a few more cookies, then coming down from his sugar high, it didn't take Matty long to fall asleep. He was on a barrage of medications, most of which made him drowsy. Julian carried him into his bed while I placed all of his presents from Santa under the tree.

I was sitting on the couch trying to figure out how to put batteries in one of Matty's presents as Julian sat down next to me, taking it from my hand, figuring it out right away.

"Thanks for making this Christmas special for him," I said.

"No need to thank me, Kat."

I sighed deeply, thinking of Matty and how sick and frail he had looked tonight.

"What's wrong?" Julian asked.

"I'm just so scared, that he's not going to make it through this." My eyes flooded with tears.

"Why would you think that? All of his tests are coming back perfect, and his levels are right where they should be."

"I'm just scared of this transplant, I'm scared of him being in pain and being all alone. If anything were to happen to him, I wouldn't be able to go on. I would die right along with him." I broke down, allowing the tears to flow freely.

"The transplant isn't going to be easy for him, but you have to stay positive." He moved closer and wiped away a tear that was rolling down my face. I stared up at him, hypnotized by those spellbinding eyes I had dreamed of so often over the past five years. He moved in closer, and I stretched my neck to meet him, our lips gently skimming each other's. Before I knew it, our simple little brush on the lips had turned into a full-blown, passionate kiss. He pushed me down on the couch, and those butterflies in my stomach that had been locked away for so many years were finally freed. As his hands moved about my body, I pulled him closer, needing him emotionally—wanting him physically. His lips trailed down my neck and my insides awakened from their long slumber. As my body eagerly waited in anticipation for his next move—he stopped, sitting up, leaving me wanting more.

"I'm sorry Kat, I just—" He shook his head, still trying to gain control of himself.

"It's okay." I sat up and kissed him again, letting him know, I was perfectly fine with it. Only this time instead of responding positively, he pushed me away.

"We can't do this," he said.

"Why not?"

He raked his hands through his hair, and stared straight ahead. "I don't want to make things complicated between us."

"I think we're way past complicated, Julian."

"Look, what just happened was a mistake."

I bit my lower lip and took a deep breath. "I won't expect any promises." I didn't want to sound desperate, but I wanted him badly.

He let out an exhausting breath before meeting my gaze. "This isn't about us anymore–it's about Matty."

There I had it. His words hit me like a ton of bricks, but he was right. He was here for Matty, not to re-claim any unfinished business between us, and I needed to come to terms with that. We seemed to be in a pretty good place now, and I didn't want to ruin that, but I still couldn't deny that I was still so attracted to him.

"I'm sorry," I whispered.

"No, I'm sorry," he replied, standing up and walking over to the window to look at the falling snow.

My eyes focused on the dancing flames in the fireplace, trying to remove what had just transpired from my mind. Tomorrow was Christmas. I would soon be feeling the same joy I had felt every year, seeing the look on Matty's face as he woke up to find his presents from Santa. I was going to cook a nice dinner for the three of us and just focus on enjoying the day. Even though I had caught another glimpse of the old Julian tonight, I knew that he was long gone as I tried my hardest to convince myself that Julian was just Matty's dad–not the man I had once loved so deeply.

Chapter 32

The day I had tried to put out of my mind was finally here. Julian was already in for the extraction. His part was fairly simple, but he would be in some pain for a day or so. Even though the doctor performing the extraction recommended an overnight hospital stay–Julian was adamant that he would not. I tried convincing him several times, to no avail.

Matty was receiving one more round of chemo and the transplant would take place the next day. He was in a regular room for now, then once the transplant took place, he would be moved to a specially filtered room with isolation requirements and a strict hygiene regimen.

I sat next to Matty as he was poked and prodded. His little arm was so black and blue from all the needles that it didn't even seem to bother him anymore. It was as if he was numb to it all.

"Where's Daddy?" His blue eyes were so inquisitive.

I explained as best I could about what was happening, reassuring him that Julian would be fine.

I spent the entire morning with him, waiting for all of the testing to be complete. When he finally gave in to his tired eyes and took a nap, I decided to use that time to check on Julian.

I entered his hospital room, surprised to find him already dressed and studying something on his phone–work emails no doubt. He seemed paler than usual, and his normal bright blue eyes were dull and flat–the same color as Matty's when he was under the weather.

"Look at you, up and working already," I said with a smile.

He immediately put his phone down. "I told you I'd be fine. I'm just waiting for my discharge papers, so I can get the heck out of here." He bent down to tie his shoe and flinched in pain. He tried to play it off when he knew that I had seen.

"Did they give you pain medication?" I asked as I sat down on the chair next to his bed.

"I don't need it," he said in a dismissing tone.

"Well, by the looks of it you are in some pain," I insisted.

"What's going on with Matty?" he deflected.

"He's sleeping right now, just waiting to get all his tests back."

"Thank you," I said.

"For what?"

"For possibly saving Matty's life. If it weren't for you, Matty would still be on the list, waiting for a match."

He gazed at me, not saying a word. The silence was finally broken when the doctor who performed his extraction entered the room.

"Good Morning, Dr. Young," I greeted. We were introduced previously, at one of the many meetings with Matty's medical team.

"Good morning," he responded before turning his attention back to Julian. "You know this is against my better judgment, but I do feel a little better, knowing you have Dr. Vallia here to take care of you."

Julian raised his eyebrow. "I'll be fine. I don't need anyone to take care of me." He was short and bordering on downright rude.

"I can assure you that you're going to be in a lot more pain tonight," Dr. Young warned.

Julian took the discharge papers from him and signed them, walking out of the room while I stayed behind.

"I'm sorry for that, he's just stubborn," I apologized.

"That's quite okay, I understand, doctors make the worst patients." Dr. Young laughed it off. "Just make sure you're around to keep an eye on him tonight."

"I will," I reassured him.

"Good luck to Matty tomorrow," he said with a warm smile.

"Thank you," I said, walking out the door.

As I made my way to Matty's room, I tried to brush off Julian's rude behavior with Dr. Young. I knew his nerves were finally getting the best of him. He was sleep deprived, in pain, and worrying about Matty just as much as I was. I heard Matty's voice even before entering the room. He and Julian seemed to be having a serious conversation. I peeked in to see Julian sitting on the bed next to him as I stood just outside the doorway listening.

"Am I going to die?" Matty asked, his voice quivering while my heart sank.

"No, Matty, you're not," Julian reassured him.

"Well, my mommy cries a lot. She thinks I don't hear her, but I do, so she must think I'm going to die. I don't like it when she's sad," Matty cried.

"She's not crying because she thinks you're going to die. She just gets sad because she loves you so much, and she doesn't like how sick this medicine is making you," Julian explained.

"Well if the medicine makes me sick then why do I have to take it?" Matty asked.

"Because even though it's making you sick right now, eventually it's going to make you better. Did you ever take medicine for a really bad sore throat or an ear ache?"

"Yeah, Mommy always gets mad at me because I try to spit it out. It's really yucky!"

"But even though it tastes yucky, it makes you feel better, right?"

"Yes," Matty answered.

"Well, this medicine is kind of like that, but only instead of tasting yucky, it makes you feel yucky before you get better," Julian explained. I remained outside the door amazed with the way he was handling the situation.

"So am I going to get better?" Matty asked.

"Of course, you're going to get better," Julian replied.

"Oh," Matty said sadly.

"Why do you sound so sad about that?"

"Because once I get better, you're going to go away again." Matty cried once again.

"Matty, I will never leave you, I promise."

"But don't you have to go help other sick kids far away, once I get all better?"

"I will only be in Chicago, and you're going to come and see me all the time. You'll have two houses—one in Chicago and one with your mom."

"But I want you and Mommy to live in the same house."

"Mommy has her job here, and I have mine in Chicago," Julian tried to explain.

"Don't you love my mommy?" he pleaded.

I didn't know what to do, unsure if I should interrupt and help

Julian out. I waited a couple seconds longer to see if he had it under control.

"Matty, it's not that simple," he started to explain.

"Well, I love you, and I love Mommy, and I want us all together," Matty interrupted.

I walked into the room acting as if I hadn't heard the entire conversation that had just taken place. "Look who's awake!" I exclaimed, hoping to change the topic of conversation. Matty clung tightly to Julian as tears streamed down his face. I sat at the edge of the bed, trying to comfort him.

Dr. Fowler entered the room, causing a welcome distraction, seeming surprised to see Julian up and about. "Weren't you having the procedure today?" he asked.

"Yes, it's done," Julian said, using the same tone that he had with Dr. Young.

"You should be sleeping that anesthesia off," he lectured.

Julian ignored him and took Matty's test results from his hand to read them over—once again, making me feel like I needed to apologize for his dismissing demeanor.

"Everything looks good to go," Julian said, giving them back to Dr. Fowler.

"Julian, I know you know the drill, but I wanted to let Kat know," Dr. Fowler began to explain, focusing his attention on me. "The transplant is scheduled to begin at six a.m. tomorrow. You'll be able to stay with him overnight until he's moved to the other room. If he starts showing any signs of infection, he will be put in total isolation." I nodded, trying to keep my mind from wandering to the dark side.

We spent the rest of the day and night with Matty. He was handling the meds well, thanks to the anti-nausea medication. It was getting late, and Matty had just fallen asleep. Julian made sure to check his medication one last time before we left.

It felt a little strange, having him spend the night without Matty there to act as a buffer, especially after our kiss the other night, and I sensed he was feeling the same way too.

"You can just drop me off at your house, and I'll head over to James'," he said as we reached my car.

"It's late. You haven't gotten any sleep after being under anesthesia, and you're in pain." I was finally able to think logically and put the other night out of my mind. "Plus, you're not supposed to be driving for twenty-four hours," I added.

"I will be–" He tried getting the words out, but I wouldn't allow it.

"Really, Julian, we have to be at the hospital early tomorrow." I was firm, and his silence indicated to me that he knew I was right.

Julian remained quiet the entire car ride home, responding to emails on his phone. I was amazed that he was still coherent after the day he had. We arrived back at my house and I went into my room to change into my pajamas, while he was still typing away on his phone. When I came back into the kitchen, I noticed his painful reaction as he got up from the kitchen chair.

"Will you please go sit down on the couch and relax?" I requested.

He obliged. Silently walking over to the couch.

"Take these," I said, taking a seat next to him and handing him two *Tylenol* and a glass of water. Much to my surprise he didn't put up a fight. "You really overdid it today."

"I'm fine," he answered.

"Have you even checked the extraction site?"

"It's fine!" he snapped, using the same short tone he had with everyone all day.

"Let me see," I persisted.

He shook his head and let out an annoyed breath.

"Julian–now!" I shouted, feeling more like I was talking to Matty.

He raised his eyebrow at me as I glared at him, not giving in. He finally relented, lowering the waistline on his pants to reveal the site on his hip, covering it back up so quickly, I couldn't see a thing.

"Julian, honestly let me see," I pleaded.

He reluctantly revealed it to me again, and I gently removed the bandage.

"It's fine," he insisted.

"No, it's not fine. It red and swollen!"

After rolling his eyes at me, I stood up and pulled him off the couch, leading him into the bathroom.

"You know, I'm quite capable of doing this myself," he said sarcastically as I cleaned it thoroughly with soap, water, and peroxide. This time, I was the one who was ignoring him. I just continued putting some antibiotic cream on it, slapping the bandage on just a little harder than usual.

"Geez, are you this rough with all your patients?" he asked with a boyish grin.

"Only the bad ones who won't listen." I was very matter-of-fact. "Now go to bed! You look like a zombie."

"What?" he chuckled at my stern demeanor.

"You should have been resting all day," I lectured.

He rolled his eyes again. "I'm not one of your patients."

"Well, if you're going to act like a child then I'm going to treat you like one."

I pushed him in the direction of the guest room and turned down the covers. He shook his head, and I sensed he realized he wasn't going to win this battle.

"Now, Dr. Kiron, can I get you anything else before you go to bed?" I joked.

"Yeah, a new doctor." He tried to hold back his smile.

"Oh, sorry, I'm the only one on duty tonight." I gave him a sarcastic grin. "Sleep well, Doctor." He shook his head as I shut the door behind me.

I was super tired, but at the same time wide awake. I decided to head out to the living room and watch some TV in hopes of falling asleep, but as I walked past Matty's room something compelled me to go in. I sat down on his bed and grabbed one of his stuffed animals, hugging it tightly as I lay down, and breathing in his scent that was still on his pillow. There was nothing in the world that I wanted more than to be cuddling with him right now. I missed my baby boy so much. That familiar painful lump formed in the back of my throat, thinking about the long journey ahead. I tried remaining positive as I thought of what tomorrow would bring, taking comfort in knowing that Julian was here, and Matty had the best doctor in the world caring for him. Closing my eyes, I whispered, "thank you" to the special angel who I knew was watching over his grandson and would never leave his side—my dad.

Chapter 33

I sat in Matty's room on the day of his transplant looking at the bag of blood hanging from his IV pole. It was hard to fathom that this was what his life had come to. This was what was going to keep him alive. He wasn't eating much of anything. Even his usual sweet tooth was curtailed. I was warned that this would happen, but the sight of him turning down a brownie was as painful as watching him lying in that hospital bed.

It was now a waiting game. The first few weeks were the most critical. The intense regimen of chemo that he received prior to the transplant had crippled his immune system. Julian and I were the only visitors he was allowed as he was highly susceptible to infection. The transplanted bone marrow had to set up inside his body and start producing normal blood cells, and I was taking it one day at a time. Every day he got through without any major complications was a victory.

My world now consisted of this hospital room. I hadn't seen Charles and Claire or Tricia in weeks. I missed them so much and would call or text them each day with updates.

We were now two and a half weeks post-transplant. Matty had been showing flu-like symptoms, which was common for any patient receiving a transplant. He was weak and irritable, and nothing seemed to appease him. I was amazed by Julian's diligence to stay by his side. He had totally put work on the back burner, letting his associates temporarily take over for him, and I was grateful for this. There was no way I would have been able to go through this alone.

Matty picked up his favorite book from the table beside him. "Can you read this to me?" he asked Julian with his gruff little voice now sounding very weak.

Matty listened closely, taking extra time to look at the pictures as Julian read to him. I watched and smiled, thinking he was finally showing an interest in something—maybe this was a good sign. As I looked on I began to notice his eyes moving about strangely. He let out a hoarse cry, and his body shook uncontrollably as he began to seize. This was another side effect that I was told could possibly happen, although it was very rare. I was paralyzed in fear as I stood there watching it unfold. Julian quickly turned him on his side to help keep his airway open.

Snap out of it!

I was finally able to move myself over to his bed as he started to come out of it. Julian was comforting him while he got his bearings. He was trembling and crying, hugging Julian tightly. I sat down on the bed next to him, and he began to cry harder when he looked down and realized he had lost control of his bladder.

"Matty, it's okay," Julian reassured him.

"I'm scared, I want to go home." The tears streamed down his face.

"I know. Soon, buddy," Julian said as he rested his lips on the top of his head.

My heart was breaking. I didn't know how much more I could take. I sat down on the other side of the bed. "Matty, everything is going to be okay, sweetie," I said, rubbing his back.

Julian waited until Matty had calmed down a bit before getting up. "Damn it!" he shouted, looking over Matty's chart and slamming it on the table before heading out of the room. A few seconds later, I heard Dr. Fowler being paged, clueless as to what was going on.

Matty's little body was so frail, I was afraid I would hurt him when I changed him into clean clothes. I offered him some water, and he took a small sip as tears streamed down his face. He lay back down, and I rubbed his back until he started to fall asleep as I watched him closely.

"What's the matter?" I asked when Julian returned.

"I specifically told Dr. Fowler that I wanted Matty on anti-seizure medication as a precaution. Apparently, it was never done."

I wasn't sure who he was more upset with, Dr. Fowler or himself for not double-checking his medications. Knowing Julian, it was more than likely the latter.

"Please don't blame yourself. You've been doing everything humanly possible for him," I reassured him.

"If he had been on this before, this would have never

happened."

"It's over with now, and he's okay." I tried my best to calm him down, but I could tell he wasn't going to let it go. He sat down in the chair alongside Matty, watching him sleep, carefully observing every breath he took, almost as if he was afraid he would seize again.

"When do you have to go back to Chicago?" I asked, trying to take his mind off it.

"Next week for some meetings–just for a couple of days."

A heightened sense of alarm came over me. I was so afraid of dealing with this on my own.

"Call me if you need anything," he said, apparently sensing my apprehension. "I'll have my phone on me at all times."

Dr. Fowler entered the room along with Dr. Taylor, another doctor who was assisting with Matty's treatment. Julian immediately stood up as if all the anger that had just diffused was resurfacing.

"Why was he not put on anti-seizure meds like I asked?" he demanded.

Dr. Taylor began to explain. "Dr. Kiron, being that there was such a slight chance of a seizure, I felt it would be best to not subject him to any more medications."

I could see the rage in Julian's eyes. I sat down next to Matty and prepared myself for what was to come.

"*You* felt it would be best?" His voice grew louder. "Do I have to remind you, I'm overseeing his treatment, and I said I wanted him to have it, so it doesn't matter what you felt was best!"

"He only thought that–" Dr. Fowler tried to speak in Dr. Taylor's defense, but Julian quickly stopped him.

"Well, he thought wrong! My son had a seizure because my request was not followed."

I remained quiet and cringed at the fury in his voice. This was a side of Julian I wasn't used to. He always remained so calm and cool. Even when he was angry, he hardly ever raised his voice.

"The nurse will be in shortly with the medicine," Dr. Fowler said.

He and Dr. Taylor apologized, and I gave them a nod of acceptance. Julian didn't acknowledge them at all, walking over to the window and looking outside as they exited the room.

"Why don't you go back to my house and get some rest?" I said as I went over to him. "You're beyond exhausted."

He immediately shook his head. "This has nothing to do with me being tired. One simple thing could have prevented this from happening today."

I rubbed his arm lightly as he continued to stare out the window. I could tell he was upset with himself, and I wanted to comfort him. I wrapped my arms around him to give him a hug, and he pushed me away.

"Kat, just stop!"

"I'm sorry," I responded, confused by his harsh reaction.

"You can't just think that a hug is going to make everything better."

"Julian, I only thought—"

"Matty had a seizure because I let my guard down and didn't double-check his chart."

I was afraid to respond, afraid that I would only be cut off again. "Julian, he's fine now, he's going to get the medication he needs and it won't happen again. It's not your fault."

"Yes, it is, Kat. This is why I can't stop thinking like a doctor for even one second. Because God knows you sure as hell aren't."

My eyes widened. I was both furious and hurt over his harsh words.

He ran his hand through his hair and looked away almost as if he was preparing for what he had coming to him.

"You are the most pompous, insensitive ass I have ever met!" I shouted.

"Really, Kat, he was having a seizure and you just froze up. What if I wasn't here, what would you have done, let him choke on his own vomit?" He was using the same harsh tone now with me that he had with Dr. Fowler and Dr. Taylor.

I began to cry, which was the last thing I wanted him to see. "I honestly don't know how I ever had a child with someone like you— or how I could have ever even loved someone like you." I was on emotion overload, and the words slipped out before I could stop them.

His eyes widened over that admission, and his tough demeanor softened a bit. "Kat, I'm sorry." He took my hand and I yanked it away.

"Just leave me alone because right now, I really hate you." In typical Julian fashion, he abided by my wishes and walked out the door.

I sat by Matty's bedside, trying my best to stop crying but I couldn't. *Why did I let him get me so upset?* The nurse came in with Matty's medicine, and I dabbed my eyes with a tissue, knowing it was a lost cause.

"Are you okay, Dr. Vallia?" the nurse asked.

"Yes, just an emotional day," I responded.

She looked at me sympathetically. "What's the medication that you're giving him?" I asked.

"Diazepam, five milligrams," she clarified.

"Diazepam? Why didn't he order Gabapentin instead?" Which was always my first choice in anti-seizure medication.

"I believe Dr. Fowler said that the Diazepam is what Dr. Kiron had requested," she replied.

"Oh," I said, rolling my eyes.

"I could double-check with Dr. Fowler if you'd like," she said.

"No, that's fine. I'm okay with the Diazepam." I didn't want to start a whole new argument by questioning Julian's judgment.

Julian was gone for quite some time. When he returned, I didn't acknowledge him in any way and just focused my attention on Matty, who was still sleeping.

"I'm sorry, Kat," Julian said as he sat down in the chair next to me.

I continued looking straight ahead until he took my face in his hands and turned my head forcing me to look at him. "You're a great mom and a great doctor."

"Why do you have to be so mean?" I asked. "I was only trying to make you see that it wasn't your fault that this happened. I didn't know it was going to make you so upset."

"I know and I shouldn't have blown up on you like that. I was just so angry at myself that I took it out on you." His tone was soft and gentle.

"It's okay," I said as he handed me a tissue to wipe away a stray tear that rolled down my face. "And I'm sorry for what I said to you."

"That's okay, you're not the first girl to tell me they hate me. I'm used to it," he joked. I shook my head and gave him the best smile that I could manage.

Matty finally woke up around dinnertime, not taking one bite of his food. "Matty, you have to try to eat," I pleaded as I tried giving him a spoonful of applesauce.

"How about some ice cream?" Julian asked. Matty shook his head. "That's okay, maybe tomorrow you'll feel like some," Julian said as if trying to put both Matty's and my mind at ease.

We spent the rest of the night watching movies. Matty remained quiet the entire night, falling back asleep around ten o'clock. The room he was in now was a lot larger than his other one. There was a pullout sofa so the parents could stay overnight. Julian and I had been taking turns staying with him. Tonight, Julian was adamant that he stay, and I wasn't going to put up a fight. I knew that he would be much better with handling another seizure in the middle of the night than me.

"Are you sure you don't want me to stay instead?" I asked.

"No," he responded quickly. "I want be here to make sure that he's given the proper medications."

"Do you need anything before I go?" I asked.

"No, I'm good."

He got up from the chair, looking over at Matty, making sure he was asleep. He wanted to check his voicemail and was unable to use his cell phone in the room, so he decided to walk me to my car. I immediately zipped my coat up when we stepped out into the cold January air.

"It's freezing!" I exclaimed. "You don't have to walk me all the way to my car."

"That's okay, I could use some fresh air," he said.

I felt guilty about leaving, but Julian was insistent that he stay. He assured me he would call me right away if anything were to happen in the middle of the night.

We finally reached my car, and I shivered from the cold. "Get in and get warmed up," he said.

"Okay," I said with my hand on the door handle.

I looked at him again with gratitude as he gazed back at me. For a brief second I thought he was going to kiss me, but instead he pulled me close and hugged me tightly. I quickly removed my hand from the door handle and wrapped both my arms around him as well. Closing my eyes, feeling so at peace when he kissed me on my head and rested his lips there for a few seconds. The frigid temperature outside as well as the coldness inside of Julian was suddenly replaced with warmth. He finally released me from his embrace and took my cold hands in his.

"I'll see you tomorrow," he said as he opened the car door for me.

I got in my car and started it, waiting for it to heat up, already feeling warm inside as I watched him walk away.

Chapter 34

Another week had gone by, and thankfully Matty didn't have any more seizures. Julian went back to Chicago for a few days for a series of meetings and would be returning in two days. He didn't want to leave Matty, but it was mandatory he attend the meetings. I was counting the days until he returned, beginning to feel helpless without him around.

"Good morning," Dr. Fowler greeted when he came in for Matty's morning checkup. Matty was running a fever and had been clingy with me all morning. Dr. Fowler took his temperature again, and it had gone up from earlier. Matty whimpered upon hearing he would need more blood work done.

"It will be really quick," Dr. Fowler tried to reassure him, but Matty wouldn't even look at him. His personality had changed so much since starting this harrowing treatment. I couldn't blame him, he had had more blood tests done than I could even count. My biggest fear was that he may have contracted an infection which would then require him to be put in total isolation.

I followed Dr. Fowler into the hallway at his request. "I wanted to discuss with you and Dr. Kiron about the possibility of putting Matty on a feeding tube."

"A feeding tube?" I knew Matty hadn't been eating properly, but I didn't think it had come down to this yet.

"It would only be for a few days, just so he can get some nutrients back into his body to make him a little stronger," he explained. "Let's wait and see how these tests come back before we discuss that."

Matty was sleeping when I walked back into his room. I caressed his cheek, wanting so badly to hug him, but now feared his fragile little body. Flinching only a bit when the nurse came in to take his blood work, I was relieved that he remained sleeping through it, sparing him from yet another traumatizing blood test. The walls in that hospital room were closing in on me. I had never felt so helpless in my life, wishing I could be going through this in place of him. I closed my eyes, trying to clear my head and dozed off.

"Kat." I opened my eyes and stood up immediately at the sound of Dr. Fowler's voice. "I just got the blood work, and he does have an infection," he confirmed. "I have a call in to Dr. Kiron, but I'm sure he will agree with starting him on a high dose of antibiotics."

I hadn't called Julian yet. I wanted to wait until the results had come back. I was hoping in the back of my mind that it wasn't an infection. I nodded in agreement, giving him permission to start the antibiotics.

"I'm also going to suggest that we start the feeding tube," he said.

I looked over at Matty who was still sound asleep as I battled with tears in my eyes and the lump in my throat. "Okay," I whispered.

"I'm sorry, but he's going to have to be quarantined until we get this infection under control."

I shook my head and looked over at Matty who was now awake, but still very out of it. The infection was starting to take hold. His skin was pale white and dark circles encompassed his beautiful blue eyes. It was as if I didn't even recognize the child in that hospital bed, and it scared me to death. I sat down on the bed next to him, holding back my tears.

"Matty, they're going to give you special medicine to help you get better." He stared at me blankly. "Mommy can't be in the room with you for a few days while you take this medicine. I promise I will be right outside though."

"No, Mommy, don't go," he said, his bottom lip quivering, too weak to even cry.

"This medicine is going to make you better, Matty. Don't you want to feel better so you can come home?"

He nodded.

"I need you to be brave. It's only going to be a few days." My eyes were stinging, holding back the tears. I couldn't let him see me cry. I had to be strong for him now more than ever.

I hugged him gently, feeling the heat coming off him as his body trembled.

"Hi, Matty, I'm Barbara." An older nurse who had just entered the room introduced herself. "And guess what? You're such a special guest here, that I'm going to be assigned to just you." She gave him a warm smile and gently rubbed his arm. He listened to her carefully as he clung to my arm, and I could tell that he instantly trusted her.

"Now, Matty, you're a big boy, right?" she asked.

He nodded.

"As soon as this is over, you'll feel so much better, and Mommy will be back, I promise." Her calm and caring voice even put me somewhat at ease. "The nurses will be here to take care of anything you need. Do you think you can be a big boy for a few days?"

Matty nodded once again.

She focused her attention on me. "I promise you, Mom, we'll take good care of him."

"Thanks." My voice cracked with emotion.

She flashed me a sympathetic smile, and I knew that was my signal to leave. I hugged Matty as tightly as his little body could handle and kissed him on the forehead. "I love you so much, and I promise I will see you in a couple of days." I wiped the tears off his face as I did my best to hold mine back.

"Will Daddy be here too when you come back?" Matty's normally gruff voice was barely a whisper.

"Yes, Matty, I will make sure that he is." His face forced the best smile that he could, and I felt my heart leap out of my chest as I tried not to break the dam that was holding my tears back. "I love you, sweet boy," I said as I gave him one last kiss.

I made my way through the hospital, allowing the tears to flow when I got outside. I finally had a signal on my phone, and it started beeping like crazy from inside my purse with the messages that had come through all morning. I sat in my car, trying to chase away my horrible thoughts, Matty lying in that bed–would that be the last memory I had of my son? Had he come all this way just to lose his battle now? When I was finally composed enough, I took my phone from my purse to check my messages. There were several voicemails from Claire and Tricia, but I bypassed them to get to the one from Julian:

"Kat, I just spoke with Dr. Fowler. Just sign off on everything he's recommending. It's best for Matty right now–he's going to be okay. I'm cancelling my meetings for tomorrow. I'll see you in the morning."

I played his message over and over, just hearing his voice strangely put me at ease. I didn't know what to do next, so I started my car and just began to drive, blasting the radio with the windows rolled all the way down, paying no mind to the cold winter air blowing in.

Not even remembering the drive, I found myself in front of Charles and Claire's house. I walked through the front door and found them both in the kitchen preparing dinner.

"Kat, what's the matter, honey?" Claire asked, seeing the expression on my face.

"Matty's developed an infection and they're starting him on a feeding tube as well." I managed to get the words out without breaking down.

Charles sat down next to me, placing his hand on my shoulder. "Do they have him isolated?" he asked. I nodded and began to cry. Claire handed me a tissue and rubbed my back slowly.

"It's very common—just give the antibiotics a chance to do their job," Charles said. "Is Julian in agreement with all of this?"

"Yes," I replied. "He'll be back tomorrow morning." Charles nodded, seeming relieved.

"Stay for dinner," Claire insisted.

Even though I didn't have much of an appetite, I agreed because I didn't want to be alone.

The sound of my ringing phone startled me. I didn't even want to look to see who it was, afraid it would be the hospital with more bad news. I excused myself from the kitchen upon seeing it was Julian.

"Julian," I answered, sounding relieved.

"Hey, I just talked to Dr. Fowler, they put the feeding tube in," he advised.

"I'm going back up there after..." My voice cracked, and I couldn't finish talking. All I could do was cry.

"He's going to be okay," Julian tried to reassure me.

"You didn't see him lying in that hospital bed when I left. I just can't get the image out of my mind."

"Kat, just go home and get a good night's sleep. There's nothing you can do for him tonight."

"I just want to be there with him. He looked so scared and alone."

"I know, but you just have to let him get through these next few days," he said compassionately. "He'll be well taken care of."

He was right. I wasn't allowed to see him, and if anything were to happen, Dr. Fowler would notify me immediately. I needed to get some rest to be able to deal with the days that lay ahead.

"Please just stay positive. I'll meet you at the hospital tomorrow. Promise me you'll go home and get some sleep," he coaxed.

"I will," I whispered before hanging up.

Sleep was something that wasn't coming easy to me lately, and it was beginning to show. As I looked in the mirror hanging in Charles and Claire's foyer, I realized the dark circles under my eyes were almost as big as Matty's. I hadn't had much of an appetite and was withering away to nothing as my clothes hung from me like a bag lady.

It amazed me at how much calmer I was after talking to Julian compared to just a few minutes ago. I was grateful and scared at the same time. Once Matty was better, things would be back to normal. Julian would be in Chicago, and I would be here, splitting our time with Matty over holidays and summers. I was finding myself needing Julian more each day, realizing that it wasn't all due to Matty's sickness. Each time I was around him, old feelings began to stir up inside, and the more that I tried to ignore them, the stronger they became.

***

I was up and out the door by 7 a.m. Despite my best efforts, I didn't sleep well. I took the brisk walk from my car to the hospital, burying my freezing hands deep within my coat pockets after realizing I had forgotten my gloves. When I entered the hospital, I took in the warm air for a brief second before finally moving forward.

I reached Matty's floor and checked in with one of the nurses on duty. "He had a very good night, Dr. Vallia." She smiled. "His fever has gone down as well." I smiled back, hearing the news.

I was happy to see the curtain open on the big picture window that looked into his room. I pressed my head against the cool glass, never wanting to cuddle with him more than I did at that moment.

Why did this have to happen to him? He didn't deserve to suffer like this. I had lost both my mom and dad to cancer. I couldn't lose Matty too.

"Kat."

I turned around to find Julian's beautiful eyes gazing at me.

"Julian, what are you doing here so early?"

"I caught an early flight," he said as he looked in the window at Matty.

"Thank you," I whispered, knowing he hadn't a clue as to how much his presence meant to me right now. All my emotions began to course through me at once, and it was just too much for me to take. I didn't try to hold back the tears, I let them flow.

"He's going to be okay, I promise you." Julian did his best to comfort me.

"I just hate seeing him this way." I wiped the tears from my eyes.

"I told you this wasn't going to be easy, but he will get through it."

I trusted Julian more than anyone when it came to Matty's care, and I wanted to believe more than anything that he was going to be okay, but still it was hard for me to fathom seeing him so helpless. I was taken off guard when Julian pulled me close and hugged me tightly. I rested my head on his chest, breathing in his fresh clean scent, feeling so at ease for just a brief moment.

"Excuse me, Dr. Kiron, here's a report on Matty from the last twelve hours." I pulled away from his embrace when the nurse who had given me the update on Matty earlier handed him a stack of papers. She looked at me compassionately as I tried wiping the last of the tears from my eyes.

He sat down on the large leather couch just outside Matty's room, reading his records thoroughly, reaching around in his pockets, looking for a pen. I pulled one from my purse and handed it to him, and he began to mark up some things in the report. He ran his hand through his hair, looking like he was deep in thought, and I waited until he was done before speaking.

"The nurse said his fever's gone down," I said.

"It has, but his blood count isn't going up." He finished writing up a few more things before walking over to the same nurse who had given him the report. He spoke to her briefly, and she nodded her head.

"Is everything okay?" I asked.

"Yes," he replied. "I just want Dr. Fowler to adjust his medicine.

Everything is going to be okay, Kat, this is just a setback. The survival rate in a child Matty's age is more than ninety percent."

My stomach was in knots, and I was amazed by Julian's ability to remain so calm and focused, hardly showing any emotion at all. I wasn't sure if he was trying to remain strong for my benefit or if that's just how he viewed the whole situation—the same way he would with any of his other patients.

"I realize that you can't get attached to your patients and need to keep it all clinical, but it's okay to break down that wall and show emotion where Matty's concerned. He's just as much your child as he is mine. He's not just a cancer case, he's a little boy who happens to love you very much. Stop giving me statistics and lecturing me, and let's just focus on *our* child and his survival," I said gently.

"This is all so new to me, Kat."

"I know, and I realize that you want to be perfect at everything you do—and you are. You're a great doctor and Matty's father—you can be two things at once, it's okay."

"I'm just so afraid I'm going to screw up with him."

"The wonderful thing about being a parent is you *can* screw up and your child will still love you unconditionally—and Matty does love you very much, Julian." His eyes glassed over, and I could tell that I was finally breaking through to him. I was becoming more emotional as well, feeling the overwhelming need to convey my feelings to him. "Thank you so much for everything. I know we've had our difference of opinions, but I truly don't know what I would do if you weren't here." He gazed at me intently as I continued. "I need you to know, I am so sorry for doing what I did to you."

"Kat, please just—" He held up his hand and tried stopping me.

I completely ignored him. "I never wanted to hurt you. I just wanted you to be happy, and I thought that's what I was doing. It killed me inside not seeing you and not talking to you. There was no one in the world that I wanted by my side when Matty was born more than you." I swallowed hard, fighting back the tears. "What if he doesn't make it, Julian? All that time I took from you and now—" I couldn't finish.

"Kat, stop thinking like that. He's going to get through this."

"I need to know that you forgive me, Julian. Please forgive me," I cried.

His eyes softened as he moved closer. "I do," he whispered.

Thank you. I mouthed the words to him as he took my face in his hands, wiping away a tear.

"We'll get through this together—I promise."

I rested my head on his shoulder and intertwined my hand with his. Closing my eyes, I was suddenly filled with an inner peace, allowing me to put my fears aside. Something deep inside of me was telling me Matty was going to be okay. I didn't know if it was Julian's words or maybe a sign from my dad, but from that moment on I knew Matty would pull through this.

Chapter 35

After three long, harrowing months, Matty was finally being released from the hospital in the morning. I was planning on spending the night, prepping his room for his return home. I had just finished changing his linens when I heard my phone beeping with a message, I picked it up from Matty's dresser to see who it was from:

Tricia: There's a ticket for you at the door if you change your mind.

James had coordinated a big fundraising dinner for the hospital and had roped Julian into being the guest speaker, and Tricia had been preparing excitedly for it for weeks. I had no interest in attending, given the circumstances with Matty, and the fact that I didn't feel comfortable hobnobbing with the higher-ups. But I had to admit, the thought of seeing Julian did excite me a little. I hadn't been seeing very much of him now that Matty was recovering. He basically only flew in on the weekends to spend time with Matty. I knew we had to sit down and work out a schedule for Matty soon, but I didn't want to think about that now, I was much too happy about Matty coming home tomorrow. I didn't want to spoil my bliss by thinking about Julian being back in Chicago and me being here. As much as I was going to hate sharing holidays and juggling Matty back and forth, I hated the fact that Julian would be gone from my life again even more. Sure, he would always be Matty's father, but in the back of my mind, I wanted it to be more. We had gotten even closer over the past few months, getting through Matty's sickness together. There was no doubt in my mind how I felt about him. He had warmed up to me so much, and now he was back to being distant. It was almost as if he were reminding me again that he was here for Matty's sake only and didn't have any intention of rekindling what we once had together. I was angry at myself for falling for him all over again, and deep down I wondered if I ever really did get over him the first time.

I looked around Matty's room when I realized there really was nothing left to do. I had just changed his sheets, vacuumed, and dusted just two nights ago, so I decided to jump in the shower, order takeout and relax for the rest of the night. After getting out of the shower, I threw on my sweats and pondered over the takeout menus. Still undecided on pizza or Chinese, I decide to take a few minutes to decide. I was feeling so anxious as I flicked on the TV and channel surfed endlessly, having as much luck finding something to watch as I was deciding on dinner. I glanced at the clock to find it was 6:15 p.m., the dinner started at 7:30 p.m.

If you really want to go, you still have enough time to get yourself together and make it.

I erased that ridiculous thought from my mind, flicking through the channels once again before turning off the TV and tossing the remote control on the couch.

Wandering into the bathroom, I plugged in my flat iron and applied my makeup while I waited for it to warm up. When I was all done, I looked in the mirror at the girl staring back at me, not even recognizing her. My wavy hair was poker straight, and I was wearing more makeup than usual. "Not bad," I said to myself as I smiled at my reflection.

I went into the back of my closet and grabbed the long champagne-colored halter dress that I had fallen in love with some time ago. It had been sitting in the back of my closet with the tags still on it, just waiting for an occasion like this. I stood in front of the floor-length mirror as I slipped it on—it was a perfect fit. The sequins on my strappy sandals were the perfect match to the sequins on the neckline of my dress. I threw on some earrings and gave myself one last look in the mirror. "Here goes nothing," I whispered before heading out the door.

I arrived at the upscale banquet facility, watching everyone shuffling in. The men all dressed in top of the line suits—some even in tuxedos. The women dressed in an array of different ensembles. Some with just little black dresses—others with all-out ball gowns.

I quickly sent Tricia a text, letting her know I had change my mind and was coming, so she would be on the lookout for me.

"Hi, I believe a ticket was left here for me, Dr. Vallia," I said to one of the two older women, collecting tickets at the door.

One of the women fumbled through the pile, looking for my

name while the other woman looked me over. "You look absolutely stunning, dear."

"Thank you." I smiled as the other woman handed me my ticket. I prepared myself to enter the huge ballroom already filled with people, hoping that Tricia got my text and was looking for me. I took a deep breath and walked in, making my way through the crowd, trying to find a familiar face.

"Kat, wow, you look amazing!" I turned around happy to see Patrick—my so supposed boyfriend.

"Thanks, Patrick, you don't look so bad yourself," I replied as I looked him over. Yes, he was quite handsome. Not quite as tall as Julian and his eyes weren't as blue, but nonetheless he was very good-looking.

"How's Matty doing?" he asked.

"Very well, thank you. He's coming home tomorrow."

I couldn't contain my smile at the thought of Matty coming home or the glimpse of Julian I had just caught out of the corner of my eye. He looked to be deep into conversation with the chief of staff and another bigwig from the hospital. Patrick continued talking, but I was no longer paying attention. Julian finally met my gaze, doing a double take to make sure it was me. I watched as he excused himself from the conversation and made his way over to me. *Could he get any more handsome?* He was dressed in a perfectly tailored suit with a crisp white button-up shirt underneath, looking as if he had just stepped off of a *GQ* magazine cover.

"Hey!" I said, trying to contain my excitement and failing miserably.

"I thought you weren't coming."

"Changed my mind, besides, I heard the guest speaker is phenomenal," I joked.

He smiled as he assessed me up and down. "You look beautiful," he said as the butterflies began to flutter hard in my stomach.

"Thanks. Oh, Julian, this is Dr. Patrick McGinn," I said, almost forgetting that Patrick was standing there.

Julian extended his hand to Patrick who seemed enthralled at meeting him. "Dr. Kiron, it's really a pleasure to meet you."

Julian nodded, seeming a little cold toward Patrick.

"Well, Kat, I have to go find my seat. Please tell Matty hello and remember, anytime you're ready for that drink…" Patrick flashed me a smile and walked away.

"So, I finally get to meet your boyfriend," Julian joked.

"Haha, very funny." I smiled.

"Anytime you're ready for that drink," Julian mocked Patrick in his best Irish accent. I was a little surprised by his childish behavior but couldn't help but laugh, and then it dawned on me– he was jealous. "Tell Matty he says hello," he carried on. "You know, Kat, he's the type of guy who tries to win over a girl's affection through her kid."

"Really?" I raised my eyebrow and grinned. "Is that what you do too?"

"What?" He looked confused.

"Try and pick up women by winning over the affection of their kids?" I clarified.

"No, I don't date women with kids. But, there is this one girl who I would be willing to bend the rules for." He smirked.

"Really, and who's that lucky girl?" I asked.

"You." He had a much more serious look about him now.

"Me? Oh, I'm sorry, but I don't date guys with kids." I tried my best not to laugh.

He smiled and shook his head. "Yeah, but my kid is really cool," he countered.

"So is mine. Plus, he's super adorable–looks just like his dad."

"Well, I'm not going to argue with you there." He chuckled.

I was so happy to see this side of him. For the past few weeks he had been so distant and now here he was joking around. So much like the man I fell in love with years ago.

"Excuse me, Dr. Kiron, but they're ready for you," Dr. Martin, the chief of staff said.

"Alright, I'll be right there." Julian sounded annoyed by the interruption.

"You better go. Your fans are awaiting for you." I moved closer and straightened his tie. "There, that's better," I said as I headed off to find my table.

Relief washed over me when I finally found table number fourteen.

"Kat! There you are," Tricia greeted, looking absolutely beautiful in a long, yellow taffeta gown. "Look at you! You look gorgeous," she said running her fingers through my silky straight hair.

"So do you."

"Kat, you look hot!" James said as he took his seat.

"Oh, gee thanks." I wasn't really sure if I should take that as a compliment or not.

Tricia and I sat down as the room became quiet. Dr. Martin, the chief of staff, stepped to the podium and gave his spiel about how much money the hospital had made this year, along with all the changes that had been implemented. He lost me about three minutes into it, painfully reminding me why I hated coming to these types of things. He was finally finishing his very long-winded speech when my ears perked up at the sound of Julian's name. Dr. Martin read Julian's credentials and announced him as if he were a major celebrity.

Julian approached the podium cool, calm, and collected, which was so like him. I admired his courage to speak so eloquently in front of all these people–this was something I knew I would never be able to do. After the applause finally died down, he began to speak. Unlike last time, I was totally engrossed in what he had to say.

"I was once told to not go on and on and brag about my accomplishments in my speech, and I've tried to use that advice wisely over the years. So, if I'm putting any of you to sleep or talking too much about myself, please feel free to stop me and let me know."

The room filled with laughter as Julian looked over at me and smiled. I shook my head and smiled back.

"I was asked to come here and speak tonight about closing the gap on childhood cancer and being a hero in a child's life. I had a speech all prepared for that, but, I've decided to go a little off topic, because the true heroes are the children I encounter every day who are living through cancer. The ones who are enduring the rigorous treatments each and every day and never giving up. We can only give them the medicine to make them better, but they have to have the will and the spirit to keep going. I guess I never realized this. I was always like a robot programmed to give the right doses of chemo and radiation and move on to the next patient. I never looked at the big picture of it all until I was able to see it from the other side, when my son was diagnosed with leukemia."

There were some gasps from the room, and a few people who knew about Matty's situation looked over at me, finally putting the pieces together. Tricia took my hand, and I could see she was starting to get as choked up as me. I did my best to pull it together as Julian continued.

"Nothing in medical school, and no amount of training, prepares you for the true pain that it puts on the child, the parents, and everyone who loves them by watching him suffer and knowing there was nothing else in the world you could do for him—he had to have the will to fight it, and he did. So, I want to say thank you to Matty for making me realize this. He's one of the bravest kids I know. I also want to say thank you to his mom, who opened up my eyes in so many ways and made me see what really matters most in this world."

There was a loud round of applause. I wiped a tear from my eye and looked at Julian, who was staring at me.

"Oh my goodness, Kat, I can't believe he did that. That was so sweet," Tricia said, wiping the tears from her eyes as well. I shook my head, unable to speak. I had never expected Julian to express himself in such a way, and it really meant a lot to me. James and Tricia headed off to the dance floor while I remained at the table, deep in thought over Julian's speech.

"Did you pay attention this time?" Julian came up behind me, making me jump.

"That was a great speech," I said.

"Do you want to dance?" he asked.

"But I thought you didn't dance," I teased.

"I've been known to make exceptions." I stood up as he took my hand and led me to the dance floor. Pulling me closer, we began to move.

"Well I'm happy to see that your dancing has improved over the years," I mocked. He just smiled and shook his head. "I can't believe Matty's coming home tomorrow." I was beaming with happiness just thinking about it while Julian remained silent. I looked up to meet his gaze, making me feel as if it was just me and him on the dance floor.

"What's the matter?" I asked. He shook his head, but I could tell that he had something on his mind. "I guess we need to sit down soon and figure out a schedule for Matty." I tried to break the silence to no avail. He sighed deeply and pulled me closer, so close that I could feel his heart beating. I was in a trance, being in his arms, inhaling his delicious cologne, feeling his body touching mine. If there was any doubt in my mind before, it was now gone—I was still so very much in love with him.

His warm soft hands moved up my bare back as my stomach fluttered and my knees weakened. He lowered his head until our lips were just inches apart. I wanted to feel them pressed against mine so badly, but I didn't think it'd be appropriate to kiss him in the middle of the dance floor in front of all our colleagues. Besides, I wanted more than just a kiss—I wanted all of him.

"Can you leave?" I whispered in his ear, wondering if he was done with his part of this dinner.

"I really don't care if I can't," he replied as he pressed his forehead against mine.

I took his hand and led him off the dance floor, grabbing my purse from the table as we maneuvered our way through the crowd of people standing around talking. In the back of my mind, I was beginning to think of the emotional impact this may have afterwards, but I didn't care—I would deal with that after. For right now, I just knew that I wanted him more than anything.

Chapter 36

"Julian Kiron," a woman's voice shouted as we were almost out the door. I turned around to find a tall, very well-endowed blonde, wearing a short black dress that left nothing to the imagination. I was quite certain that both her hair color and breasts were fake. Still, I couldn't help but feel a little inadequate in her presence. She was assessing Julian up and down while Julian stared at her blankly, clueless to who she was.

"Don't you remember me?" she asked with an over confident smile.

"I'm sorry, but I don't," Julian answered.

"Remember, we met at a benefit dinner back in Chicago a few years ago–Stacia Doberman," she said raising her eyebrows.

"Oh–" he said with a nervous look on his face as if the light bulb in his head finally turned on.

"That was a great speech you gave, but I didn't realize you had a son," she said, glancing my way with a phony smile.

Julian nodded as he nervously raked his hand through his hair. "Well, it was nice seeing you again. Come on, Kat, let's go."

"Oh wait, I'm sorry, are you his wife?" She was smug with her inquiry. I was just about to answer, but stopped myself as she continued.

"Dr. Martin just told me your little boy is five years old and that she's the mother of your child," she said as she pointed at me.

"And?" Julian snapped. I could see that his patience was running thin.

"Well, when we had our little one-night thing, two years ago– you failed to mention that you had a wife and a son–but then again there wasn't much talking going on that night, was there?" A sly satisfying grin stretched across her face.

I took a deep breath and looked at Julian who seemed

flustered–which was so out of character for him. I wasn't quite sure if it was from running into this woman or because he was afraid of what my reaction would be to her. I knew I couldn't really tell her what I thought of her in front of all of these people without making a scene, even though I wanted to. I took the high road instead, deciding to kill her with kindness and ignoring the little voice that was telling me otherwise.

"Oh no, I'm not his wife," I clarified. "My name is Kat, very nice to meet you…Stacia, is that your name?" I asked in an overly sweet voice. She nodded with a perplexed look on her face. "Now if you'll please excuse us."

"Well, don't be expecting anything from him after tonight, he'll be done with you and move on to the next. But then again, you should know all about that, he knocked you up and still couldn't stay committed," she shouted loud enough so the people standing close by could hear.

"What?" I turned around, feeling my anger building up inside me.

"Kat, just come on," Julian coaxed. He grabbed my arm and tried to pull me away, but I broke free.

My sickening sweet persona was completely gone. "You have no clue what my relationship is with Julian!" I snapped, getting right in her face. Truth be told, I wasn't even sure of what our relationship was.

"Oh, honey, surely you're not that naïve to think you're special just because you're the mother of his child," she rebutted.

"You know what, that's enough," Julian snapped "Just because you're–"

"Because I'm what? Some woman you had a one-night fling with and then never called again," she said, cutting him off.

I could see the hurt in her eyes, and I almost felt sorry for her. I wondered how many other women out there were taken by Julian's good looks and charm. If we didn't have Matty together, would I have been one of those women who he had just checked off a list? I immediately began to think of the repercussions if I were to sleep with him tonight. I was in love with him, and I knew I wouldn't be able to handle the aftermath if he didn't feel the same. I wanted something beyond physical with him, and my heart couldn't handle taking that risk tonight.

"You know what–I'm gonna to go. I'll meet you at the hospital in the morning," I said to Julian.

I glanced over at the woman. "Sorry." She shrugged with a triumphant grin plastered on her face.

"Kat!" Julian shouted as he came chasing after me, finally catching up to me in the parking lot. I turned around finally ready to face him. "That woman meant nothing, you have to believe me," he said.

"Well, I could certainly see that, considering you didn't even remember her. But did it ever occur to you that maybe it meant something to her?" I asked.

"I told you, I don't make promises to anyone I can't keep."

I nodded. "Yes, I know, I was the perfect example of that."

He shook his head. "No, Kat, you were so different."

"How was I different, just because we have a child together? I guess I was lucky that day I tracked you down at the hospital that you at least remembered my name." My voice cracked with emotion.

"Kat, I cared about you. I wanted to be with you. You were so different from any girl I had ever met. I thought about you all the time. I would always ask James how you were when I would talk to him. He was always so vague with his answers. I just assumed you were living happily with some other guy–never in a million years, did I imagine that *other guy* was my son." He moved closer to me and grabbed my arm. "How could you even compare what we had to her? It was so much more."

I tried to release my arm from his grip, but he held it tighter, taken totally off guard when he pulled me closer and his lips came crashing down on mine. I briefly tried to put up a fight as his tongue invaded my mouth, but he wasn't surrendering. I found myself kissing him back with the same intensity until I was finally able to gain the strength to stop and push him away. His beautiful eyes gazing at me through his dark lashes made me melt, but I stayed strong.

"No, Julian, I can't do this with you again. I know I told you I wouldn't expect any promises, but I do–promises I know you can't keep, and my heart just can't handle getting over you again."

"Kat, please just listen–"

"Hey, Julian, I've been looking all over for you," James interrupted. "Dr. Martin wants to introduce you to one of the members of the board of trustees." Julian was totally ignoring James, never taking his eyes from me the whole time.

"Is everything okay?" James asked as he looked at both of us. "Matty's okay, right?

"Yes, Matty's fine," I finally answered.

"I'll see you tomorrow morning, Julian." I tried to sound as if everything were as normal as possible. He was silent, still staring at me as I turned around and made my way to my car.

I sat in my car for a few minutes, trying to pull it together. I was so angry at myself for getting in the same position I had been with him years ago. I wanted to be with him more than anything, but I wasn't willing to risk another heartache. The tears I had been holding in began to stream down my face simultaneously with the raindrops pelting my windshield.

The rain was beginning to fall harder as I drove out of the parking lot, and by the time I pulled out onto the main road it was pouring. The teeming rain and dark rural roads made driving next to impossible. I tried my best to concentrate when my phone began ringing from my purse. I fumbled around and looked down quickly to see it was Julian. I had half a mind to let it go to voicemail, but instead I quickly switched it to speaker and answered.

"I know you're upset, and you can hang up on me, tell me to go to hell or do whatever you want. But first, will you please just listen to what I have to tell you?" Julian pleaded. I could hardly hear him over the swishing of my windshield wipers and the pelting rain.

"Julian, please just stop," I was getting emotional once again at the sound of his voice.

"No, I'm not going to stop until you know exactly how I feel about you."

I slammed on my brakes—and then there was total darkness.

Chapter 37

I wasn't sure what was more intense, the endless beeping in my ears or the pounding ache inside my head. I wanted to open my eyes so badly but I couldn't.

Where was I? Was I dreaming?

I faintly heard a familiar voice–it was Charles. I tried calling to him, but nothing came out. My whole body ached, and it hurt to breathe.

Why couldn't I open my eyes? Why was I so tired?

"Kat, please wake up." It was Julian.

I'm here, Julian. I can hear you. Why can't you hear me?

The warmth of his hand enveloped mine as his lips gently skimmed my forehead.

I need to open my eyes. I need to see him.

I tried my hardest to wake up, but my eyelids were anchored down with weights.

Where was I?

The smell of this place was so familiar, but I couldn't figure out where the heck I was.

"It's been forty-eight hours. I'm going to be honest with you, Dr. Kiron, we were hoping she would have come out of it by now," an unfamiliar voice spoke.

I'm up. Why can't anyone hear me? Why was I so tired? All I wanted to do was sleep.

"Julian, you should really go back to Kat's and get some rest, you look exhausted. Matty's been asking about you, he needs you. I'll be here, and I promise I'll call if anything happens." Tricia's voice was so monotone and sad, so unlike her normal happy self.

"I can't leave her, this is all my fault." Julian sounded shaken.

"Julian, this is not your fault in any way," Tricia said compassionately.

"If she didn't get upset with me, then she would have been with me, she wouldn't have been alone," Julian said.

"And then you would have both been lying in a hospital bed. Then where would Matty be? Stop blaming yourself for this. Look, Kat is my very best friend, and if there is one thing this girl is besides stubborn, it's strong. She's going to wake up Julian–I know it. She would never give up and leave Matty." She paused briefly. "Or you."

"What?" Julian whispered.

"Really, Julian, why is it so clear to everyone else but the two of you? She's still in love with you, she never stopped loving you. She could deny it all she wants, but I know differently. She never got over you and clearly, you've never gotten over her."

Tricia, be quiet! He doesn't feel the same for me. I wanted so badly for her to hear me but it was to no avail, the words just couldn't make it out of my mouth.

I waited in angst for Julian's reply, but I was just too tired, I couldn't fight it anymore. I drifted off into a deep sleep.

***

"Kat, please wake up. I can't do this without you. Matty needs you," Julian pleaded.

Matty–where was Matty? I had to let him know that his mommy was here. I didn't leave him.

"Please, Kat, I need you. You've opened my eyes so much and helped me see the world so differently. You've given me the greatest gift in the world, the one thing in life I never thought I wanted–a child." His hand gently caressed my cheek. "I was so stupid for letting you go so easily all those years ago. I want to be with you forever. Please, Kat, wake up. I love you." There was a sound of desperation in Julian's voice as he took my hand and kissed it.

I was slipping in and out of consciousness. I was watching Julian walk out the door. I wanted to tell him so badly that day that I loved him back, but I couldn't get the words out until he was gone. Why didn't I tell him? Maybe he would have stayed. Maybe we would have been here with Matty from the time he was born. I was so stupid.

Say the words, Kat.

I willed myself to get it out, needing him to hear me this time.

"I love you too." This time I could hear my words as I fought with everything I had to open my eyes. Everything was blurred. I finally focused on Julian's beautiful tear-filled eyes.

"Where am I?" I managed to get out.

"Kat, thank God," Julian said as he bent down and rested his lips on my head. "You're in the hospital. You were in an accident."

"Where's Matty?" I asked.

"He's fine, he's home, Charles and Claire are with him." I went to move and flinched in extreme pain. "Easy, you broke two ribs," Julian advised.

"Dr. Kiron, you hit the call button, is everything..." the nurse said as she walked in, surprised to find me awake. "I'm going to page her doctor, and then I'll be right back in."

As my eyes finally came into focus, I noticed Julian didn't look like his clean-cut self. He had stubble on his face, looking like he hadn't shaved in a few days.

"How long have I been here?" I asked.

"Three days."

A tall, African American doctor whom I had never seen before came into the room. "Dr. Vallia, it's so nice to see you up." As soon as he spoke, I recognized the voice as the one that had been talking to Julian. "You're pretty banged up," he said as he shined a bright flashlight into my eyes.

"My head is pounding," I said.

"Okay, we'll give you something for that in your IV," he said gently. "I just want to order another CAT scan as a precaution," he said to Julian.

"You're a very lucky girl." He turned his attention back to me, giving Julian a reassuring pat on the shoulder before walking out of the room.

I tried moving again slightly, but the pain stopped me. Julian rushed over to try to help me. "If you weren't here with me right now, I would be quite certain that I had died and gone to hell. I have never been in so much pain," I said.

"It's going to take a while to heal," Julian said gently.

"Am I going to have to check into a rehab when this is all over?" I joked as I looked up at my IV pole, trying to make out what kind of medications they had me on.

Julian smiled and shook his head. "Does Matty know anything?" I asked.

Julian's smile faded. "Yes, he was pretty upset, but he's okay now. I did it Kat, I was able to talk to him like a dad and calmed him down," he said proudly.

I could feel an enormous smile stretch across my face. "I knew you could," I said as I took his hand in mine.

It was all starting to come back to me now. With the rain pelting down, I didn't see the deer until the last minute. My first instinct was to just slam on my brakes and swerve to avoid it, and instead I hit a tree.

Julian pushed my hair out of my face and tenderly kissed me on my lips.

"I'm sorry for getting so angry with you the other night, Julian. I was just afraid of putting my heart out there again. I didn't want to be *that* girl who meant nothing to you."

"Never. You *are* so much more, it scares me." I smiled at him with tears in my eyes. "I'm in love with you, Kat. I've been trying to fight it as hard as I could, but I can't anymore."

"Are you in love with me because of Matty? Because you feel like that's the right thing to do because I'm the mother of your child?"

"Absolutely not. I'll always be Matty's dad, and I'm going to be in his life and there to support him with whatever he needs, regardless if we're together or not. I've wanted you from the day that you showed up at the hospital. It was as if all of those old feelings came rushing back." I swallowed hard and listened intently. "Then this happened, I thought I was going to lose you again forever. I don't know what I would have done if—" His voice wavered and eyes glassed over. I put my finger over his lips to stop him from talking.

"It's okay, I'm fine." I caressed the stubble on his face. "I like this look," I said, trying to lighten the mood.

"I don't want to waste any more time. I want you and Matty to come to Chicago with me to live."

"Chicago? Wow!" I was in shock, this was what I had wanted from the day I found out I was pregnant—for Julian to want to be with Matty and me. Still, I couldn't help but feel a little hesitation at the prospect of moving halfway across the country, away from everything and everyone I loved so much. Then it dawned on me—I would be with the two most important people in my life.

"I know it's a big decision, and I want you to take your time to think about it," he said.

I thought about how much I wanted to be with him. It didn't matter where we were, I just wanted the three of us to be a family. "I don't need to think about it–I'll go," I answered without hesitation.

His blue eyes widened. "I don't want to push you into anything."

"You're not pushing me into anything. I want to be with you. It doesn't matter where, as long as it's with you." I wanted to hug him so badly, but I couldn't, I was in too much physical pain. Emotionally it was a different story–I had never been happier.

He looked up at my IV and chuckled. "Do you want me to ask you again when you don't have all those drugs pumping into you?" He laughed.

I managed my best smile, and shook my head.

"I love you, Kat." He bent down and kissed me on the forehead.

"I love you too," I answered, making sure he heard me loud and clear.

Chapter 38

It had been three weeks since my accident, and Julian hadn't left my side. I was feeling much better, still a little sore and bruised, but nothing compared to the pain I had been in when I first came home. Matty was out of the hospital and doing well. He and Julian had been taking such good care of me in the past few weeks.

My car had been totaled in the accident, so Julian and I were spending the entire morning car shopping. Usually, I'd give in and take the first price they threw at me just to avoid playing their stupid game, but Julian was the opposite, he loved playing this game–and he played it well.

"You know, we could have been out of here hours ago," I said as the salesman got up to talk to the manger.

"No way, Kat. You never take the first price they give you."

"Well, that was just a ridiculous figure you threw at him, they're never going to accept it." I was getting anxious over the thought of wasting the rest of the beautiful day in this place. I wanted to be over at Tricia's, spending time with everyone at her barbeque.

I watched as the manager got up from his desk with the salesman. "Here we go," I whispered to Julian.

"Congratulations, Dr. Vallia," the manager said with a Cheshire cat grin.

Julian smirked, and whispered, "You see, that's how it's done."

After signing all the papers, I was finally free to enjoy the rest of the afternoon, not even caring that I had to wait two days for the color car I wanted. I jumped into Julian's rental car and sighed with relief. Pulling my phone from my purse to find a text from Tricia:

Please bring Matty a change of clothes, he and James had a little mishap.

I shook my head, wondering what kind of mischief he and James had been up to now. I showed Julian the text as we made our way back to my house to get Matty's clothes.

Julian's phone rang as we were just about to enter the house. I could tell it was a work call and went in ahead of him to gather Matty's clothes. After grabbing Matty a pair of shorts and a T-shirt, I went into my bedroom and sat down on the bed for a moment. I had so much to do to prepare for this big move to Chicago. I was hoping to have my house on the market within the next week, which made me sad. This had been my home my whole life. I had so many happy memories here, and it was hard for me to fathom living anywhere else. When those thoughts crept in, I reminded myself that I would be with the two most important people in my life and would be making new memories.

I still had to give my notice to work and then work on finding a job in Chicago. Julian kept telling me to take my time with it, and that I didn't even have to work if I didn't want, but that wasn't an option for me, being a doctor was part of who I was. I would never be happy just sitting at home all day. I let him know I had every intention of working and would find a job all by myself, without any outside influence from him.

We still hadn't made love, and I wanted him more with each day that passed. He was so afraid that I was still in pain and didn't want to hurt me. What he didn't realize was that it was hurting me more by not being with him. It had been six long years since I felt his touch, and I yearned for it more than anything.

"Are you ready to go?" Julian asked as he stood in my bedroom doorway.

I tapped lightly on the bed, signaling for him to sit down next to me. "I want you to make love to me, Julian," I requested as he took a seat next to me.

"Kat, you're still healing. Believe me, there's nothing I want more, but I don't want to hurt you."

"Please, Julian, you're not going to hurt me, I promise."

Doubt clouded his eyes, so I decided to be bold and make the first move, stretching my neck and meeting his lips. It didn't take him long to respond back just as eagerly. When our lips finally parted, he pressed his forehead up to mine. "Are you sure you're okay, Kat?" There was still a little uncertainty in his voice. I didn't reply with words, instead I stood up, lifting my sundress over my head and removing my bra and panties. He stared up at me, standing before him naked. Wrapping his arms around my waste, he pulled me closer, trailing his lips up my stomach before standing up and kissing me. I removed his shirt and pressed my lips against his bare chest. His breathing became heavier as I unzipped his shorts, wasting no time in helping him remove them. Our tongues collided while our hands became reacquainted with each other's body. As we lay down on the bed, I sensed him taking extra care in making sure he didn't press his weight up against my ribs. Every touch, every kiss, and every move he made was so familiar, yet so new. He rolled over, pulling me on top of him, gazing at my naked body closely while he softly caressed my breasts.

"You're so beautiful," he whispered. My stomach did a somersault at the sound of his voice.

I let out a pleasurable gasp when he entered me, never breaking eye contact as he looked up. I moved about slowly, watching the pleasure on his face as he placed his hands on my hips. Everything in that moment was so perfect—so right.

I bent down to kiss him and was filled with a rush of excitement when he whispered, "I love you." I was enjoying every single second of being with him in this way once again. I had longed for this forever.

He was breathless, sitting up and switching positions. He hovered over me, and we connected once again. I didn't want to close my eyes because I was afraid that if I opened them, it would only be a dream. All those years apart, comparing every guy I met to him, dreaming of being in his arms—and here we were together again as if there was never any time lost between us. I couldn't hold out any longer, gently digging my fingers into his back, my hips rose one last time to meet him before letting out a gentle cry of sheer pleasure. He began to move quicker and harder now before expressing his own pleasure and losing himself inside of me.

I was on emotional overload. My body began to quiver, never feeling so fulfilled in my whole life just by being with him again in this way. I was overjoyed and at the same time inexplicably crying as all of the emotions I had bottled up for the past six years finally surfaced.

"Are you okay? Did I hurt you?" Julian looked at me alarmed, when he saw the tears coming down my face.

I pulled him closer, hugging him as tightly as I could. "No,

Julian, that was absolutely perfect."

I nuzzled up into his chest and we rested quietly in each other's arms. "I missed you," I whispered.

"I missed you too," he responded.

"I never thought I'd be here with you again in this way." I gazed up at him, stretching my neck and planting a gentle kiss on his cheek. "I love you."

A beautiful smile stretched across his face. Pushing my hair behind my ear, he lifted his head to meet my lips before rolling me over and working his way down my neck.

My body was still overly sensitive and the touch of his lips on my neck tickled me, I began to giggle. "Julian, we have to get going–" He pressed his lips against mine. I didn't put up much of a fight and we ended up being just a little late to Tricia's barbeque.

Chapter 39

Summer

Matty was back to looking and acting like the child I knew before he had gotten sick. He was still being monitored very closely and getting stronger each day. His thick dark hair was starting to grow back in and he would be starting kindergarten in the fall.

I was finally feeling one hundred percent myself as well. So much had happened in just a few short months. I had met Julian's family and felt immediately comfortable around all of them. His mother and father were so warm and accepting, instantly falling in love with Matty, and vice versa. His mother was amazed over the resemblance between Julian and Matty, expressing her gratitude to me for helping her son realize that there was more to life than just work. His sister and I became fast friends. I felt like I could talk to her about anything from the moment I met her. The same way I had felt when I had first met Julian.

We had just returned from visiting Julian in Chicago for a few days. It was Matty's first time there and he loved it. I actually enjoyed myself as well. The circumstances were a lot happier compared to the last time I had been there. Julian's home was breathtaking. It was a magnificent four-bedroom townhome, about four times the size of my home. Matty was mesmerized by the fact that it had three floors after living in a one-story home his whole life. My favorite part was the beautiful patio area off the dining area. It overlooked the perfectly landscaped courtyard giving it a very Parisian feel—I could definitely get used to living there. I closed my eyes thinking back to our visit:

We were winding down from a very busy day of sightseeing around the city. We finished the day with dinner and then returned to Julian's. We were enjoying a glass of wine on the patio while Matty was absorbed in a chocolate milkshake.

"So, do you like it here?" Julian asked Matty.

Matty nodded. His eyes crossed as he tried sucking the thick milkshake he was drinking through the straw. Julian laughed at his persistence.

"Do you like it here?" he asked with a cute boyish smile.

"Of course, I do—because you're here." I took his hand in mine and kissed it.

It was a perfect early summer evening. Even though I knew I could get very used to living here, it was still going to be a big adjustment for me, but I was looking at it positively. I didn't care where I was, as long as it was with Julian and Matty. I smiled thinking about being able to wake up with Julian every morning.

"What are you smiling about?" he asked.

"You," I said, kissing him softly on the lips.

I closed my eyes and smiled as I reminisced back to that night and what followed after Matty was fast asleep. My stomach fluttered just imagining how many more nights like that I had to look forward to once we were finally together.

Surprisingly, my house sold quickly, and we would be moving in a month. It worked out perfectly—Matty would be in Chicago by the time school started. It was bittersweet for me to be leaving the place I had lived my whole life. But I knew my home would now be wherever Matty and Julian were.

Tricia was trying her best to help me pack while James and Matty had gone to pick Julian up from the airport. "I can't believe you're leaving me." Tricia sighed.

"Tricia, I'm not leaving you. I'll be a two-hour plane ride and a phone call away."

"It's just not going to be the same."

"Come on. I'll be coming back a lot to visit. You know I can't be away from the ocean for too long."

She still wasn't smiling. She seemed to be taking this harder than anyone. Even Claire and Charles were handling it better. They were upset, but they knew how much I loved Julian and this was the only way for Julian and me to be together.

"Well, I still say you shouldn't be going anywhere without a ring on your finger," Tricia lectured as she taped up one of the boxes.

She had been on my case about making such a big commitment without being engaged since the day I told her I was moving. I reminded her that she had been engaged for almost two years and still had not acted on it.

"I pushed him full force into being a dad, I'm not going to push him into being a husband too," I said. "I know he loves me. I don't need a ring to tell me that."

She rolled her eyes. "Yeah, but he's like your knight in shining armor. I'm just shocked that he didn't get down on one knee with a beautiful diamond, but instead just asked you to shack up with him."

I shook my head at her fairy-tale way of thinking. "Tricia, I'm not shacking up with him, we love each other.

"While we're on the subject of marriage..." I started.

She put her hand up to stop my lecture about setting a wedding date. I laughed it off, making my way into Matty's room to pack up his closet. After pulling everything out, I finally reached the back when a stack of boxes caught my eye, and I instantly recognized them as the presents I had bought for my dad on his last Christmas. I didn't have the heart to donate them back then, so I shoved them in the back of the closet and forgot all about them. I smiled through the tears that were forming in my eyes. I could almost feel his presence in the room.

"Thank you, Dad, for watching over Matty, and bringing Julian back to me," I whispered. "Are you okay?" Julian asked, leaning down and kissing me on the cheek.

"Yeah, I'm fine. I didn't even hear you guys come in." I stood up, rubbing my eyes and giving him a hug.

"That's because nobody else came in. Matty talked James and Tricia into taking him for ice cream."

"So, I guess Tricia is officially off duty." I sighed, looking around at the mess.

"I'll help you," he said, pulling me closer and kissing me on the lips. "But first, I want you to come with me."

"What? Where? Julian, I have to..."

He wasn't hearing any of it. Instead he took my hand and led me to the front door, grabbing my car keys that were hanging on the hook along the way.

"Where are we going?" I asked with confusion. He didn't respond. We drove a few blocks up the road along the bay front before he finally parked the car and we got out.

"Let's go for a walk," he said, taking my hand.

There was nothing I would have loved to have done more than go for a walk with him. But at present, I had my house ripped apart and was in desperate need to get back to that mess, if I had any intention of moving within a month.

"Okay, but only for a few minutes," I said.

He took my hand in his and we walked for a while. I still didn't get the point. He was quiet the whole time, so he obviously didn't have anything that he wanted to talk about.

"Okay, are you ready to go back?" he asked after we had walked for about five minutes.

I shrugged, looking at him strangely, totally confused by his odd behavior. We exited the beach a few blocks up from where we had started. I stopped for a second to admire the beautiful new home right across from where we were standing. It was built to replicate an old Victorian house. Matty and I would peek in the windows, trying to get a glimpse inside as it was being built. It now looked like it was finally complete.

"Wow, that's beautiful," Julian remarked.

"I know," I agreed.

I pulled his hand leading him in the direction of the car, but he wasn't moving, instead he walked up to the house. I was shocked when he turned the handle on the front door and it opened.

"We can't just go in there," I said as he walked in, ignoring me. I was a little wary about trespassing. Finally giving into my curiosity, it didn't take me long to follow him.

I was awe-struck when I walked into the huge entryway. The living room was open and airy with a huge fireplace. The kitchen had all top of the line appliances and beautiful granite counter tops. There were pristine hardwood floors throughout and bay views from every window. We walked upstairs to find four bedrooms. The first three bedrooms were all similar in size. We saved the master bedroom for last. As I entered I was overwhelmed by the size. There was a fireplace and two enormous closets. The huge master bath was intricately tiled with a double sink, a shower, and Jacuzzi tub. After taking every single detail in, I stepped outside the French doors that led to a balcony overlooking the bay.

"Wow, could you imagine waking up to this every morning?" I asked.

"Yeah, it's pretty nice," Julian replied.

"Pretty nice? It's gorgeous!" My eyes widened.

He smiled at my enthusiasm. "So you wouldn't mind living

here?" he asked.

"Umm, sure." I laughed at that ridiculous thought. "But I'm moving to Chicago with this pretty handsome guy." I grinned.

"Okay, if you weren't moving to Chicago, would you want to live in this house?" he asked more seriously.

"Are you kidding me? Of course."

"Well, that's good to know because they accepted my offer today."

"What are you talking about?" I creased my eyebrows.

"You love this house–it's yours," he said.

"Okay, now I'm really confused. What? Are you going to keep commuting back and forth to Chicago? As much as I love it here, I want to be with you more and not just a few days out of the month." I tried to catch my breath. He began to laugh at the state of panic I was getting in. I didn't find any humor in it. I thought we had it all figured out and here he was changing the plan.

"What's so funny?" I snapped.

"You," he replied.

"I thought we agreed that we weren't going to do the long-distance thing."

He kissed me on the lips to stop me from talking. "We're not."

"Then, I'm confused."

He pulled me close and wrapped his arms around me. "I've been offered a very lucrative position that I just couldn't turn down. And guess what–it's only forty-five minutes away from here."

I looked at him in disbelief.

"I just need a guarantee before I uproot my whole life and buy you this big expensive house…" He reached into his pocket and pulled out a small box. My heart fluttered when he opened it, revealing the most perfect diamond ring I had ever seen.

I had to catch my breath–I was in shock.

"Kat, I love you and Matty more than anything in this world."

My head was spinning as I tried to register everything that was happening.

"Will you marry me?" His eyes never looked more beautiful.

I was speechless. I needed to be pinched to make sure this wasn't all a dream. "Yes," I finally managed to get out through my tears. He slipped the ring on my trembling finger, and I wrapped my arms around him. "Is this really happening?" I asked.

"I told you a long time ago, you were the girl for me and I meant it," he said.

"I love you so much, and I would have gone anywhere to be with you."

"I know." He smiled.

"You're really leaving Chicago? That hospital is your life."

"No, Kat, you and Matty are my life."

"I just can't believe you did all this. This house is beautiful. How did you know how much I loved it?"

"Matty." He grinned.

"Did Matty know all about this?"

"Of course. Who do you think helped me pick out the ring?"

I shook my head and smiled, shocked that Matty was able to keep it a secret. The ring was exactly what I would have picked out for myself—a beautiful princess-cut diamond in a platinum bezel setting.

"Did you have any help with this ring besides Matty?" I asked, impressed with his keen sense of style.

"Nope." He was trying his best to keep a straight face.

"Tricia?"

He nodded, finally admitting defeat. I thought about Tricia and the great acting job she had done earlier when she gave her lecture about not going to Chicago without a ring.

"Does anyone else know about this house?" I asked.

"Just you and Matty."

"How did I get so lucky?" I wrapped my arms around him tightly.

He pulled me closer and kissed me on the head. "I love you so much," he whispered.

My stomach fluttered. My dreams were all coming true. I had everything that I ever wanted—a beautiful child and my handsome prince. I was actually going to have my happily ever after.

Epilogue

Julian and Matty sat at the table working on a puzzle as I lay in my hospital bed coming out of a deep sleep. I began to think back on what a whirlwind the past year had been. Matty reached his one-year cancer-free milestone. He had come so far from that little frail boy from not that long ago. He was growing so quickly, and I was having a hard time believing he was already in the first grade. We moved into our new home and Julian had started his new job. He was still one hundred percent committed to his career, but he was even more committed to Matty and me. We had just celebrated our one year anniversary, and I had never been happier in my life. I smiled as I thought back to one of the happiest days of my life:

It was the perfect autumn day. Claire's already meticulous backyard could have been pictured in a home and garden magazine. The leaves on the trees were ablaze in vibrant shades of red, gold, and orange. Yellow and burgundy mums were meticulously placed throughout the yard, adding to the perfect palette of hues. I wanted to get married on the beach, but Claire was insistent that we have the ceremony in her backyard. I knew how much she wanted to do it, and since I was the closest thing to a daughter that she had, I gave in. It was a small wedding with just a few close friends and family, but it was exactly how I wanted it.

I gave myself one last look in the full-length mirror of Charles and Claire's guest room. I wore a plain white strapless sheath-style dress accented with pearls at the waistline. It was a lot simpler than the intricate wedding gowns I had always dreamed of when I was a little girl, but when I tried it on for the first time, I just knew it was the one for me.

I got butterflies in my stomach when I looked out the window, taking a sneak peek at Julian. I truly was marrying the handsomest man in the world. He was dressed in a black suit, looking just as beautiful as the first day I had met him. Matty was his best man, and he too was dressed in a suit similar to Julian's. His dark hair had grown back and his blue eyes sparkled, looking like a miniature clone of Julian as the two of them stood together.

How I had wished my mom and dad could have been here sharing this special day with me. I knew that my dad would have been beaming with pride walking me down the aisle. I also knew that he would have been equally as proud with my choice of husband.

"Are you ready?" Charles asked as he entered the room.

I took a deep breath. "Yes," I replied without hesitation.

"You look beautiful," Charles remarked, tearing up.

"Thank you. Thank you for everything, I don't know how I would have gotten through everything if it weren't for you and Claire."

"Well, we couldn't have asked for a better 'daughter' than you," he said.

Now it was I, who was beginning to tear up. "Let's go before my mascara starts to run," I laughed.

Charles took my arm as we made our way out the door. I looked up at the bright blue sky scattered with big puffy clouds throughout. The last thought I had before I walked down the aisle was—my dad had been right. Everything did happen for a reason. I thought of everything that Julian and I had been through. My dad's death led Julian to come and comfort me, resulting in Matty—the greatest gift of all, and it took something as horrible as Matty's sickness to bring us back together again. I smiled up at the sky, touching the diamond pendant hanging from my neck. I knew my mom and dad were there with me—I could feel them. "I found my 'one,' Dad," I whispered.

My knees began to tremble as we made our way down the aisle, concentrating on the one person who could always put me at ease—Julian. He had the biggest smile I had ever seen as my eyes met his. My heart raced as I smiled and cried at the same time—feeling so blessed. All of my fears washed away as I focused on nothing else but the two loves of my life—Julian and Matty.

I was hastily broken from my daydreaming when I felt a contraction.

"Ouch," I said, trying to breathe through it.

Julian quickly got up from his seat and sat down on the bed next to me.

"Are you okay?" he asked.

"Yeah, they're just starting to come a little closer now," I said, catching my breath.

"Where's Matty?" I asked, realizing he was no longer in the room.

"He went with Charles and Claire to get lunch," Julian answered. "You go easy on your mom." Julian put his head on my belly giving it a kiss. We didn't find out the sex. Julian didn't want to know. Matty was so excited about being a big brother, even though he wanted a little brother, he said he'd love the baby just as much even if it were a girl. I didn't care one way or the other. After everything Matty had been through, all that mattered was that the baby was healthy.

I laughed at Julian as he lifted his head from my belly. "I was just having the best daydream ever," I said.

"Oh yeah, what was that?" he asked.

"Our wedding day." I smiled.

"Thank you," he said.

"For what?"

"For opening my eyes to what really matters. You guys are the most important thing in my life."

I pulled him closer and kissed him on the cheek. He rested his head on my shoulder and rubbed my arm lightly. I thought back to the day Matty was born, and how I yearned to have him by my side.

I squeezed his hand through another contraction. "That was a bad one," I said, releasing his hand once it was over.

He gently rubbed my back, and before I knew it, another one was coming, this one even stronger than the last.

"I think you better go tell them to get my doctor," I said, now having an intense desire to push. Julian was able to handle anything, but for some reason this scared him to death. He stood up staring at me blankly.

"Julian, it's time," I said calmly, working through another contraction. He finally broke from his trance when the nurse entered the room.

"How are you feeling, honey?" She checked the monitor for my contraction activity.

"Oh boy, I think you're ready," she said, running out to get the doctor.

I looked at Julian who was standing there, dazed. "Are you going to be okay?" I asked. "You look like you're going to pass out," I managed to get out just before another contraction came on.

"No, I'll be fine," he reassured me as he rushed over to comfort me through it.

My doctor finally arrived. After examining me, she confirmed I was ten centimeters dilated. "Are you ready to push this baby out, Kat?" she asked.

I nodded, grabbing Julian's hand and bearing down as hard as I could. The pain seemed more intense than it had been with

Matty. I tried to get my breathing under control, catching a quick glimpse into Julian's eyes–so full of emotion.

"Come on, Kat, you're almost there," Julian reassured me.

I took a deep breath, never breaking eye contact with him, and pushed as hard as I could until the cries of my newborn baby filled the room.

"It's a girl," the doctor announced, holding up the baby.

Julian was beaming as he leaned over to give me a kiss. "I love you so much, Kat."

"I love you too," I replied, anxiously waiting to see my baby.

I didn't think it was possible to love someone as much as Matty, but as the nurse put her in my arms, I realized it was. I stared at her intently and kissed her head–she was perfect.

"Meet your daddy," I said, placing her in Julian's arms for the very first time. He was unable to wipe the smile from his face.

"She's so beautiful," he said, kissing her head.

I smiled in delight, enjoying every second of his bonding time with his daughter. I had denied him this moment with Matty, so I had every intention of making sure he got to experience this now. He couldn't take his eyes off of her, and she seemed so content in his arms. I could tell he was instantly in love.

He sat down on the bed next to me. "Olivia Hope Kiron," I said, looking down at her in his arms.

Julian smiled in agreement. "Thank you so much," he said, kissing me on the forehead. "I have two beautiful children and a beautiful wife. I don't need anything else."

"But that was *my* dream, Julian." I smiled.

"You helped me realize that it's mine too. You were the exception to the rule. You were the one person who made me rethink everything I ever believed in, and I'm so happy that you did."

The exception to the rule–I was taken back in time for a brief moment to a handsome blue-eyed stranger who I had just met, comforting me over losing a patient. So much had happened since then. It seemed like a lifetime ago. I took his hand in mine and kissed it. "I love you so much, Julian."

"I love you too." He squeezed my hand gently.

Julian gave the baby her first bottle, never taking his eyes from her. Matty finally appeared in the doorway, with Charles and Claire behind him.

"Matty, meet your sister," Julian said, bringing the baby over to him.

His smile lit up the room. "Wow!" he exclaimed as he sat down in the chair and Julian placed her in his arms. I felt myself tearing up watching him with her–my brave little boy with his new baby sister. It didn't get much better than this.

"Hi, baby sister, I'm your big brother, and I love you so much." He leaned down to kiss her. Julian seemed to be just as touched by this interaction as I was.

"We need a picture," Claire shouted, taking her camera from her purse. She began snapping pictures of Matty and Olivia as Matty posed so proudly for every photo. "Let me get a family picture." Claire placed the baby in my arms while Julian sat next to me on the bed with Matty on his lap.

"Everyone ready?" she asked just before snapping the picture. "Absolutely beautiful," she said as she looked at the screen on her camera.

"Let me see," I requested. I couldn't take my eyes off of the photo when she placed the camera in my hand. I had a family, it was a long harrowing journey to get there, but I was living out my dream. I had two precious children with the love of my life–my life was finally complete.

The End

ALSO BY BETH RINYU

Drowning In Love

Blind Side Of Love

An Unplanned Lesson

An Unplanned Life

A Cry For Hope

A Will To Change

Easy Silence

When The Chips Are Down

Two Of Hearts

Straight To The Heart

A Right To Remain

Keepin' The Faith

Thursday Afternoon